The Serenity Murders

· MEHMET MURAT SOMER ·

PENGUIN BOOKS

PENGUIN BOOKS
Published by the Penguin Group
Penguin Group (USA) Inc., 375 Hudson Street, New York, New York 10014, USA · Penguin
Group (Canada), 90 Eglinton Avenue East, Suite 700, Toronto, Ontario M4P 2Y3, Canada (a
division of Pearson Penguin Canada Inc.) · Penguin Books Ltd, 80 Strand, London WC2R
0RL, England · Penguin Ireland, 25 St Stephen's Green, Dublin 2, Ireland (a division of
Penguin Books Ltd) · Penguin Group (Australia), 707 Collins Street, Melbourne, Victoria
3008, Australia (a division of Pearson Australia Group Pty Ltd) · Penguin Books India Pvt
Ltd, 11 Community Centre, Panchsheel Park, New Delhi – 110 017, India · Penguin Group
(NZ), 67 Apollo Drive, Rosedale, Auckland 0632, New Zealand (a division of Pearson New
Zealand Ltd) · Penguin Books (South Africa), Rosebank Office Park, 181 Jan Smuts Avenue,
Parktown North 2193, South Africa · Penguin China, B7 Jiaming Center, 27 East Third Ring
Road North, Chaoyang District, Beijing 100020, China

Penguin Books Ltd, Registered Offices:
80 Strand, London WC2R 0RL, England

First published in Penguin Books 2012

1   3   5   7   9   10   8   6   4   2

Copyright © Mehmet Murat Somer, 2004
Translation copyright © Amy Marie Spangler, 2012

Originally published in Turkish under the title *Huzur Cimayetleri*.

Publisher's Note
This is a work of fiction. Names, characters, places, and incidents either are the product
of the author's imagination or are used fictitiously, and any resemblance to actual persons,
living or dead, business establishments, events, or locales is entirely coincidental.

LIBRARY OF CONGRESS CATALOGING IN PUBLICATION DATA
Somer, Mehmet Murat, 1959–
[Huzur cimayetleri. English]
The serenity murders / Mehmet Murat Somer.
p. cm.
ISBN 978-0-14-312122-0
1. Transvestites—Turkey—Fiction. 2. Murder—Investigation—Turkey—Fiction.
3. Istanbul (Turkey)—Fiction. I. Title.
PL248.S557H8913 2013
894'.3534—dc23   2012030581

Printed in the United States of America
Set in Dante MT
Designed by Elke Sigal

The Serenity Murders

MEHMET MURAT SOMER was born in Ankara in 1959. His *Turkish Delight* crime series hit number one on Turkey's bestseller lists, where it remained for months, and has since been published in fourteen countries (UK, United States, France, Italy, Spain, Poland, Greece, Germany, Sweden, Bulgaria, Bosnia-Herzegovina, Brazil, Egypt, and Turkey). He is a screenwriter for both film and television, and a classical music critic for various newspapers and magazines. He lives in Istanbul, Rio de Janeiro, and occasionally in other corners of the world, as long as there is enough sunlight.

Cast of Characters

Burçak Veral	The Turkish Delight protagonist
Sofya	Ex-stage star, retired but still impressive, has dark relations
Ponpon/Zekeriya	Transvestite drag star, best friend
Figen	Secretary in the office
Cüneyt	Bodyguard at the club
Hasan	Maitre'd of the club
Osman	DJ at the club
Şükrü	Barman at the club, loves twinks
Yavuz	Young man from suburbs, customer at the club, usually dancing topless
İpekten	Transvestite friend, very chic, elegant, out of *Harper's Bazaar*
Selçuk Tayanç	Childhood friend, now a department director for the police
Hüseyin Talip Kozalak	Taxi driver at the neighborhood, has a crush on Burçak
Satı	Cleaning lady, maid
Refik Altın	Gay poet, lyricist
Ayla Tayanç	Childhood friend, once a nemesis, now wife of Selçuk

Belinda D.	Very famous and powerful DJ, music critic, guru of Turkish pop
Jihad2000/Kemal Barutçu	Computer hacker, doomed to wheelchair, with bizarre sexual drives
Cem Yeğenoğlu	Hypnotherapist
Ricardo	Drag star from Brazil
Hümeyra	Neighborhood woman who works at the bank
İsmail Kozalak	Hüseyin's father, ironmonger
Kevser Kozalak	Hüseyin's mother
Tarık	Another taxi driver from the neighborhood, buddy of Hüseyin
Sermet Kiliç	Aikido and Tai chi master
Hilmi Kuloğlu	Square-faced commissar of the Homicide Department
Aykut Batur	Ex-chorister at the opera, now going onto pop
Alberto Maggıore	New York mortician, makeup master
Andelıp Turhan	Tarot master, always in queer dresses
Bahadır	Young and fresh lover of Gül
Bedirhan ender	Health food and diet master
Buket	TV programmer
Cavit Ateş	Reiki master
Cemil Kazancı	Mafia head
Gazanfer	Grocery wholesaler, usually silent customer at the club
Gül Tamay	Reiki master
Hakan Akincı	Tantra master
Haydar Hocaev	Bioenergy master from Azerbaijan
Koral Kohen	Gossip columnist
Mehmet Murat Somer	Bestselling author
Morlu Kadın	The angelic woman

Nılgün Kutlu	Yoga and meditation master
Nımet Hanoğlu	Faruk's wealthy widow
Süheyl Arkın	TV programmer
Vildan Karaca	Crystal and feng shui master, always in hurry
Yılmaz Karataş	Small and dark Mafia bodyguard
Wimpy Ferdı	Weird neighbor
Alı	Money-counter, freelance computing employer
Afet	Red-haired Reiki expert
Melek	Young girl from the Kozalaks' neighborhood
Genteel Gönül	Tranvestite acquintance, lower class than most but tries hard to sound classy
Şırın Güney	Yoga and meditation specialist, girlfriend of Cavit Ateş

The Girls at the Club

Beyza (Dumptruck Beyza)	Overweight transvestite at the club
Demet Kıllı (Hairy Demet)	Transvestite at the club, no waxing, kind of kinky
Elvan	Ignorant transvestite at the club
Karakaş Lulu	Hot-tempered transvestite at the club
Mehtap	Tall and red-wigged transvestite at the club
Müjde	Chubby transvestite at the club
Pamir / Yahya	Aggressive transvestite at the club
Sakallı Barbi (Bearded Barbie)	Transvestite at the club

*"In order to commit murder with relative ease,
one must harbor an idyllic love, almost puritan in nature."*

MICHEL DEL CASTILLO,
La tunique d'infamie (The Tunic of Disgrace)

The Serenity Murders

1.

I've always enjoyed being watched, but the idea of going on TV, talking in front of hundreds, maybe thousands of people, and playing the know-it-all expert, saying levelheaded, inoffensive things while discussing the reality of transvestitism without seeming to "promote" it—the prospect of which made the producer break out in a cold sweat—had put me on edge. I was dreadfully nervous.

The other guest on the show was the author Mehmet Murat Somer, who had artfully augmented my adventures, using them as fodder for his novels. We had been invited onto the most popular talk show of Turkey's most prestigious TV channels. And it would be live!

I had prepared modestly. I looked neither too plain, that is to say ordinary, nor as decked out and fancy as I would have looked in, say, one of Ponpon's stage costumes. Refined makeup, short but well-kept hair, slightly supported breasts, a pair of black leather trousers of the latest fashion, and a transparent shirt with a low neck that reached all the way down to my belly button, allowing me to display my lace bra and porcelain-like décolleté. Admittedly, I wasn't exactly in my best Audrey Hepburn mode. But I could hardly be faulted. After all, it wasn't every day that I hit the small screen. In fact, this was, officially, my first time; I mean, if I *had* appeared before, if I had happened to be caught on camera accidentally at some point, well, I could no longer recall it.

"We're going to raise hell in every sense of the word! Our ratings are going to rocket sky-high! But still, don't go overboard. If things do start getting nasty, if anything inappropriate slips out of our mouths, my friend the director over there is going to cut to a commercial break. Still, let's be careful . . ." the producer and presenter Süheyl Arkın cautioned us.

Nothing would slip out of *his* mouth, that's for sure. The "us" was actually "us two"; in fact, it was really just me. The host was an old hand at this game; he was on-screen with different guests almost every day of the week. I was sure he fed the same "our ratings are going to rocket" cliché to all of his guests. As we were waiting for the show to begin, he had said only a few words to the author and had cautiously avoided addressing me directly. As for the red-bearded media consultant who also acted as Mehmet Murat Somer's manager, with him Süheyl Arkın appeared to be engaged in a deep, meaningful conversation. It was obvious who was going to get preferential treatment here. Still, I kept my spirits high.

We were ushered into the studio. I immediately set my sights on the chair in the middle, the one that would be in the camera's view from every possible angle. If I were to sit there, though, the coffee table with the silly vase on top would hide my legs, in which case my John Galliano–designed Dior "Swinging Bombay" shoes, which I'd spent a fortune on and purchased especially for the show, wouldn't be visible. Well, in that case I'd just have to cross my legs and make sure to flash them at every possible opportunity. Otherwise I would surely regret having shelled out so much cash for such incredible footwear.

Süheyl Arkın seated himself behind the desk. Since his feet wouldn't be seen, he wore comfortable sneakers; as for the rest of him, he had smartened up with a blazer, a white high-collar shirt, and a dark tie.

After receiving his final orders from his media consultant, Mehmet Murat Somer walked over to me. "My right-side profile's just dreadful," he said. "I look twice my age and bald as an eagle." Just when I had made myself comfortable, there he was, trying to usurp my seat!

Left or right—what did it matter? As if he would actually look the twenty-seven years he claimed to be if they shot him from the left. Did he think he was Tom Cruise from the left, and Woody Allen from the right? I didn't want to escalate the tension by making a big deal out of a petty seat-swapping issue. I look good from every angle. I did as he asked.

And it was, ultimately, for the better, since my new position afforded the camera an unobstructed view of my Swinging Bombays, with their sequins, stones, tiny mirrors, and cashmere patterns, clearly displayed in all their glory, for all the world to see. Not to mention my six-inch heels . . .

Though most women and some of our girls claim to be perfectly comfortable in high heels, the same cannot be said of me. Far from it. As a child I would put on my mother's high-heel slippers, which were normally reserved for when we had guests, and first try to keep my balance, before attempting small steps. It was hard! Later, when I unabashedly started shopping at women's stores, I immediately bought myself a pair of high-heel shoes, and then promptly stuffed them into the wardrobe after wearing them only twice. If you ask me, such shoes are not for walking in or standing on; at best, they are for posing, as I was doing now.

My new chair was lower and less comfortable than the previous one, but I kept my mouth shut.

The set technician lad came up to me with a look in his eyes that shouted, *I know you and your kind*. He attached a microphone

onto my décolleté, careful to keep physical contact to a bare mini-
mum. As if touching me would give him a *bad* name, or, I don't
know, as if he'd catch the incurable transvestitism bug, as if it
would possess him, gradually taking over his entire being! I responded with a similarly patronizing, stern gaze. Once he had
completed his task, I grabbed hold of his hand and thanked him. Of
course he jumped back in a fright.

When the countdown for the live broadcast began, Süheyl
Arkın, with his carefully mussed-up hair—each and every strand
styled separately—put on that mask I was so accustomed to seeing
on the screen: an expression that was equal parts Lothario and
genuine curiosity.

I watched the monitor in front of me. After making his usual
opening remarks and bidding his viewers a good evening, Süheyl
Arkın introduced the topic and that day's guests, which were us.
He reminded viewers who might have questions of the studio's
telephone numbers and then turned to Mehmet, asking him for a
definition of transvestitism. Mehmet proceeded to expound in his
know-it-all tone. The camera had zoomed in on him, capturing
only the left shoulder and knee of yours truly, who was sitting to
his right.

I had meant to take one last look in the mirror before we went
into the studio, but out of sheer nervousness I had forgotten. I wondered if my hair and everything else looked okay. I could feel the
outer corner of the fake eyelash on my right eye rising a bit, but I
didn't dare touch it. The last thing I wanted was to get caught on
camera like that; after all, one never knew when they might switch
to a master shot, and then there I would be, for all the world to see,
fussing with my makeup! I knew all the girls from my club would
be glued to the television, on the prowl for the slightest imperfec-
tion, which they would then rattle on about for days. While I myself had gone to no great lengths to announce the event, my

photos, acquired from God knows where, had appeared in the television pages of the newspapers and all day long during ads for the show. Before I left the apartment my dearest friend Ponpon had called to wish me luck.

"Ayolcuğum," she said, "I can't tell you how proud I am of you! I believe with all my heart that you'll represent us in the best possible way."

My right-hand man Hasan, the headwaiter at the club I ran, had offered to come with me, an offer which I had politely declined. I thought it best not to arrive with a crowded entourage.

And then all of a sudden Süheyl Arkın turned to me and asked, "So, Burçak Veral, how did you become a transvestite? Would you like to share your story with us?"

This question wasn't among those we had discussed backstage. I was caught completely off guard. Over the previous two days I had rehearsed, albeit surreptitiously, everything I was going to say, thoroughly preparing myself for what was to come. But I was not prepared for this! The camera was on me. I smiled, blinking my eyes like Audrey Hepburn.

"I am sure you do not mean in terms of sexual development, Süheyl," I said, wondering if I should have addressed him by his first and last names. But wouldn't that have been a bit too *cool*? Besides, by addressing him as I did, I had, in my own way, expressed a kind of reserved intimacy. "If you like, I could tell you about my influences, and about how I find inner peace despite so many problems in the world."

I told them everything—from Reiki, which I had recently taken an interest in, to Thai boxing and aikido, which I had already mastered, to my high school days when I insisted on becoming an actor and made my parents hire a private tutor to give me acting lessons. But what I told them was really more about the things that had made me who I was than about how I achieved inner peace. I think I was talking a bit too fast, and had forgotten all about the lessons I'd learned from Alberto, a New Yorker who had taught me the fine points of makeup application, and from that mysterious woman, the marvelous Sofya, whom I followed slavishly back when I was filled with ambition to become a TV star.

The three of us talked about the crime novels penned by Mehmet, about how much of what was described in them was really true, and how none of the crimes in question could have been solved without the help of the police, and so on and so forth. It was smooth sailing, as we passed the ball to one another without a hitch.

"Of course, I get support from the police when I need it," I said.

"So you have a police connection," Süheyl responded, trying to corner me. The fake expression of surprise on his face must have looked more sincere on-screen, because close up it wasn't in the least.

"You could say that, but I wouldn't want to make his name public."

"Oh, look, we have an incoming call," he said, wearing a naughty smirk. "Hello?"

The caller was my childhood friend, my man, my police connection: Selçuk Tayanç, who never denied me his help, and who always showed great concern for my silly caprices. In complete disregard for his position as a member of the force, he proudly announced on national television that, yes, he was my friend. Although, in order to keep his name clean, a couple of times he highlighted our relationship as that of "childhood friends." I felt my eyes well up. I was already grateful for all he had done, for all I had made him do, and now this. Selçuk's courage, the way he proudly stood by me, warmed the cockles of my heart.

As soon as we cut to a commercial break, I quickly pulled a mirror out of my bag and checked whether my mascara had smudged. No, it hadn't. And the fake eyelash was still in place too.

Then we spoke of metrosexuals, of David Beckham, who paints his finger- and toenails, the new feminine trend in men's fashion clothing, flower prints, transparent tops, and facial skin-care products, which Süheyl announced that he used too. We talked about how transvestites aren't necessarily homosexual, explaining that sometimes transvestitism might simply be due to a particular fondness for women's clothing.

There was an incoming call from a lady, a psychologist who offered up scientific explanations. Everything she said confirmed all that I had already said.

We talked about the Ottoman tradition of male belly dancers and boy dancers, about the fact that men had worn dresses in the past, about how the jewelry we saw in sultans' portraits from centuries ago wasn't worn by even the most over-the-top homosexuals of today. A painting of Yavuz Sultan Selim wearing a pearl earring popped up on the monitor. This was followed by a discussion of famous transvestites, and then images from the RuPaul and Elton John video clip "Don't Go Breaking My Heart." A couple of Boy George photos, famous Turks, movie scenes in which men were disguised as women . . . the stunning Jack Lemmon and Tony Curtis in *Some Like It Hot*, Kemal Sunal in *Şabaniye*, Ali Poyrazoğlu in the Turkish theater production of *La Cage aux Folles*, and the final scene in the Hollywood version of the latter, *The Birdcage*, when Gene Hackman moans, "No one will dance with me. It's this dress. I told them white would make me look fat." We smiled as we watched. Clearly they had conducted extensive archival research to come up with a short, fast, effective series of clips. I was truly impressed. Jihad2000 and Ponpon were both recording the program, so it was nice to know that I would possess a copy of such a fine documentary. Süheyl Arkın punctuated the conversation with pleasant yet prudent comments.

Now it was time for viewer phone calls. I had finally gotten used to the atmosphere and loosened up a bit. There was a call from the father of a young transvestite. He told us the heart-wrenching story of how difficult it had been for the family to accept their son as a transvestite, given the humiliating gaze of the neighbors. He said that he knew his son wasn't doing anything wrong; he wasn't selling drugs, he wasn't stealing from the state, he wasn't a murderer, he just had different preferences when it came to clothing. Once again, my eyes grew damp.

"I can't wear what I want here," said a lass calling from the countryside. "Do you think I should come to Istanbul? Could I wear whatever I wanted there? If I came, could you help me out?" Her frantic questions set my teeth on edge.

A woman caller, her voice vibrating with tension, remarked, "You could actually be quite an attractive man. Women would be interested in you"; and finally posed the question, "Are you afraid of women?"

Another caller asked, "Do you see yourself as superior to women?"

Censoring my true feelings about those who ask such questions, I responded with polite, noncontroversial answers.

The next viewer's question was for both me and the author. "You snobs, you look down on everyone. Who the hell do you think you are?" he said, in a perfectly calm voice. "You don't have an ounce of respect for society, or for the values of the Turkish people. Living in a society that you're not even really a part of, whose values you hold in complete disdain, that's how you find inner peace? It's time somebody put you in your place. You're a total disgrace, the both of you, nothing but threats to society."

We were stunned into silence. The director had cut to the ads as soon as the first sentence was out of the caller's mouth, but the phone connection inside the studio hadn't been cut, so we were still listening.

"Who are you?" Süheyl said, the tone of his voice reminding us just who was in charge around here.

"And you, watch your step! You're promoting these assholes!"

"Find out where he is and cut that line!"

Süheyl's command wasn't carried out immediately. The abusive caller made his final threat just before the line was cut.

"I dare you to find me! And until you do, each week I'm going to kill someone near and dear to you, until I've put an end to your precious 'inner peace' once and for all!"

We froze, staring at each other with wide eyes.

"Who was that?" asked Süheyl. There was some commotion in the glass soundproof management room opposite us.

"Who was it?"

A worried look on his face, Süheyl listened to the voice transmitted through his earphones. Unable to hear what was being said, naturally, both my author and I watched him with keen curiosity. We waited for an explanation.

"We have to go back on air," he said finally, as if nothing had happened. "Just some sick psycho."

"I've been threatened before," said Mehmet. "At first I panicked a bit, but they turned out to be empty threats. Anyone able to dig up my phone number or e-mail address thinks they can say or write whatever they want. It really isn't worth worrying about."

I'm not the type to be outdone.

"I've been threatened before too," I said. It was true. And in every way you could possibly imagine.

At last we finished the program. I was almost glued to my seat, so profusely had I sweat. Süheyl thanked me by kissing my hand. The looks, the moves . . . there was something about this guy . . . One had to hand it to him, he certainly hid it well. Either that or he hadn't yet gotten the memo himself.

I have years of experience and observation. Rarely am I wrong.

2.

When the program was over I went home and relieved my feet of my Swinging Bombays, which had the appearance of miniature Eiffel Towers covered in Christmas decorations. I'd listen to the congratulatory messages on the answering machine later. I took a quick shower and put on a white knee-length dress with a petticoat skirt and strapless ornate top adorned with thin ribbons of the same color. It was one of my fabulous, flamboyant, elegant 1950s costumes, identical to that worn by Audrey Hepburn in *Roman Holiday*. I headed off to the club, where I would accept congratulations in the flesh. I looked like a true princess.

My always reliable, ever ready taxi driver Hüseyin had already arrived and was waiting at the door. And my nosy neighbor, Wimpy Ferdı, was peering out his window. I was beginning to feel annoyed at how he appeared at the window and watched me every time I entered and exited the apartment.

When he saw me step out of the apartment, Hüseyin got out of his car and opened the door for me. I was shocked. I wasn't used to such behavior coming from him. He had never displayed such habits, such courtesy before.

"I saw you on TV, ma'am. You're pretty much famous now."

I thanked him.

"Your breasts looked fuller, ma'am," he said.

Yes, my La Perla bra had needed a little support to fill it out, but I needn't explain that to him. Once upon a time, we'd accidentally slept together. He had told me then that he disliked big breasts, and that he loved my masculine contours.

Gathering my layered skirt, I got in the car without responding.

"You haven't had silicone implants or anything, have you?"

There you go, he had dropped the ma'am, *and* he was asking the most private of questions. A big no-no in my book!

I didn't want us to get stuck on how he addressed me, or the size of my tits. Once Hüseyin got stuck on something, he refused to drop it, and even if he was made to drop it, he'd grow sour, and when he grew sour, he caused trouble, and so on and so forth. Plus God only knows what stories Ferdı was inventing as he watched us. I was in the car, and nosy Ferdı couldn't see me, even through his Coke-bottle glasses. I grabbed my elastic strapless top and pulled it down to reveal my breasts. There they were: flat, muscular even.

I could see him staring, aroused. I pulled my top back up.

"Nice," he said, with a twitch of the lip he must have mistaken for sexy.

The club wasn't packed but there was a crowd. The congratulations started pouring in as soon as I arrived. Our security guard, bodybuilder Cüneyt, bowed down before me, almost kissing the floor.

"You were magnificent, boss! Can we have a picture taken together? I'll show it to the guys at the gym."

I didn't ask him whom he'd want to show a picture of the two of us to at his local gym, or why. If he were to show them and boast, *This is my girl, lads*, he knew I'd tear him to pieces if ever I caught wind of it. He'd probably tell them that he worked with me, or that he was my bodyguard. Cüneyt, who never feels in the least embarrassed to be working in a transvestite club, and who, unable to resist the girls' pleas, every now and then ends up going to the cinema or shopping with them during the day, is one of the purest souls I know. He lives in that delicate balance between naïveté and imbecility. And it is to his naïveté that he owes his sincere and cheerful nature.

DJ Osman had the trumpet-led opening music ready for my grand entrance. At first I paused, and, smiling, gave my community the once-over. And they did the same to me. There they were, all standing before me: Hasan, who had made a habit of exaggerating the whole concept of low-rise jeans to the point that he barely concealed his crotch anymore, stood there clapping. The bartender Şükrü, who had climbed up on something behind the bar so that he could see me over the crowd, gazed upon me as if seeing me for the first time in his life. Chubby Müjde, Elvan the queen of ignorance, Hairy Demet, Dump Truck Beyza, Mehtap with her tomato-red wig, flashy Pamir, Çise displaying her newly installed porcelain teeth, which were two sizes too big for her mouth, numb Lulu with the bushy black eyebrows, Sırma, who never missed an opportunity to show off the gold hoop piercing on her right nipple . . . There they were, my girls, standing before me.

"Oh, you were so striking . . ."; "You were wonderful, *abla* . . ."; "I loved it, dear, I hope I get to go on TV someday too . . ."; "Your shoes were fabulous, I couldn't take my eyes off of them. In fact, I couldn't really concentrate on you, I was so busy staring at them." That last sentence could have come from none other than bushy-brows Lulu. It suited her perfectly: a woman of spite and envy, yet smart enough to cover her insults with pleasant ingratiation.

The few early bird customers applauded, even though they had no idea what was going on. They probably thought it was my birthday or something. Yavuz, who loved taking his shirt off and showing off his ripped muscles once he was up on the floor dancing, but who was so broke the girls only slept with him for fun, came over and gave me a big hug. He was sweaty. I politely distanced him from me. He must have thought sweat was something pleasant, arousing even. I, however, am not of that opinion. He'd had a tattoo done on his right shoulder since I'd last seen him. It appeared to consist of Japanese letters.

As Şükrü slipped me a Virgin Mary, DJ Osman started playing "It's Raining Men" by The Weather Girls. He knows it's my favorite dance song. So I cut the greetings and good wishes short and quickly got on the floor and danced a little, displaying polite moves that befit my costume.

It was almost time for customers to start invading the club.

The first to arrive: a mixed group, among them my Reiki master Gül Tamay; Cavit Ateş from the same Reiki group; Cavit's relaxed lover, a yoga and meditation expert named Şirin Güney; Haydar Hocaev, a new arrival from Azerbaijan whom they introduced as a bioenergy expert; and a young man called Bahadır, who dazzled me with his good looks, and whose area of expertise I couldn't have cared about in the least. He had a bony face, strong fingers that grasped tightly as we shook hands, and shiny, pitch-dark eyes. His plump lips were enticing.

"How do you like my new boyfriend?" Gül whispered into my ear as we touched cheeks. It was pretty obvious monobrow Haydar wasn't the new boyfriend. I felt like a child whose toy has been taken away.

"Careful, I might steal him from you," I told her, laughing it off.

Even though she has a grown son from her first marriage, Gül has maintained a slim figure; with her sleek blond hair and her finger always on the pulse of the latest fashion, she is one elegant, attractive woman. Besides that, she's funny. She laughed, quite sincerely, at the idea of me stealing her lover.

Our regulars, those with a perpetual sweet tooth for our girls, were slowly filling up the club. There, cozily perched between two girls he had invited to his table, was the literary critic with the bushy mustache. Initially he only came to the club with the poet Refik Altın, but later he became a frequent visitor on his own, after Refik stopped coming following some minor disagreements between us. Once, out of curiosity, I had tried reading his poems, but they were so insufferably boring that I gave up. When such a mass of cultural knowledge remains undigested, it leads not to refinement but to tedious constipation. From what the girls told me, he wasn't bad in bed, but he did have fantasies that even they qualified as weird, such as having cigar smoke blown up his ass.

As usual the fruit and vegetable dealer Gazanfer was trying to pass off his quietness as politeness, occasionally lifting his *rakı* glass to greet the girls. He's a good customer, generous with his tips, reserved in his demands. He tries each girl one by one. The girls like him. His record is spotless.

At one point, Şirin Güney, the yoga expert, walked up to me in a panic and asked, "Where's the ladies' room?" The truth is, we have no ladies' room; we have only one single restroom. In protest against sexual discrimination, we had not separated the toilets. Besides, it saves us space.

She giggled upon hearing my reply, as if I had said something funny. "Well, let's give it a go, then," she said. I've always found her to be a bit shallow, and although I've known her for years, I've preferred to keep my distance.

She caught up with me again on her way back from the toilet. She was still giggling. It seemed she'd had a generous helping of alcohol.

"What a fabulous idea to have mirrors fitted behind the urinals! And no screens either . . ."

What she thought was a mirror was actually stainless steel, but it served the same purpose. After all, ours was a venue that, striving to be *cool*, bore the marks of a designer's touch. We deserved that extra bit of quality. She had clearly found it difficult to take her eyes off of what she had seen, and had immediately begun comparing it to her boyfriend, Cavit Ateş. Cavit was a man who not only had a big build, but was overweight with a fat belly to boot. No matter what size it was, it was going to look small in proportion to his body. For God's sake, didn't these women ever watch porn, look at pictures, buy a *Playgirl* magazine? Even when you're buying tomatoes from the market you look, touch, compare, and *then* choose.

As I walked about conducting my managerial duties, my gaze frequently landed upon Bahadır, and each time it did, our eyes met. Sure, he was holding Gül's hand, stroking her long blond hair, but he emitted a covert signal that did not escape my attention. Best not to give it a name. I had utmost love and respect for Gül. But I just could not keep my eyes off the lad.

Later that night Belinda D. and her husband Naim arrived. Belinda D. was an indisputable authority on Turkish pop music, and her most recent book, her most comprehensive to date, was titled *Superstar*. It was she who decreed which songs sank and which songs swam. Some called her the Herodotus of Turkish pop, others a reaper, due to her fine, highly selective taste. My personal favorite nickname for her was Hammurabi, which she was awarded owing to her declaration of the standards and rules of Turkish pop. The singers, composers, and production companies that feared Belinda D.'s malice had their books kept by her invisible husband, and rumor had it that he earned his keep solely from those who'd been touched by the magic wand of his wife.

I rushed over to greet them.

Belinda D., always high in spirits, was nervous. She gasped for breath as she spoke.

"Darling, I just found out, I don't know what to say. Someone shot Süheyl."

Yes, Süheyl, the very same Süheyl Arkın whose program I had been on that night.

3.

t was quite natural for Süheyl, who made a habit of probing controversial topics, to have lots of enemies. But it certainly wasn't natural for him to have been shot. He wasn't dead, but he was seriously wounded. He had been taken to the hospital, and the shooter had of course fled without leaving a trace.

I would go visit him with a huge bunch of flowers first thing in the morning. In my mind, I quickly struck a bargain and decided to buy carnations if they were cheap, and if not, anemones.

I was alone when I woke up. Bahadır had accompanied me in all my dreams. We ran together hand in hand in the countryside, squabbled over games of Scrabble, lit fires on the beach and watched the sunset in each other's arms, animated *Kama Sutra* positions, sloppily ate spaghetti bolognese out of the same bowl; in brief, we did everything that lovers do together. The strange thing was, I couldn't recall his face or other important attributes.

I sat at the computer, coffee in hand. I hadn't yet pulled myself together, even though it was already past midday. I'd received a slew of messages, as per usual. The group of hackers called the Web-Guerrillas, of which I was an active member, had wasted no time posting messages, half of which were filled with useless clues; the other half, however, were promising.

My eternal fan and rival, Jihad2000, who had recently become my friend as well, had sent me three messages, the last of which was clearly marked "urgent" in the subject field. I read that one first.

"What's going on? What are all these threatening messages pouring in for you? If there's anything I can do, I'm at your disposal," it read. What threatening messages was he talking about? What was pouring in? I knew he liked reading my messages. Although he had promised several times never to do it again, he was incapable of controlling himself, or of reining in his curiosity, or of restraining his sense of rivalry. And so he hacked into my account and logged in to read my messages before I had a chance to do so myself. Although this did give me a sense of protection, it also annoyed the living daylights out of me. I had a few addresses he still hadn't managed to access, but with his talent and patience, he'd access those too soon enough. Of that I was certain.

Jihad2000's other messages pointed to the source of the threat. The psycho viewer who had called the show had found my e-mail address and sent me a threatening message every hour. Apparently there was no room on this earth for me and my kind. He was going to wipe us out. Those who influenced me, those who had made it possible for me to achieve inner peace (this bit he had typed in capital letters and put in quotation marks), would get their due too. He had copied all the names I had published on my Web site, and heralded the fabulous news that he would murder someone each week until I found him.

The one sent at 3:16 in the morning was a notification of his accomplishment.

"Strike one! I shot Süheyl Arkın, the closet-case faggot who flaunts you and your kind in front of the public as if you were some kind of hot shit. I'll have more news for you soon!"

A cramp gripped my stomach as I read his words. What a truly wonderful start to the day. I headed straight for the shower. By the time I got out, my remaining coffee was cold.

Still wearing my bathrobe, I sat back down at the computer. My stomach was growling, but my curiosity outweighed my hunger. First, using classic hacking methods, I tried finding his address, his connecting computer. Our psycho was smart. He had connected from a different area, with a different computer, each time. Clearly, he was using Internet cafés. That's what I'd do if I were him: the best way not to leave a trace. The messages had been sent from providers such as Yahoo, Hotmail, Freemail, and so on, where you could create an account easily without providing any sort of personal information whatsoever.

"Let's see if you have the guts to find some 'inner peace' now," it said. He addressed me as an "enemy of peace," which I didn't believe I deserved at all. "It's you and your kind that disturb the peace."

My head had started to ache. I looked at the list of names; it was a veritable who's who of my illustrious life. On my Web site, besides those whose names I had mentioned on the program, I had listed the names of people I didn't know, of whom I was just an admirer or whom I held in high regard. Instead of taking the easy route and simply copied and pasted the list, he had actually examined it and copied one by one only those names he deemed appropriate targets for his cause.

My site was actually dedicated to Audrey Hepburn. It had her photographs, biography, filmography, in short, everything about her. John Pruitt was also prominently featured as the ideal man. Besides these two, there was of course my Reiki master Gül Tamay; my aikido tutor, the tai-chi master Sermet Kılıç; my gushing fount of love and joie de vivre, Zekeriya "Ponpon" Güney; and the one and only hypnotherapist in the country, NLP[1] expert Cem Yeğenoğlu, who was only on there because he had insisted.

---

1 Neuro-linguistic programming

From the list in his threatening message my menace had specifically excluded foreigners like the mortician from New York, my makeup master Alberto Maggiore, and my personal development guru Will Schutz.

I checked the program that tracked visitors to my Web site. There had been visitors whom I knew; but for the most part, it revealed dozens of anonymous addresses. Scanning all these from start to finish, tracking them, would be enough to make one lose one's wits.

When Jihad2000 failed to respond in his chat room, I decided to give him a call. I was sure he would have thought of everything I had, and done even more than I had already done. His private line, the one his mother didn't answer, rang and rang. He was probably in the bath or using the toilet. I sent him a message coded "urgent urgent urgent" which read, "Call me," and got off the computer.

I suddenly realized why I'd been feeling empty all morning: There was no music! Wimpy Ferdı downstairs hadn't yet begun blasting his music yet. He may have been a nosy neighbor, but devoid of manners he was not. I'd had a run-in with him once when he moved in the previous year, and that had done the trick. He does not commence with his roaring, wall-shaking rock music until he's heard noises coming from my apartment first.

Silence wasn't doing me any good. I quickly reached out to the Handel shelf and pulled out the *Athalia* oratorio. The beauty of baroque music filled my home like sunlight. Emma Kirkby's angelic tone, Joan Sutherland's nightingale soprano, little Aled Jones's hair-raising, prepubescent soprano together with Anthony Rolfe Johnson's tenor; it was simply perfection. The conductor Christopher Hogwood, the man responsible for launching the authentic instruments movement, had once again made a recording that would be a milestone in classical music.

Accompanied by this angelic group, I could now sit and think, and begin making plans.

If this psycho was serious, I mean, if he really was the one who shot Süheyl Arkın, then we were in deep shit. As Süheyl Arkın had considered it his duty to turn over stones that were not meant to be touched, there was of course the possibility that he had been shot by some other offended soul, in which case my psycho would be taking credit for someone else's work.

When someone like Süheyl Arkın, the apple of the media's eye, was shot, the police would waste no time in finding a suspect.

I answered the ringing phone thinking it would be Jihad2000, but it wasn't; it was Ponpon.

"*Ayolcuğum*, darling . . . You can't possibly imagine how proud I felt as I watched you. You spoke just as fluently as myself. I just watched the video recording again and, believe me, I couldn't find a single flaw."

"Stop exaggerating, *ayol*," I said. "For one, the lights were completely wrong. Whenever I turned my head you could see the sagging skin on my neck. Plus, I was nervous, and so I spoke in a rush. What's more, the shadow of my eyelashes fell on my face."

The girls had told me all this one by one last night. I hadn't forgotten, and was now reporting it all to Ponpon.

"Oh, you're exaggerating," she said. "Come on, get up and get yourself over here. You can pick up your cassette and we can eat together. I made delicious courgette *börek*. It'll be out of the oven in a short while. I put yogurt . . ."

Ponpon sure knew how to make a girl's mouth water. The way she described courgette *börek* . . .

"I'm expecting a phone call."

"Just redirect it, *ayolcuğum* . . ."

"And then I have to go to the hospital. You know they shot the program host, Süheyl Arkın."

I was doing my best to bid that courgette *börek* a tearless fare-well.

"All right, you have no intention of coming. It's up to you, cream puff. I'm not going to insist. Come if you want, don't if you don't. I've issued my invitation."

And slam, she hangs up on me. You can never tell when or at what Ponpon will be offended. My hand reached out to the phone to call and try to make it up to her, the smell of courgette *börek* filled my nostrils, and my stomach growled, but my distress over what to do about the threat hurling psycho outweighed all else.

I called Mehmet and suggested we go to the hospital together. After all, he too was one of the three people to be threatened.

"I'd like to, but unfortunately, I don't have time," he said. "I'm flying to Rio de Janeiro tonight."

I knew he lived there six months a year.

"It won't take long, just fifteen, twenty minutes."

"Still, I can't."

"But you've been threatened too . . ."

"Exactly, that's why I'm leaving. There's no need for me to walk around here like a target. I was going to leave anyway, now I'm just leaving two days earlier than planned. Write to me if you find any-thing. I'll be checking my e-mail. I'm sure you'll have solved the case and tracked down the psycho by the time I'm back."

"And all you'll have to do is write about it . . ."

"Of course, if it's exciting enough."

I turned the television on. The channels were broadcasting news about the attack on Süheyl Arkın. And what were they using as visuals? The moment the threatening call was received in the studio. So there I was, on the screen again, and on every single channel. The phone call, which hadn't originally been broadcast in full but which had been recorded, was now on air for the world to see and hear. And Süheyl Arkın being carried on a stretcher, the emergency entrance at the hospital, a doctor commenting on his condition, and then us again . . . They had identified the location from which the phone call had been made. It was a phone booth in Bakırköy. No suspects had yet been taken into custody. The police were doing their best to track down the criminal. The shadow of my eyelashes really did fall on my face. And the Swinging Bombays truly were dazzling.

The doorbell rang. No one comes to my place without notice, except for the grocer's delivery boy and the apartment caretaker. I looked through the peephole. My frail downstairs neighbor was at the door.

"Good morning," he said, scratching at his greasy, shoulder-length hair. "I saw you on TV last night. I wanted to congratulate you."

I thanked him, smiling politely, getting ready to close the door. At times like this I feel like Audrey Hepburn in *Roman Holiday*, or Grace Kelly, the princess of Monaco, shaking hands with the plebeians.

In his extended hand he held a CD-ROM.

"I recorded the whole thing."

It was a polite gesture. I thanked him once more.

"I might have missed the very beginning, though . . ." he said.

He wiped his palm on his faded T-shirt, as if it were sweaty. He was a graphic designer or a cartoonist, or something like that. His hands were stained with ink. He was terribly skinny. You could count his ribs.

He had fixed his gaze on me, and was waiting to be invited in.

As a matter of principle, I like to keep relations with my neighbors at a minimal level of sociability, lest familiarity give rise to that notorious offspring.

And so I gave him a look that told him I would not be letting him in.

"Well, I should be going."

I tried Jihad2000 again.

"Wow, well, if it isn't my famous friend," he answered. "What have you got yourself into this time?"

I hadn't especially got myself into anything. I asked him what he'd found.

"Not much," he said. "I think we've got a professional on our hands."

He had said "we," thereby claiming the problem as his own too. This was a good sign. It meant he'd look under every stone, put tracers on the menace, and finally discover where he had logged on from. Sitting in a wheelchair all day long, he had nothing better to do.

"I haven't really searched that hard. I just had a look around . . ."

Hmm, this meant he'd need to be bribed into looking harder.

"So what are we going to do?" I asked.

"I'll catch him, all right. First I just need to know how you'll reward my efforts."

"Tell me straight, what is it you want?"

"You . . ."

His feelings for me were not mutual. I didn't like sadomasochistic relationships. I had sent him Pamir, one of our girls who shared his proclivities, and she'd managed to keep him entertained for some time.

"Out of the question," I said. It really was.

"I got really horny watching you last night. The leather trousers . . . And those shoes you were wearing . . ."

I knew these could be fetish objects, but I had by no means intended to make Jihad2000 horny.

"We're friends, *ayol*! Plus it would be rude to Pamir."

"So what . . . Friends fuck too . . . I jerked off watching the recording."

I had no intention of continuing this conversation. If I did, it would turn into bad phone sex.

Television was going to make me a newly sought-after celebrity. From Hüseyin the taxi driver to Kemal Barutçu, a.k.a. Jihad2000, it seemed my past dalliances had remembered my attractions and now couldn't get enough of me.

I was so hungry my stomach was in cramps. I couldn't help but think of Ponpon's invitation. I got ready and left my apartment in a dash. My stomach was craving courgette *börek*. I'd stop by the hospital afterward.

4.

My stomach full of delicious courgette *börek*, I arrived outside Florence Nightingale Hospital in a state of semi-lethargy, to find before me a doomsday crowd. One celebrity after another was walking in to visit Süheyl. There were several cameramen posted outside every door. Nesting at appropriate angles, they did their best to capture every person who entered or exited, celebrity or not. Considering my recent rise to fame, if I hadn't come sans makeup, dressed in ordinary, rather modest men's clothing, I would have had no chance of escaping them. In this guise, though, I was sure to pass unnoticed. Alas, my fifteen minutes would be over before the day was through.

A hand touched my shoulder.

"Hello."

It was the famous gossip columnist Koral Kohen. There he was, staring at me, with his coal-black curly hair, chubby face, and eyes that always showed an expression of surprise no matter what he was actually looking at. I smiled when I recognized him. I've known Koral Kohen for years and he always makes me laugh. He visits all sorts of venues and is buddies with all yet intimate with none. Whatever he hears, he writes in his column or goes on TV and recounts, without questioning the truth of it in the least. And then, within a week tops, he is able to win back the hearts of those he offended with his slanderous gossip. That, in a nutshell, is Koral Kohen.

He was after a story and he had caught me.

"I watched the show last night," he said, rolling his eyes. That meant he was impressed. "I think he's fine. It's meant to give the ratings a little boost, that's all."

"You mean it's all a lie?" I asked, astonished. I was used to Koral generating conspiracy theories, but this, to be honest, seemed a bit far-fetched.

"Don't you see?" he said. "He's on every television channel, on the front page of every newspaper today. What could be better for a program that's taking a plunge in the ratings?"

Oh, so the program I had been on was a dead bird, its ratings plummeting!

"So what about the images on TV?" I asked. "He was wounded . . . rushed into emergency . . . And all the things the doctors said . . ."

"He's in showbiz, hon. He could easily arrange all that."

And to indicate that his explanation was final and that the topic was closed to further discussion, he quickly turned his head toward a different direction.

"But I'm still being threatened," I said. "I received dozens of threatening messages last night. There's a psycho out there saying, *Catch me if you can, or else I'll kill everyone you love, one by one.* Or do you suppose that's fake as well? To make it more realistic, perhaps?"

The expression on his face told me that he thought I was being silly. What I had just said ran completely counter to his theory. He looked as if he couldn't believe his ears, as if I had said something wrong. He made a wry face, the kind one makes after gulping down a spoonful of disgusting cough syrup.

"Are you worried about Süheyl?"

"Yes," I said. "Of course I am. No matter how you look at it, it's an unpleasant situation. Plus, I was there. I heard it all. The threat was pointed at me too."

"Have you called the police?"

"No," I said. "I can take care of myself."

"You have a lot of confidence in yourself, don't you?"

"I wouldn't say *a lot*, but, yes, I do."

He was rescued from having to respond when a navy BMW drove up to the hospital door. He, along with the other journalists and reporters, gravitated toward the vehicle. The commotion continued as the members of the press thrust forward toward their target, constricting the circle that had formed around the car.

I had met the newcomer before and knew him to be Süheyl Arkın's friend. Dr. Bedirhan Ender, the health diet specialist who had also proclaimed his expertise in the field of herbal therapy. After generating a mass of readers and followers thanks to his books, he started writing a weekly column for one of the mass circulation newspapers, and had recently begun hosting a program on Süheyl's channel. He explained how to make medicine from herbs, and which herb is good for which illness. He also hosted guests he had cured and listened to them as they conveyed their eternal gratitude, an expression of fake modesty plastered on his face. In truth, he was as proud as a peacock.

He spoke into the microphones that were shoved in his face, saying how upset he was, describing the incident as a genuine tragedy, and explaining that everything possible would be done to cure Süheyl, but that ultimately, at the core of everything was inner desire and divine ordinance. The aura of sterility radiating from Bedirhan Ender was too much for me. He was always clean-shaven, his hair always perfectly styled, his gold-framed glasses sparkling clean and resting at the exactly correct position on his nose, his shirt starched and white as snow, his jacket stiff, his trousers ironed. Perhaps worst of all, anyone with half a brain could see the herbal remedies he claimed as his own dated back centuries, millennia even. It pissed me off even more when he claimed that he had lived in a Tibetan monastery for some time, and that he was a messenger sent to spread the knowledge that he had acquired in Tibet. Even my grandma knew at least half of what he preached, and besides that, there were those with similar interests and knowledge in our Reiki group too. What's more, they had learned all that same stuff without having to go all the way to Tibet! In short, I detested the guy. Although I did believe in what he taught, I detested the way he presented and promoted himself.

I wonder, if I were to give the psycho his name, might he give priority to Dr. Bedirhan Ender and rub him out first? I was frightened by my own thoughts!

Because of the crowd and commotion, it seemed I wouldn't be able to get in to see Süheyl Arkın after all. Frankly, I wasn't all that bothered. The sluggish feeling that follows a serving of *börek* was slowly wrapping me in its warm embrace.

At this point, a little physical activity could only do me good. I decided to go see Master Sermet for our usual program: tai chi to warm up, unwind, and balance my energy, followed by aikido. I hopped into a cab and headed for his apartment, which he always says is in the classy neighborhood of Ulus, but which I would describe as being just up the hill from the rather more ordinary Ortaköy. It was an old building, in which he occupied two apartments on the same floor. One he lived in, while the other he used to hold his classes. He led groups that came at a fixed time on certain days of the week, but I didn't belong to any of those. I had started off as a private student, and as the relationship between master and disciple transformed into friendship, I became someone who stopped by whenever I felt like it, someone who sometimes popped in sim-

ply for a chat, and who had also equaled his master's mastery of aikido and perhaps had even come to surpass it, as the master
occasionally admitted.

While the side of the road looking onto the Bosporus bore all
the hallmarks of prosperity and sophistication, the opposite side
appeared equally middle-class. And there, on the middle-class side
of the road, was where Sermet Kılıç lived, bitterly calculating ways
in which he could upgrade to the other side. "I'd double my fees,"
he said. "Think about it, the whole of high society would come
rushing!"

In order to attract new customers, he himself had started taking jujitsu lessons. "It's a completely different discipline," he would
say, trying to tempt me into learning it.

Due to a recent increase in hair loss, he had had his head shaven
and then proclaimed, "See, I look like a real Tibetan monk now."
He certainly was as skinny as one. He wore baggy trousers and
cotton jackets or tunics that he secured by tying a belt around his
waist. And he always wore his specially made soft shoes. He was
super-sensitive when it came to animal rights and so he preferred
not to use leather. Naturally, he was also a vegetarian.

The lock on the metal entrance gate was broken, so I pushed it
open and walked in. They had planted grass in the minuscule garden, but it had failed to flourish due to neglect.

As I walked up the stairs, I felt the courgette *börek* I had had at
Ponpon's weighing me down. Ponpon was an excellent cook. She
could knock the socks off any housewife. She never skimps on in-
gredients, especially butter: "That's what gives it its flavor," she ar-
gues. The third slice of *börek* I had eaten out of sheer gluttony was
now giving me a guilty conscience. But Master Sermet always has
green tea. I'd feel much better after a cup of warm green tea.

I stopped at the landing on the third floor. I could hear the
sound of a familiar tune. The soft music was coming from the

apartment opposite his home, but the door to the studio was wide open. I wondered if I had arrived during class hours. But then who would come at this time of the day? People prefer sessions either in the early hours of the morning or after work.

In case they were doing tai chi, which requires intense concentration, I let out an unobtrusive, "Hello, it's me," as I walked in through the studio door, doing my best not to make any noise. There was no answer. They might have been in one of the back rooms, where he preferred to work with me as well. The apartment where classes were held didn't have any furniture, so that people could move around easily. I walked in to find the thin gymnastics mats folded up and piled against the wall. The room was completely empty.

"Master . . . it's me . . ." I called out again.

I then swiftly strode down the short corridor and into the room where we always had our sessions.

Master Sermet was lying on the floor, next to him a cup of unfinished green tea. He was motionless. His eyes were wide open. He was staring at the ceiling. He was dead.

5.

I knew that I wasn't supposed to touch anything, that I was meant to call the police right away. But, shocked and devastated, I collapsed onto the floor next to him. I tried to lower his cold eyelids like they do in the movies, but the soft stroke that I applied was not enough to do the trick. I didn't want to fiddle around with the body too much. I left it as it was.

A storm brewed inside of me. I wanted to scream, shout, beat the crap out of someone. I had learned to remain calm in the face of death, but inside, I still hadn't gotten used to it. A wave of fury swelled inside of me, nearly engulfing my sanity.

There was no blood or wound on his body. So he hadn't been shot. It was up to forensics to find out how he had died. It could have been a heart attack, or something else entirely. But if this was the work of that threatening psycho, he was going to suffer at my hands when I found him.

I sat next to my master for God knows how long. I wanted to reach out and hold his hand. I didn't. Those hands had struck me in various parts of my body, and had taught me how to dodge and avoid such blows. He had veiny hands, knobby fingers, and square fingernails. They reminded me of a book I had recently read: *Who Are You? 101 Ways of Seeing Yourself.* The book covered the 101 physical, intellectual, and spiritual ways of seeing oneself, and it said that hands and nails of this type symbolized elegance and energy, a taste for beauty and harmony. They were described as philosophers' hands. They belonged to people who were analytical, philosophical, compliant, tolerant, who had a strong sense of justice, and who sought the truth. All characteristics that described Sermet Kılıç. He hadn't deserved to die.

The truth was, I just could not bear that he was dead. I wondered if the feeling of injustice I felt inside was because he had died, or because of my own loss.

I waited with him until the police arrived. The skinny and short-tempered police chief was anything but pleasant. From the way he looked me up and down, it was obvious from the start that we weren't going to get along. I decided that I wouldn't back down if he were to make things difficult. After all, my old friend in the police department, the great Selçuk Tayanç, had my back, plus there were the dozens of letters of gratitude I had received from the police.

I told him how I'd found the body. And who I was. I slipped Selçuk's name in once or twice. From the way he reacted, though, it seemed that he wasn't familiar with the name.

"Well, I guess I'll be off now," I said. "I've given you my address. You know how to find me if you need me."

"Impossible," he said, grinning.

"Why, *ayol*?"

"You're the only person we have."

He had slim, well-kept hands that I would consider small for a police officer. I always take notice of people's hands. His nails appeared to be manicured. Could it be that metrosexuality was catching on among cops as well?

"You don't even know for sure if it's a suspicious death," I said, switching to defense mode and getting ready to call Selçuk.

"I didn't say you were a suspect. I said you're our only source.

Does he have friends or family? Who do we need to inform? Who is going to arrange the funeral?"

Right, these were all valid questions. It was then that I realized I didn't know much about Sermet Kılıç, even though we had been working together for years. He was divorced when I met him. He had a daughter who refused to see him. She lived someplace down south, like Antalya or Mersin. I think she was married. This place belonged to Sermet Kılıç. I didn't think he was particularly wealthy. Although he did have fantasies about moving to the other side of the road, he was in no way a money-grubber. That was it. I really wasn't much help.

The square-faced police chief was fast, energetic, stubborn, and by the book. Those with forehead and chin of equal height and broad cheeks were hardworking, judgmental, strict, and intolerant. And that was precisely how this specimen was acting. Suddenly I realized how deeply *Who Are You?* had influenced my subconscious. But then again, the book was proving to be correct.

"So what are we going to do?" I asked. "Are you going to keep me in custody until the forensic results arrive?"

"Oh, no, hardly," he said, trying to laugh. "We don't even have a place to detain you."

"So?" I said, implying with my sarcasm that he should get this over with a.s.a.p.

"I don't know," he said in a mocking tone. "This has never happened to us before. I need to call and ask my superior."

"Okay, fine, and I'll call Selçuk Tayanç."

I wasn't going to sit around and wait for him. Selçuk's secretary, who by now was able to recognize my voice, put me straight through. First I thanked him for his kind gesture the previous evening when he'd called in to the show. I told him how moved I was. The square-faced police chief had his eyes fixed squarely upon me as he listened intently to every word that came out of my mouth.

"I have a problem," I said.

"You wouldn't be calling me otherwise, would you?"

This wasn't an expression of reproach. He always had a lot on his plate as it was.

"I know how busy you are. You're an important man. I hate to disturb you."

"I understand," he said. There was a hint of sarcasm in his voice. After all, if I was so concerned about disturbing him, then why the hell was I calling him out of the blue like this right now?

I explained the situation.

"Give him to me," he said, meaning square-face.

"He wants to have a word," I said to the chief, as I handed over my mobile.

He took it, making a sour face as he did so and thereby indicating that he did not think me worth the time of day, and that since he did not know the man on the other end of the line, he had no intention of taking this Selçuk Tayanç, whoever he was, seriously.

In a smug and smirky, just short of insubordinate, tone, "Yes," he said, introducing himself.

Square-face's name was Hilmi Kuloğlu. He was chief of the Homicide Division.

Now it was my turn. *I* was watching him. Whatever it was that Selçuk was saying, square-face's posture had changed instantaneously. His body shot into an upright position. His face first turned white and then red. I leaned against the wall and crossed my arms as I continued watching him, deriving indescribable pleasure from the view. Unexpected paybacks are the source of small satisfactions.

Whatever Selçuk was saying, it was punctuated only by the occasional "Yes, sir," on the part of the square-faced chief.

Having been put in his place, the latter was receiving orders about how to treat me.

"Chief would like to speak to you," he said, as he respectfully passed the phone back to me.

Selçuk gave me an unconvincing scolding for stirring up trouble, and asked if it had anything to do with the threatening message on television the previous night. I didn't know. I hoped it didn't. It was my sincere wish that Sermet Kılıç had died of a perfectly polite, run-of-the-mill heart attack.

"I'll look into it," he said as he hung up. "Don't go poking around too much. The case is complicated enough."

I hung up the phone and slipped it into my pocket. I was deliberately dragging my feet now.

"Right," I said cheekily, "so what now?"

"Whatever you wish," said square-face, choosing his words carefully lest he fail to show me the respect I was due. "And, I do apologize. I didn't recognize the chief's name when you said it, but of course I know him. I mean, I wouldn't want to be misunderstood . . ."

Right, he was trying to cover his ass now. He was alarmed, thinking that if this faggot made any complaints about him, he might end up in a rather unpleasant situation, or with an unnecessary appointment, or on an exile assignment. It was nice to know what he was thinking, but I dislike it when those who are not faggots call me a faggot, or in fact even think it. I assume that they do so in an attempt to degrade me.

"Now, now, no reason to get upset. Or do you think this faggot might just get you in trouble?" I said. Having witnessed his pathetic state at being confronted by a superior, in my eyes he had already been demoted to the status of pathetic cop.

"No, no, sir, I would never use such a word," he said in all sincerity.

"You were thinking it, though."

He'd been caught, and he knew it.

"But aren't you?" he asked, in a tone of surrender.

"That's a different matter," I replied.

You know how I said that according to the personality analysis he was stubborn and narrow-minded? Well, he was, and he insisted.

"I saw you on TV today. In a news report about Süheyl Arkın being shot."

I quickly took back the adjective "pathetic" that I had previously ascribed him. "Pathetic" square-face was not. No, he was a total fool. And an obstinate one, at that.

"My sexual preferences are my private business and mine alone," I said, raising my head. "And yours are yours."

"But I don't go on TV dressed like a woman and announce it to the whole world."

His obstinacy was worthy of a flogging.

"I'm leaving," I said. "Let me know whatever you find out. Don't make me have to call Mr. Tayanç again."

On my way back I thought about Master Sermet, about our respectful and loving relationship, about how polite and refined he was despite his profession, which was to teach people how to fight and protect themselves . . . How he lay there on the floor. The arrival of the police. And then I pictured Officer Hilmi. I imagined him wearing lace pink underwear under his uniform. Net tights . . . Secretly shaving his whole body, smothering himself in makeup, and walking around in high-heeled women's slippers when he was at home alone . . . I couldn't help but laugh. I wouldn't be able to forgive myself for days for getting carried away like that with such thoughts, to the point of laughter even, when Master Sermet had just died and I had just discovered his body. As punishment to myself, and to impose some discipline upon my body, soul, and will, I forswore sex for five days.

Five days, I thought. Five whole days! Day and night . . . It was a

long time. Suddenly those five days, a number I had randomly conjured up, loomed large. But I could start the countdown beginning
from last night. I hadn't slept with anyone last night. Yes, in fact,
my fast had begun yesterday morning at five a.m. Dreams didn't
count.

6.

My beloved Master Sermet Kılıç had been poisoned. A mite of *Actaea spicata*, a.k.a. baneberries, had been slipped into his green tea, triggering heart failure and resulting in death. This information I had gathered not from the police but from the threatening psycho himself. He was already busy boasting, and had sent me an e-mail detailing his accomplishments. I tracked the address to an Internet café in Ortaköy, which meant that, once again, I was left without a good lead.

The bastard was playing dirty. He'd said he would kill someone every week, but, apparently unable to contain himself, he'd started killing someone every day. He must have been really, truly pissed off, to go breaking his own rules like that.

I sent e-mails of vehement protest to each and every one of his e-mail addresses, just in case he did check them. And if he did, at least he'd know what I thought of him.

Jihad2000 hadn't been able to turn up anything. He kept writing about how desperately he wanted me, about the visit I was to make to his place in my leather trousers, and what exactly he wanted me to do during my visit. Not a chance in hell. But I could tell that his time with Pamir had done him good; he was now able to identify with some clarity what exactly it was that he wanted. He wanted rough sex, a bit on the nasty side. But nothing too painful. My visit was never going to happen. I was absolutely adamant about it. First, I don't like S&M. Second, although I do admire his genius when it comes to computers, as a man Jihad2000, that is, Kemal Barutçu, does not make my heart, or any other part of me, stir in the least. And by the looks of it, he never would. Plus, I was fasting. Out of respect for my master . . . I had to remain resolute, firm—a veritable will of iron!

The very thought of fasting was beginning to agitate me, to yank at my nerves, pulling them taut. It turns out I had underestimated our psycho, who, in just two deft moves in less than twenty-four hours had gone from being a perv with homicidal tendencies to a straight-up murderous monster.

My phone beeped, reminding me that I had a Reiki meeting in half an hour. I'd completely forgotten. I had promised I would be there. We were going to treat a young MS patient. Reiki, which initially I'd had not an ounce of faith in, turns out to be marvelously effective against numerous illnesses and diseases, among them multiple sclerosis. I had attended a meeting upon the recommendation of a friend of mine from the beauty salon, Afet with the ketchup-red hair. "Reiki can't make an illness any worse," she had said. "And good for us if it provides some relief."

Afet, who was actually a French teacher, had been introduced to Reiki by a colleague of her husband. She had immediately embraced it and quickly seen its benefits.

"The migraine that plagued me for years is gone!" she had told me. "For years I tried every medicine in the book, every folk remedy available to humankind; none of it worked. But Reiki did the trick! Now I can drink as much orange juice as I like and eat as much chocolate as I can, and nothing happens."

During a lengthy skin-care and full-body seaweed massage session one day, she had worn me down going on and on about Reiki, until finally I agreed to give it a go myself. After all, it wouldn't *kill* me, now, would it? "Everything on this earth, from the table we are lying on to the seaweed covering us, from the pavement we walk on to our very bodies themselves, *everything* is made up of atoms, of energy particles. All Reiki does is adjust the energy in our bodies to create a balance. After all, it's the imbalances in our body's energy that give rise to mental and physical illnesses. Our channels might be shriveled, crinkled, or blocked. With Reiki, we open those channels back up to create a proper balance," she had summarized. Since I didn't like taking drugs and I believed that scientific medicine developed its treatments by practicing trial-and-error methods upon us, this idea hadn't struck me as odd at all. I simply had very little faith in modern medicine, which banned medications widely used just twenty years ago, ridiculed operations carried out only thirty years ago, and as recently as the 1940s had disastrously practiced barbaric lobotomy surgeries. As she polished her designer glasses that matched her red hair, Afet had explained, "I think it's absolutely ridiculous that we should ignore Chinese medicine prescriptions dating back thousands of years and the healing methods of Tibetan monks when they can cure certain illnesses like psoriasis that scientific medicine simply still can't." That did the trick—I was in.

Today's meeting was at Gül Tamay's apartment in Emirgan. It was one of those deceptive apartments that, seen from the outside, makes you think it must have a view of the sea, whereas the truth is, it doesn't have a view at all. It was Bahadır, the man who had been haunting my dreams, who opened the door for me. He seemed even better looking now in the daylight. He had pink shiny lips that looked as if they had just been sucked. He looked me up and down straightaway, and smiled.

"Welcome. Please, come in," he said.

His sexy Adam's apple moved up and down as he spoke.

And his voice, which I hadn't been able to hear very well in the noise of the club, was awfully sexy too. Now, why had I gone and developed a crush when the guy was Gül's boyfriend and I had just started fasting? And what about this newly found coyness of mine, the kind more befitting a young girl? Doing my best to keep up a cool appearance, I stuck my hand out, and, as soon as we had shaken, quickly pulled it back.

"You know, there's an old actress named Audrey Hepburn, you look just like her."

I was undone, arrested, melting away. It was my favorite compliment. I even forgave him for calling Audrey an old actress. By some amazing feat of self-control, I managed to stay on my feet and not collapse into his arms. And then in I sailed, walking on air.

Gül was interviewing our patient in the back room in preparation for the session. Permanent fixtures of the group, the quiet Cavit Ateş and the tarot-reading expert Andelip Turhan, had already arrived.

With hands joined on his stomach and eyes squinted, Cavit Ateş sat there smiling like a Buddha who had already reached Nirvana. He greeted me from where he sat, bowing his head. The smile on his face remained serene.

I was surprised when I first heard the unusual name Andelip, which is another word for nightingale in Turkish, but it grew on me fairly quickly. As for the incessantly twittering Andelip Turhan herself, if you asked me, she had more than a few screws loose. She was a fairly short, plump brunette who constantly flipped her curly hair from side to side whenever she was in motion. As for her clothing, she wore absolutely, positively anything and everything, wrapping herself in layers of odd clothes, just like an onion, and adorning herself with an assortment of outrageous jewelry. When I first met her she was wearing a lace petticoat over her clothes and had puckered the cuffs of her pajama-like baggy trousers using massive curtain tiebacks.

"She does it on purpose," Gül had said, after noticing the look on my face. "She thinks people will take her more seriously as a fortune-teller if she looks like a freak."

And today she had decorated her curly hair with what appeared to be a white bonnet, but which upon closer inspection was revealed to be a pair of cotton men's briefs. That's right, *underwear*. Andelip had pulled the undies over her head like a bonnet, leaving her hair to stick out of the leg holes. The waistband came all the way down to her forehead, and read "Calvin Klein" upside down. Of course, she noticed where I was looking.

Wearing her sweetest smile, "I bought it online," she said, in that chirping voice of hers. "They belonged to Kevin Spacey. He wore them for at least a day. I paid a fortune for them in an auction. I'd simply die if I didn't parade them around a bit."

She chuckled, her entire body jiggling.

I knew of Web sites that claimed to be selling celebrity clothes and underwear. Once, I too had bid in an auction, for the *Colt* magazine model John Pruitt's original stained boxer shorts, but then had come to my senses upon Ponpon's warning and withdrew from the bidding. "They're probably fake, *ayolcuğum*," she had said. "If people are stupid enough to buy them, I'll start manufacturing celebrity boxers and bras myself." Although I could hardly stomach being classified as stupid, by Ponpon, no less, I acquiesced; she was right.

I wondered what Andelip would think, what she'd say if I told her all of that.

She had already turned around to share the details of the briefs with Bahadır.

"They even had his scent on them when they first arrived. A masculine body odor, mixed with a little perfume. They arrived in a firmly closed plastic bag. But then the scent vanished. As you've probably guessed already, I absolutely *adore* Kevin Spacey. My heart skips a beat whenever I see him. I don't even know anymore how many times I've seen *American Beauty*. I've read my tarot cards a million times, but alas, he isn't in my destiny. Oh, well. I'll just have to make do with his briefs."

As she said that last line, she stroked the briefs as if Kevin Spacey were in them.

I didn't tell them about Sermet's death. I highly doubted any of them knew him anyway. Besides, I didn't want them to panic.

Our patient was a twenty-six-year-old woman who worked at a bank. She had been suffering from MS for four years. During her MS attacks, she experienced excruciating pain, which she could no longer bear to live with. She had contacted Gül upon recommendation.

We chatted as we sipped the tea that Bahadır had brewed and served. I like men who do housework. But I didn't approve of the way Bahadır had settled in and become a member of the household in such a short time. It was too soon for him to be assuming the role of the host.

We had almost finished our tea when the feng shui and crystal healing expert Vildan Karaca arrived. As usual, she was late and anxious. She shook hands with one person as she spoke to the next, left her bag in one corner of the room and her jacket on a chair in another. Then she went over and started rummaging through her bag, only to return without having taken anything out. In no time at all she had successfully demonstrated her tremendous talent for spreading her anxiety like a contagious disease. She claimed that the balance of energy wasn't right and asked everyone to stand up, and then she changed all of our places. She sat me and Bahadır down on the same couch, side by side. So our energy had been deemed balanced and compatible by a professional. I could have gotten carried away with this idea and ended up God only knows where, but, alas . . .

The seat-swapping exercise did nothing to alleviate her point-less anxiety. To the contrary, she'd only succeeded in infecting the rest of us. "I'll calm down now . . . Calm down . . ." she repeated, pulling out a huge pink quartz globe from her bag and closing her eyes as she held it tightly in her hands. Under the influence of the pink quartz we all slowly calmed down. Or it felt good to believe that we did. Whatever comes to pass ultimately happens thanks to belief, to faith. Whatever we believe will make us feel better, does.

Our healing session lasted approximately forty-five minutes. We saw our patient off and then began to chat.

Vildan, the feng shui expert, started the conversation by saying she had seen me on TV. They all confessed one by one that they had watched me too.

"Sweetie," said Vildan, "as long as you've started going on TV shows, why don't you join Buket's program as well? She mentioned it the other day. She wants to invite the tantra practitioner Hakan Akıncı and me. I'd rather be on the show with you than with that sex-crazed pervert. We'd have a much better conversation. The man won't stop going on about tantra and he sees sex as the pur-pose of everything."

"How delightful . . ." Andelip sighed.

Vildan, considering the remark nothing short of impertinence, responded, "*Ayol*, I've been there, done that . . . It takes hours."

"Even better!" said Andelip, ogling. "What more could one possibly want?"

"It's not at all like you think, darling. The male doesn't ejacu-late. And in the meantime, you end up contorting yourself into a million and one acrobatic positions. Your back, your hips, your shoulders . . . The next day you're stiff all over."

"Yes, but sweetie, that's all perfectly fine with me . . . And if it makes *you* stiff, perhaps that's because you're too out of practice . . ."

"Yeah, right! *Ayol*, believe me, it's nothing like wearing a man's undies on your head and prancing around with 'I'm horny' written all over your forehead. I've tried it, I know, and I'm telling you, it's unpleasant. But you won't believe me!"

The invitation I had just received to the new TV program got lost in the muddle of Andelip and Vildan's quarrel. She'd call me if she was really serious about it. And I'd think about it. I'd been on television once, and look what had happened; I didn't want to even begin imagining what would happen if I were to go on again.

Gül, unable to suppress her curiosity, intervened. "Vildan, do you mean to say you slept with that disgusting Hakan Akıncı?"

No one could possibly argue that Hakan Akıncı was good-looking, or even charismatic. The man was simply ugly and sullen.

"Yes," said Vildan nonchalantly. "To get some practice . . ."

"Might your discontent be due to the man himself?" suggested Gül, with sincere curiosity. "Because tantra is actually quite nice."

Cavit Ateş, whom I'd forgotten even existed, emitted a few strange noises to express his agreement.

What? Gül and Cavit had done tantra too? Okay, I could understand Gül. She was an attractive woman, a presentable woman, but Cavit! Cavit, who looked like the Buddha! Was I the only innocent in this fold?

"I've never tried it," I said naïvely.

"No need to," burst out Vildan, "You must," insisted Gül simultaneously. I looked at one and then the other.

As Gül reached out to hold Bahadır's hand, "My personal opinion," she said coyly.

So the two of them . . . Tantra . . . By the look of the lad's proud posture, the answer was clearly yes.

7.

On my way back home, I received a message on my cell phone. It was one of those pay-as-you-go numbers. I opened the message, hoping that it was one of the spruce but penniless men I'd given my number to, asking to be called back so he didn't run out of credits.

"I know where you are and who you're with," it read. That was it!

I immediately called back the number that had appeared on the screen. It rang, but of course there was no answer. So my psycho had gotten hold of my secret number! Considering his accomplishments so far, I could tell that he was a force to be reckoned with. And clearly he wasn't bluffing.

So he was following me around. I had never developed the paranoid habit of checking to see if I was being followed or not. So even if he had followed me, I wouldn't have noticed. I turned around and looked behind me involuntarily. We were inching forward in tight traffic. He could have been in any one of the surrounding cars. Heat rushed to my face. "What's the matter, sir? You all right?" asked the driver, who was dressed in casual apparel, as he watched me in the rearview mirror.

"Yes, I'm fine, fine!" I blurted, in an utterly unconvincing voice.

The state of inner peace and tranquillity at which I had arrived during the Reiki session was no more. And the evening traffic was terrible. We were moving at a snail's pace.

I needed to concentrate on something else. I needed to think of other things and shake off the suffocating feeling of panic that was engulfing me. The easiest way to do that would be to count Audrey Hepburn films like I always did. Who she costarred with, what she wore in each one, and so on and so forth. The first film to come to mind was the last one I wanted to be thinking about at that moment: *Wait Until Dark*. In it, Audrey played a blind woman, and there's this psycho killer who is after her. The psycho killer breaks into her home and poor blind Audrey has to try and save herself. Alan Arkin played the psycho killer. It was particularly annoying that, from among Audrey's corpus of films, the majority of which I had watched dozens of times, I should first recall this particular, dark movie, which I had seen only twice. It was one of Audrey's later films, a low-budget B movie. Sure, by then her youth may have faded a bit, but she was still as charming as ever, and she was perfectly convincing as a blind woman. The only problem was, she spent the whole film wearing the exact same clothes. Plus the film was nerve-racking. A house with a psycho killer in it!

It was already getting dark. I thought of how early it got dark this time of the year. I didn't feel like going home and posing like Audrey Hepburn in an empty house, filled with fearful emotions evoked by the thought of *Wait Until Dark*. I felt dreadfully awful, and awfully anxious.

From what he had said, I deduced that my psycho's intention was not to kill me (if it had been that he would have done so already!), but to let himself be caught by me. Which meant there was no need to be afraid. But then again, Mr. Psycho was no longer abiding by the one-person-per-week rule that he himself had set. His already malfunctioning mind could go completely haywire, and he might decide to bury me too. If it meant fighting, I could handle him any day. I could hardly withstand poison or bullets, though. But then, who could? If he wanted to, he could lie in ambush and shoot me, or come into the club like any stranger and slip whatever he wanted into my drink; if he really wanted to, he could even use explosives to wipe me and a whole load of the girls out at once. What could I do to stop him? Cüneyt at the door was just there for display. All he was good for was to stop obvious troublemakers and resolve minor conflicts that arose inside. If someone were to bring in poison or explosives, no one would notice.

Though the fact that the killer had declared he wasn't going to kill me did make me feel better, it failed to dispel my uneasiness at the thought of going home alone. I had a sneaking suspicion. And my instincts are sometimes very strong. And that day's Reiki practice must have made them stronger.

No, I didn't want to go home.

I could go back to Ponpon's. Her cheerfulness would do me good. Or it might be too much and simply do me in. I crossed that one out.

I could go to İpekten if she was at home. She'd gossip about absolutely everyone. Even the thought of it exhausted me. I crossed that option out too.

I could have made the visit to Selçuk and Ayla that I had been postponing for a long time now, but it was too early to visit them. Neither Selçuk nor Ayla would be back from work yet. I knew Selçuk worked until late. This option was automatically eliminated too.

I could have treated myself to a delicious slice of cake in one of the cafés of one of these five-star hotels. That would mean adding to my body weight. None of the people I had slept with objected to a slightly buxom figure, but I didn't believe it suited me in the least. Whenever I put on even half a pound, I instantly started dieting and devoting myself to gymnastics. My current lethargic state, though, had caused me to neglect gymnastics recently. And so the idea of treating myself to a piece of cake was duly banished from my mind. I had stored enough fat at noon with Ponpon's *börek* anyway. Another option crossed out!

Traffic had begun to flow, and so we were swiftly approaching my home. I'd better make up my mind, and I'd better do it fast.

Wasn't I going to go home eventually anyway? There was nowhere to run. After all, it was my home. With this in mind, I began concentrating on my options if I went home.

I could call Hasan and ask him to come over. Two were better than one. I liked this idea. But Hasan's phone was switched off. How many times had I told him not to switch it off during the day? I'd have to get on his case about it that evening.

I called the taxi stand, my one last hope. If Hüseyin was there, I'd ask him to come over. He loved to be of use at times like this, to "play detective," as he put it. He probably thought he was some kind of Rambo or something.

Hüseyin was at the stand. Without going into the details I told him that I needed him and that he should wait for me outside my apartment. God knows what he'd envisage, what unlikely scenarios, what sexual connotations he'd conjure up as he stood there waiting outside the door, all puffed up like a turkey. As for how he'd explain things to the guys at the stand, whether he'd cringe with embarrassment or happily play the "uncle" to my "aunt," who knew?

My taxi driver was all ears. Clearly he was doing his best to make sense of what I was saying. I smiled coldly into the rearview mirror. He knew how to take a hint. He quickly looked away.

Hüseyin had pulled his car up in front of the apartment building like I had told him to and was waiting for me there. He was a bit hurt to see me stepping out of a cab that he wasn't driving. Did he expect me to walk back or something?

"We would've come and picked you up, all you had to do was call," he said.

"Don't go acting all jealous on me, *ayol*. And don't be silly, of course I'm going to take other cabs when I'm out. It's not like you're my private driver!"

"Right, because you know we'd never stoop to that level," he said cheekily. "Look, you told us to get over here, okay? And so we marched straight over, no questions asked."

Something had happened to Hüseyin's manner of speaking. He was saying things I'd never heard him say before. His tone of voice, choice of words, and the way he referred to himself in the first-person plural were all typical shantytown *kahve*-speak and very unlike him. After all, Hüseyin had an impeccable reputation for minding his manners in even the most distasteful situations.

I had no intention of putting on a show for the neighbors—especially not for that nosy Ferdı, who for some strange reason fancied himself my equal and imagined an affinity between us—by screaming and shouting outside the front door. Interestingly enough, the only dark apartments in the building were mine and Ferdı's. The lights were on in all the others. I got in the car. Not in the back as I normally would, but in the front, next to him.

"I can't believe my ears," I said in all earnestness. "What's with the jargon? Where'd you pick that up from?"

He stared at me blankly, as if I had just said the oddest thing in the world. He'd normally smile at times like this. But this time he didn't.

"Say something, *ayol*!" I finally exclaimed, losing my temper.

"You should be doing the talking. You're the one who asked us to come over and said it was important."

He was right. I took a deep breath.

"I'm sorry. I'm just a little out of sorts."

I explained the situation to him. I skipped the bit about Audrey's film. I just told him I didn't want to go into my apartment alone.

"I get it. You're going to use us as bait. We're supposed to go in and see if there's a trap or something." He was really on a roll with that first-person plural, and he had no intention of dropping it.

"No," I said. "There's no trap. I just didn't feel like going in on my own."

All of a sudden his face lit up. I could almost see the dirty thoughts racing through his mind.

"No," I said again, "it's not what you think."

I wouldn't want him to get his hopes up in vain. Besides, I was fasting.

"What am I thinking?" he said, wearing a smirk.

"I know what you're thinking, *ayol*. We can sit down and have a cup of coffee. Or beer, if you'd prefer."

I don't like beer myself, but I always keep some in the fridge for visitors. It has become popular again these days. I think it's the influence of American movies. Even those men from whom you'd least expect the answer "Beer" when you ask them what they'd like to drink. And from the can, nonetheless! Whereas in the old days, only aged uncles drank beer, and even they preferred it from the bottle.

Before we'd even set foot through the door, I already regretted having invited Hüseyin over. He was going to keep hitting on me, and would do everything in his power to make me horny and seduce me. A past mistake was coming back to haunt me. But then, as far as I could recall, his performance was really too good to be categorized as a mistake. And even that was after he'd suffered a thorough beating and his entire body was in pain. But I was fasting. No way were the thoughts that crossed my mind going to come to pass.

I tried to picture Master Sermet's dead body in my mind's eye.

If I could picture it vividly enough, I would be filled with rage toward the psycho killer, and thus be able to suppress my bodily de-
sires.

If Satan did exist, he certainly worked hard at moments like
this. Seduction, deviation, denial, recklessness: it was all his doing.
Not only was I failing to picture Master Sermet, but my adventure
with Hüseyin was springing to life in my imagination, and in a
very physical sense.

I chased away my pornographic thoughts. It was times like
these that called for a will of iron. Thinking back on my past,
though, I realized that perhaps I shouldn't put too much trust in
my own willpower. My record on that front, admittedly, was
hardly impressive.

8.

Of course, there was no one in my apartment. The answering machine had recorded dozens of messages and the light on it was flashing. I quickly had a look around the apartment, with Hüseyin trailing behind me. We collided the first time I turned around. He smiled that smile he believed to be sexy. I ignored it and carried on looking. I even looked in the closet. There wasn't a soul. No one had hidden a snake, spider, scorpion, or centipede. You see, I'm not very fond of those particular hundred-legged creatures. I breathed a sigh of relief. Phew!

I gave Hüseyin, who had stretched himself out on the sofa and was scratching his chest, a can of beer.

"Switch the television on if you like," I said. "I've got a couple of things to do inside."

"Do you have any movies?" he asked. "Like DVDs . . ."

It was blatantly obvious that he was not referring to arthouse films.

One could, out of sheer spite, have presented him with a gloomy Theo Angelopoulos film in which each scene seemed to last for an eternity. But I didn't.

The phone rang before Hüseyin even had a chance to open his beer. I answered it.

"Who's the guy you're with?" said the now familiar voice.

I was startled. He couldn't be spying on me.

"Hello!" I said.

"Who is he?" he repeated.

"Who is this?"

"You know who it is. Stop pretending you don't. It hardly becomes you."

Hüseyin had understood, either from the tone of my voice or the way the blood drained from my face, that something wasn't quite right. He came to my side and pinned his questioning gaze on me.

"Hello . . ." I said timidly.

"You're not as crafty as I'd hoped you'd be. You haven't lifted a finger. I'm beginning to think you don't really care all that much for those friends of yours. You spend all your time cruising around the city. It hardly becomes you."

I held the handset away from my ear a bit so that Hüseyin could hear too. The entire studio audience had heard his voice, there was no reason why he shouldn't hear it too.

"What is it you want?"

"For you to find me. That is, if you can. When you catch me and see who I am, oh, you're going to love it . . . But then, I'm afraid you never will catch me, not at this rate."

His self-confidence was annoying. He recounted his crimes in a perfectly nonchalant tone, as if letting me know he'd had beans for lunch.

"Why should I catch you? The police can take care of it," I said, though even I didn't believe that for a minute. He burst out in hysterical laughter.

"They're not cut out for it," he said. "You're the only person who could possibly understand my clues. That is, if you're as smart as you claim to be."

"But why?" I pleaded. "Why?"

"C'mon, we're playing a game here," he answered cheerfully. "Think about it! A mind game! The great race, the grand chase! Tracking down your prey! And in the end, the big prize: me! And it's more real than any of the games we've played so far, believe you me!"

It seemed I was up against a genuinely pathological nutcase. If this really was how his brain worked, even if he was caught, he'd beat the rap in the end. All he had to do was plead insanity. They'd lock him up in a mental institution for three or four years, and then as soon as the first amnesty came along he'd be released for good behavior.

"My phone is being tracked," I told him.

"What a joke, right! I'm calling you on a mobile. You'll find the number, but not where I am. The convenience of pay-as-you-go."

But of course! It was as if the whole pay-as-you-go scheme had been created as a simple convenience for psychos like him. Picking up one of those SIM cards was as simple as buying a pack of cigarettes. After all, both were available at any local corner store. Call whomever you want whenever you want and say whatever you want. And no one can track you down.

He stopped laughing and resumed speaking in his cold voice. "You haven't answered my question. Who is he?"

"Are you spying on me?"

"What you do, where you go, who you see . . . I know all of it."

So I was being followed, watched. What was it they said? Just because you're paranoid, it doesn't mean they're not really after you. Or was it the opposite?

"I don't want to play this game," I said. "You understand? I don't want to, *ayol*!"

"Oh, he's losing his temmm-per! And doesn't he sound cute," he said, chuckling again. And then, returning to his dull tone of voice once more, he added, as serious as a heart attack, "Who is he?"

Hüseyin moved his mouth toward the handset and yelled, "What's it to you, you son of a bitch?"

That was, in my opinion, uncalled for. There was simply no need to go driving the lunatic up the wall.

"If you don't tell me, I'll find out myself. It's not that hard, not at all. But it would be a shame. He sounds young. Now you're going to make me change the order of the victim list. Watch out, sport. You're next!"

Hüseyin let out another, "Fuck off!"

"Well, well! Our gentleman's got a foul mouth on him, now, doesn't he? It's so unbecoming."

He was making fun of us, plain and simple, playing the distasteful game he himself had set up. But even cat and mouse was fairer than this. At least the mouse knew and saw who his enemy was, and could run and hide accordingly.

"I'm not playing any games with you," I said dryly. "You don't even play by your own rules. You said you'd kill once a week, but now you're doing it every day."

"That fag Süheyl doesn't count," he said, laughing. "He only got wounded. Plus, that had nothing to do with you. I shot him because I was pissed off."

So he'd kill someone whenever he felt like it, just because he was pissed off. Nice . . .

"You're still breaking your own rules. You can't play a game without rules!"

"I can break any rule I want, but if you want to catch me, you'd better get a move on. There's no time to lose."

And with that, he hung up.

I turned to look at Hüseyin. His face had gone pale and his forehead was covered in sweat.

"What is this psycho trying to say?"

I couldn't tell him he shouldn't worry. Clearly, given what the psycho had done already, there was much to worry about.

"Take a seat," I told him.

He did as I said. And I sank into the armchair opposite him. He was still holding his unopened beer, as if trying to draw strength from the aluminum can.

He let out a furious "What?" when he saw me staring.

"What what?"

"So is this punk going to come after me because I came to your place tonight? Well, fuck that! I can't believe this shit! We're out on the street all day. We pick up all kinds of people. The good, the bad, thieves, beggars . . . We've got our backs turned the whole time. All kinds of shit could happen."

"Oh, come on, don't overreact," I said, trying to calm him down.

"That's what you think. Haven't you heard of taxi drivers getting their throats slit for a few measly bucks? How their bodies are found in forests or garbage dumps? Our lives are on the line!"

I fell silent. So did he. We stared at each other, uneasy, on edge. We didn't know whether to look at each other or to look away. What could I say? Not even I knew why all this was happening. I was waiting to wake up from the whole thing, to wake up any moment and say, *Oh, it was all just a dream*. But I couldn't wait much longer.

"How about I take a few days off? . . . But that's no solution. I can't afford to. Besides, where would I hide? There's no rule that says the punk has to get me in the car. He could come get me in my sleep if he wanted to."

"Oh, come on, it's not like he's an angel of death who can move around unnoticed and then appear in front of you out of nowhere."

"Of course, you've got nothing to worry about. I'm the one who's being threatened . . . the one who's going to be sacrificed!"

I had forgotten all about this childish side of Hüseyin's. Caught up in a flood of emotion, his lower lip drooping, he sulked, confused by the entire world. For some time now I'd only seen him in the alternating roles of horny lover and melancholic romantic. Roles he played with varying degrees of success.

"What am I supposed to do?" he said, as if I could simply wave my magic wand and give him an answer.

"I don't know," I said in all earnestness. "But I'm going to check my messages immediately."

Hüseyin let out a big sigh as I pressed the button on the answering machine. He still hadn't opened his beer.

There were dozens of messages, from all sorts of people. A chaotic mix of congratulations and condolences. Alı, my partner in the computer business, had called twice and said that he had a new assignment for me. What it didn't pay in money (which was zero), it would make up for in prestige, he said meekly. I was fed up with doing people favors. Oh, please hack so-and-so's Web site, oh, please crash this site . . . I kept doing it in the hope that it would bring in customers, but the customers never came. I'd get mad and start hacking the Web sites of the thankless bastards who'd begged for the favor in the first place. Why should they get away with asking me to work for free? It wasn't like I needed the prestige. I needed the money!

Cem Yeğenoğlu, who claimed to be the first and only hypnotherapist in our country, had also left a message. "It may no longer interest you, now that you're famous, but I thought I'd let you know that there's going to be a pleasant little get-together at the Brahma Kumaris Society. But in case you are interested . . ." Then he explained that the meeting was to be held at the Brahma Kumaris, in other words the Brahma's Daughters Building in Erenköy, and repeated the date and time twice. Loud and clear. I had no intention of going. I was bored of this fascination with Far Eastern disciplines, a fad that was spreading like wildfire. I've always had a keen distaste for that which is popular. It was quite a surprise to see how hungry our people were for such things. From the most innocent feng shui books to translations of the sacred Hindu scripture Bhagavad Gita, all this ancient foreign esoterica had suddenly become fashionable. No, I didn't want anything to do with Brahma Kumaris. I'd gotten a whiff of their worldview at a couple of meetings I'd gone to. I didn't like that they seemed to want to impose it on others. I refuse to be imposed upon! Cem Yeğenoğlu could very well go if he was interested. In the meantime, I couldn't make my mind up whether to tell him or not. I knew his name had landed on the psycho killer's list as well. Then again, what was he going to do about it even if he did know?

Should I let everyone know who was on the killer's list? But then that would put everyone in a panic. What was going to happen? What was I going to do? What were we going to do?

Hüseyin finally opened his beer.

"I've got to check the computer too," I told him.

"I'm coming with you," he said, rising from his seat. He was a grown man, for Pete's sake, he could hardly be afraid of being alone, could he?

There were dozens of messages from our psycho; I say "our" because, after all, he qualified as Hüseyin's psycho now too. It seemed he'd logged on to a different computer every time he got a little bored and sent me an e-mail. In one it said, "Check out your Web site!" and in another there was the address of the location of today's Reiki meeting and a list of the names of the attendees. This guy was one busy bee. For him to know all this was equivalent to him being right inside my head. It was pretty much as if I'd been walking around with a camera planted on my shoulder.

Jihad2000 was asking what was going on, and was again making sexual innuendos. I was growing annoyed at the way he insisted upon forcing the conversation to sex at such a crucial time, when I needed his help the most. I sat down and composed a stern response. I explained to him that his behavior was simply out of line, and then went on to tell him about how I was dealing with a psychotic murderer, about how poor, innocent Master Sermet had been killed, about how everyone who had contact with me was in danger, about the grave responsibility that weighed upon my shoulders, and so on and so forth.

"Isn't that the cripple that lives in Beşiktaş?" asked Hüseyin. He had dropped me off at Kemal Barutçu's, a.k.a. Jihad2000's, house a couple of times.

"Yes," I said.

"What's he going to do?"

"He's good at tracking people down," I told him. The question, however, remained perfectly relevant. What exactly was Jihad2000 going to track down? What could he possibly track down about someone who logged on from anonymous addresses and called on pay-as-you-go SIM cards?

"You could do that yourself."

Of course I could. In a different window I opened the program that tracked my landline. The last call was from a pay-as-you-go mobile. I could find out where the card had been purchased if I tried, but what good was that going to do, when the corner store that sold it wasn't going to know who they sold it to anyway?

"There," I said, shoving what appeared on the screen into Hüseyin's face. "Nothing. One big nada!"

He moved his head closer to the screen, as if by doing so he'd understand. He studied it carefully.

"Right," he mumbled in response.

"Look at your Web site," he'd written. And so I did. He'd recorded his new achievement. The date of Sermet Kılıç's death was written next to his name. And whenever you clicked on another

name, the same question appeared on the screen: "Who's next?"
Bravo, I thought. Okay, my Web site didn't have any special protection, but it wasn't that easy to tinker around with it as you pleased.
So it seemed he'd decided to devote every ounce of his energy to
messing with me. He knew about computers. He must have had
loads of free time. What a clue indeed!

Why exactly was he so obsessed with me anyway? It couldn't
have been just an ordinary obsession with transvestites. If that
were the case, well, the streets were filled with our girls. Was it
because I had entered the public eye? Because I had helped solve a
couple of complicated cases? What was his problem with me? Everyone around me was now under threat. I had suddenly turned
into poison ivy. Anyone connected to me might be done for. The
Nazi doctor Josef Mengele had earned himself the nickname "Angel of Death," but at this rate, they'd be using it for me soon too!

"I might as well let the guys at the stand know," Hüseyin said,
reaching for the phone. "So they're not worried about me. Let me
tell them I'm here."

God knows what the guys at the stand would think, how they
would interpret it.

"You can't stay here," I said, putting down the phone. "No way."

He stared at me blankly.

"Why's that? The best way to stay safe is to be near you. If the
guy is after me and I'm always with you, our paths are bound to
cross. And you can catch him, just like that, easy as pie!"

Half of his reasoning was true. I wasn't quite sure about the
second half, the easy-as-pie bit, that is.

I let go of the phone so he could make the call.

9.

My deal with Hüseyin was simple: okay, he'd be "with" me but not *with* me.

It was high time I shook off that panicky feeling that had started to envelop me and put on an air of cool. I called the ever sensible Selçuk.

"We can't go giving police protection to everyone on your list. That's impossible," he said.

He had a point.

"So what am I going to do?" I asked.

"Not you, *us*," he said. "The police, the security forces. They're looking for clues. Whatever they can find. Anything."

"What do you mean? Are we going to wait for someone else to be murdered?"

"That's not quite how I would put it."

"But that's exactly what it means . . ."

"This is a game, a race against time," he said. He called it a game too. They'd used the same term. "If we're fast, we'll catch him before he strikes again."

"Will we be fast enough?"

"Without question!" he said.

"So what have they found so far?"

"I don't know, but I'll find out for you. They must have something. Besides, there are eyewitnesses to the attempted murder of the television host."

Right, they should have absolutely no problem at all identifying someone who fired a gun from afar in the pitch-darkness of night and then ran off. Those eyewitnesses were sure to possess a wealth of knowledge, weren't they?

"But," he added, "that case looks more like an organized crime, whereas this one seems less professional."

"But Selçuk, I'm the one who heard his threats with my own ears and then found Sermet Kılıç's dead body."

"I'm not saying it's not serious. Maybe there's some deeply rooted issue behind it. I really don't know."

"There are the voice recordings," I said. "You must have the technological know-how. Can't you identify the voice? Every voice is unique, you know. Just like fingerprints."

Right, and how would they know to whom the voice belonged? Or if they had a fingerprint, what would they match it up with? How would they find whose it was? What archive, what records did they possess? The police would have a voice and fingerprint, but wouldn't know to whom they belonged.

"If you're right, then it has to be someone who knows you," he said.

Yep. And I knew a lot of people. Not to mention the ones whom I didn't know but who still knew me.

There was nothing we could do but wait.

I ordered food from our neighborhood kebab shop. Hüseyin had lost his appetite. He didn't finish the *lahmacun* he ordered, or his one-and-a-half-portion Adana kebab. He downed two boxes of *ayran* one after the other.

It didn't take me long to get ready for the club. I was in no mood to get fancy. I went for the simplest option: black trousers with a tight black jersey jumper. And around my neck a dashing necklace of large crystals, which I had bought while in Rio. Quartz and agate sprinkled among an abundance of amethyst: attached to one another with fine wires, some of the crystals seemed to be suspended in air, a virtual doppelgänger of the galaxy.

"I'm ready," I said, as I spritzed on some perfume.

Hüseyin looked me over, from head to toe. Compared to what he was used to seeing me wear to the club, I qualified as positively homely.

"What is it, *ayol*?"

"Nothing," he said, shrugging his shoulders.

"Come on, then, we're leaving."

It was a calm night. And good thing too, because I might have exploded at any moment, like a grenade that's had its pin removed. It was only a matter of time before I projected the rage boiling inside me onto someone, anyone. Hüseyin, who hadn't said a word on the way, who believed his silence would render him invisible, went and sat in a secluded corner. Chubby Müjde, spotting an opportunity, quickly seated herself next to him. Hüseyin was *just* Müjde's type. I was spying on them as I listened to Hasan give me a full report on what drinks we were running short of and a humdrum summary of the accounts. Not long after she had sat down, Müjde rose from her seat beside Hüseyin with an ostentatious toss of her hair.

In the cacophony of the club I couldn't hear her say, "He's nuts, *ayol*!" but I could easily read her lips. She went up on the stage and began swaying her hair as she danced a dance she believed to be erotic.

"Burçak, you're not listening to me," said Hasan.

He was right. I wasn't listening. I couldn't care less whether we had used up two bottles of gin instead of three bottles of whiskey, or how many kegs of beer were sold over the weekend.

"Have you started again?" he asked, motioning with his head

toward the corner where Hüseyin sat. I wanted to slap that cynical smile off his face. Instead I tried taking a deep breath.

"Come with me," I said, grabbing hold of his arm and dragging him upstairs, into the storage room we called our office. He walked in front of me, giving the low-rise jeans slipping down his butt a yank with each step. When we reached the top of the narrow staircase, Hüseyin's head appeared at the bottom. He had come after me as if I were running away, and looked at me with an expression of concern and curiosity.

"You wait there," I said, shouting in an attempt to make my voice heard over the earsplitting music.

I ignored Hasan's giggle and made do with opening the door and fiercely shoving him into the office.

I paid no mind to his plea, "*Ay*, take it easy!" as I closed the door behind us.

"Look here, darling," I told him. When I start a sentence with "darling," and say it in that tone, he knows I mean business.

He studied my face carefully, widening his eyes. "*Ay*, you're angry, *ayol*."

"Yes, I know, don't push my buttons."

Strangely enough, Hasan too had picked up "*ayol*." Following the visit of my friend from Rio, drag queen Suzy Bumbum Ricardo, Hasan had let himself go; he'd become completely unwound. Ricardo had been in town on a dual pleasure and business trip, her itinerary consisting of sightseeing and performing at our club. The utterly feminine Ricardo and Hasan had gotten on like a house on fire. Meanwhile, Hasan had driven me mad by being at Ricardo's beck and call every minute. She hadn't had to ask for anything twice, and when she finally left, she gave her most flamboyant stage costume to Hasan as a token of remembrance. Thus this leafy green costume, which was adorned with sequins from head to toe yet nevertheless covered only a small portion of the body, hung right in front of me, in its nylon packaging. Even in the dim lighting, the sequins on it glittered.

Sharing any old gossip with Hasan and Hasan alone was enough to ensure that the masses got wind of it immediately, whether it concerned them or not. He had an extraordinary ability to disseminate such gossip at an incredible speed. He even managed to deliver it in less than twenty-four hours to people he hadn't even seen in person. And since I was aware of this splendid trait of his, my prologue ran a little longer than usual. With utmost clarity I explained to him that there was no room for joking around or sloppy gossip, and I made him repeat each important sentence after me.

"And darling, as you may have guessed by now, it could very well happen to you too," I said, to intimidate him.

Upon hearing this, Hasan put both his hands over his mouth and opened his eyes wide, but not a single sound escaped his mouth.

"You see now why Hüseyin is here?"

He nodded yes.

And then, in a hugely theatrical air reminiscent of Ricardo, he joined his hands over his heart and said in a high-pitched voice that would make countertenors green with envy: "The situation is grim!"

That sound couldn't possibly have come from the Hasan I knew. Unless, of course, he'd secretly been taking singing lessons for the last couple of months. It sounded as if he'd borrowed the shrieks of our national nightingale Sertab Erener, winner of the 2003 Eurovision Song Contest.

A knock on the door halted our conversation from reaching its conclusion. I opened the door violently, thinking it was probably Hüseyin. But instead, there in front of me stood none other than she of the colossal bushy eyebrows, Lulu. I wasn't able to rein back

in the anger I had intended for Hüseyin. Bushy-eyebrows Lulu
took a step back.

"Slow down, *abla* . . ." she said, in a deep dark bass voice, the
exact opposite of Hasan's high-pitched shriek.

"Sorry . . ." I said. I raised my eyebrows in inquiry.

"There's someone asking for you downstairs . . ."

The dull, surly, expressionless look on this girl was inexplicable. She always moved as few muscles as possible so as not to ruin
her makeup or develop wrinkles. She was like the Sphinx; sometimes she'd speak without moving her eyes, barely opening her
mouth. And she'd make fun of herself, saying, "Everyone else has
Botox done, whereas mine is natural, *abla*." I've always wondered
what she was like in bed. If it was anything like I imagined, it was
awfully hilarious. Without even batting an eyelash, or opening her
mouth too wide . . .

I must have looked blank, because she felt the need to explain.

"Hasan is here with you, and Şükrü Ağabey couldn't leave the
bar, so . . . I had to come up to let you know."

"Who is it?"

"How should I know, *abla*? He asked for you, not for me."

Although she had previously proven that she did not actually
have shit for brains, by behaving in this way from time to time she
planted a seed of doubt: Or *did* she? With those terribly blank looks,
that expressionless face, her finger-thick black eyebrows which she
refused to dye despite her corn-silk hair, her right leg bent at the
knee, and her men's size-nine feet shooting out the front and back
of her shiny silver-strapped high-heel shoes, one of which she
leaned sideways on, she looked like an imbecile.

"Don't look at me like that, *ayol*, *abla*," she said, uncomfortable
at the way I was looking her up and down. "I'm not well, you
know . . ."

To indicate she was unwell, she stroked her hair with her left hand, and then, putting her body weight on her other foot, leaned sideways on her left shoe. If she went on leaning sideways on her shoes like that, her heels wouldn't last.

"Okay. I'll be down in a minute," I said.

"Shall I wait?"

Why! Oh, why!

"No, darling," I said, emphasizing the "darling." "You go downstairs. I'll be right there."

"Okay, but what do I say to the guy?"

I summoned patience and took a deep breath.

"Tell him I'll be down . . ."

She turned around and headed down the stairs, taking each and every step with great caution. She turned again on the second step and called out to me.

"Please don't be long. I have a potential customer. I don't want to be stuck with your guy . . ."

I turned to Hasan and asked, "Deal?"

"Deal? What deal? I mean, did you tell me all this so I could warn everyone, or so I'd shut my mouth and find a place to hide?"

It was charming that he was so in tune with himself.

"You decide!" I said, as I turned around and walked out.

Strangely enough, it was that square-faced police chief Hilmi Kuloğlu. He stood in front of the bar holding a glass of whiskey on the rocks, looking around, his eyes peeled. He was wearing a poorly tailored dark suit. Not to mention the white shirt and tie.

"Hello," I said, taking utmost advantage of the fact that we were on my turf, my very own queenly realm.

"To tell you the truth, I'm rather surprised," he said, referring to the current setting.

I gave him a polite, regal smile.

"Chief ordered me to inform you should we find anything. It may not be all that important, but there are a couple of things."

He downed half the whiskey in a single gulp. He'd be footing his own bill if he failed to convey any useful information.

It became clear to me instantly: He was there to see the place. To quench his curiosity. And instead of any real dirt, he was going to hand me crumbs, just for the sake of his curiosity.

"Please, let's go upstairs to my office," I said.

He swallowed his remaining whiskey, left his glass at the bar, and tagged along behind me.

Hüseyin was at my elbow before we even reached the staircase. He had a furious expression on his face.

"Will you tell them to cut it out?" he said in a huff. "I went to the toilet to take a leak, but they wouldn't let me do it in peace. One came to watch, another fingered me . . . What the hell is going on?"

I could barely suppress my laughter. Clearly the girls were messing with him.

I motioned to Hasan from a distance, signaling that he should look out for Hüseyin.

"It's taken care of, don't worry about it," I said, patting him on the shoulder before sending him on his way.

Square-face had listened to us. Clearly in shock and unable to contain his curiosity, halfway up the stairs he asked, "Does stuff like that happen in the toilets?"

Without stopping or turning to look at him, I answered, "You can go down and see for yourself in a moment, Chief."

"No, I didn't mean it like that . . . I mean, I didn't mean it as a member of the police. Just . . . I was just curious."

"That's exactly what I meant," I replied.

I pushed open the door to the crammed storage room office and let him through. We sat down. I returned to the same seat, right opposite Ricardo's green costume.

"Yes, Chief, please, go ahead; I'm listening."

He looked at me, forcing a smile, but then soon grew self-conscious and stopped smiling; it hadn't suited his face anyway.

"Please, if you call me Hilmi instead of Chief, then I'd feel comfortable calling you Burçak."

It seemed we had on our hands yet another officer who'd learned his interviewing techniques from American television and movies.

I didn't answer him.

I began tapping on the table in front of me to let him know that I was listening.

He cleared his throat first. As if he were preparing to deliver a long sermon.

"As you might imagine, there are fingerprints everywhere in Sermet Kılıç's apartment. We are now certain he was poisoned. We're looking into what it was that poisoned him."

"*Actaea spicata*, in other words, baneberries," I said, interrupting his sermon. "The murderer sent me a message."

"You don't say! You've already found him, then!"

"No," I said, summarizing the whole story in two long sentences.

"So it's more complicated than I thought," he said finally, his voice tinged with worry.

"What else have you found besides fingerprints?"

"Um . . . there were no fingerprints on the teacup. But there is something else that's strange," he said. "We found a burned CD, without a label or anything, inside the stereo."

"What's so strange about that? Pirated CDs are available on every street corner. They've got every film you can imagine. Besides, anyone who has a CD writer can copy movies at home."

"You see, that's precisely what's so strange. There's no computer in Sermet Kılıç's apartment. Pirate copies always have labels on them so they don't get mixed up. And the CD was burned by you. That's what the root record shows."

"I don't quite understand."

"It means the CD was burned on your computer . . ."

I didn't remember burning a CD for Master Sermet. We didn't have that sort of a relationship. But preparing special CDs for people is something I would do. Still, I would have remembered if I had. Besides, I was always careful to label the CDs I burned.

"What's on the CD?" I asked curiously.

"Music," he replied, looking at me as if *that* explained everything.

"What music, *ayol*?"

"Well, classical, electronic stuff. Without lyrics . . ."

Well, that was quite helpful. Such a wealth of details to go on!

He crossed his legs and pointed his eyes to the skin that now showed under his trouser hem. I looked. There wasn't a single hair there. He couldn't possibly be waxing!

"This is all I have the courage to show at the moment," he said, giggling. "But my whole body is soft and silky!"

He displayed his joy by clapping his hands.

I felt like I was in a cheesy comedy film. The grim-faced police officer was slowly succumbing to the transvestite tendencies that secretly burned inside him!

"I do hesitate when I'm going out to work . . . I mean, if something were to happen, if I were to get hurt or have an accident and were taken to the hospital, it would be weird for them to discover me wearing women's underwear. Not only would I be discharged, but once word got out, I'd never be able to rid myself of the stigma."

He'd begun rounding his *r*'s and stressing his syllables less.

And now, yes, finally it was time for him to recount his story, which he was just dying to share. In fact, that was the one and only reason he was here, to recount all this, and to find a place where he could visit and be himself. Secretly!

He'd been married for a while but then got a divorce. It was an arranged marriage, he said. To keep his name clean. "You know how no one doubts married men, especially in small towns! Whenever my wife desired, please excuse me, *sexual intercourse*, I'd tell her I was tired, but the marriage didn't last long."

I wondered what the grounds for divorce had been. They might have gotten their divorce in a single hearing, without his wife even having to go to court, just because he was a police officer.

"I lived in Sinop before. I moved to Istanbul. I was free there. I'd walk around at home in a nightdress. I bought them in Samsun, at the Russian market. Thin straps, full lace front . . . Long . . . All the way down to the floor . . . The silky fabric. The feel of it on your skin is enough to give you the most delightful goose bumps."

I pictured a rough, synthetic, imitation Victoria's Secret. Peach or pink? I wondered.

My instincts were torn: to be or not to be a helpful, tolerant, loving, considerate person toward someone who was new, who was curious but hadn't yet come out. But did I really have the patience?

As if he could read what was going through my mind, he broke off his story and said, "If we manage to keep the fact that I'm a policeman a secret, if no one finds out, including everyone at the club, I can guarantee your safety. No one will trouble you . . ."

He had only been in Istanbul for three months but he had fallen in step with the ways of the system here pretty quick.

"We already pay people for that," I told him. "But you're welcome to come and go as you please."

"And our little secret will stay safe, right? No little birdie will go telling Selçuk Tayanç . . ."

There it was, his little pinkie erect as he spoke.

"We don't know the profession of each and every customer that comes here. It's none of our business," I told him while grinning and adopting a professional tone befitting a partner of the establishment.

Oh, those hands! Flapping around like butterfly wings.

"Well, not exactly like a customer, though . . ."

What? Did he want to jump straight to cross-dressing?

"If I could keep some of my stuff here . . ."

This was too much, even for me.

"Let's take this slow. Just have a look around tonight . . . And we'll talk again."

"If you'd introduce me as Türkanş . . ."

Whoa! Okay, everyone was free to choose their own idol, use whatever name their heart desired, but no matter how far one forced the art of makeup, square-face Hilmi would never make a Türkan Şoray, the legendary beauty of Turkish film. I bit my hand to keep myself from laughing out loud.

He was already prancing jauntily as he descended the stairs. Following a whopping ten-minute-long confession and soul-baring session, the dull police chief from Homicide had disappeared, giving way to a coquettish gargoyle. It was annoying how he hysterically cried, *"Ay! ay!"* with every step. How could one be so mindless, trusting me like that and bursting out of the closet after hardly exchanging more than two words?

"Before I forget," I said, reminding him of his job and his real reason for being here, "I want a copy of that CD."

Since I was the one who had recorded it and didn't remember, I was curious to find out what was on it. Could it have been the clue the psycho killer had mentioned and scolded me for not paying attention to?

He stopped with the hysterical *ay-ay's* immediately.

I introduced Türkanş first to Hasan, and then to Hüseyin, who was waiting for me with panic-stricken eyes. After so many years of living cheek by jowl with the girls, Hasan had grown accustomed to their ways, and so he didn't react to the name. Hüseyin, though, was a different story; he jumped at it.

"Türkanş? What kind of a name is that? Bloody hell, never heard that one before . . ."

Even though Türkanş was flirting and prancing, she was still in her dark suit and wearing a tie.

Türkanş Hilmi stared at every man with ravenous passion and at every girl with envy. Despite Hüseyin's silent objections and baf-flement, I sat Türkanş next to him. Türkanş had already started wiggling his hips to the rhythm of the music.

A giant exhalation of cigarette smoke attacked the nape of my neck. I turned around, infuriated.

"Abla, who is this trashy queen?" Dump Truck Beyza asked, tapping my shoulder with her long cigarette holder.

"Türkanş," I said.

The cigarette holder fell from her mouth. I had to repeat it again slowly to make sure she hadn't misunderstood. She started kicking and stomping in a laughing fit and almost fell off the ban-quette.

It seemed Officer Hilmi was going to find fame on his first night out, solely on account of his name.

10.

Hüseyin had stayed in the guest room, of course. He slept like a log thanks to the free drinks he'd downed one after the other all night. I cracked the door open to look at him. He was sleeping on his back like a baby, with his two arms stretched up beside his head. According to character analysis, those with inner peace slept in such comfortable positions. His cowardly behavior the previous evening was hardly a sign of inner peace, so I guessed he must have found it during the night.

He could go on sleeping, or I could wake him up. I'd had a restless night, and for him to be sleeping so peacefully was simply annoying. I voted for the second option. I reminded him of the psycho killer so he'd come to his senses more quickly. He jumped out of bed.

When one has lived alone for such a long time, the presence of a second person in the house can be a nuisance. And indeed Hüseyin, who kept getting in my way, was getting on my nerves.

"Why don't you join me . . . ?" he shouted from the bathroom a couple of times as he showered. He'd gotten his sleep, overcome his fear, and was clearly horny again. I completely ignored him.

I could hardly believe it but there were no messages on my answering machine. Not one person, not even our psycho, had called.

After assigning Hüseyin the task of preparing a grand breakfast, I headed straight for the computer. There was nothing new there either. Cleaning up the mess the psycho had made on my Web site was on my to-do list. And I would, once I'd given the situation some thought. But it wasn't something I could do right then.

There were smells coming from the kitchen: toast and omelet. It seemed Hüseyin was toiling hard, showing off all his talents in a bid to curry favor.

The phone rang.

It was Ponpon. Her voice was completely devoid of its usual joyful chirp.

"Ayolcuğum, how about canceling the call forwarding? . . . I didn't sleep a wink all night because of all your calls."

I had completely forgotten I had forwarded my landline phone to Ponpon's. If I missed or wasn't able to take them, calls were automatically directed to her phone. Now I knew why there weren't any messages on my answering machine.

"Sorry, Ponpon, dear," I said. "I totally forgot. I'm not used to using that service, it totally escaped me. I'll fix it straightaway."

"You'll never guess what happened to me," she said, turning on the waterworks with the second word.

If a threatening call had come through, Ponpon would be devastated. For Ponpon, who was inclined to perceive the most minute of matters as global disasters, a threat made directly to her person was the worst thing that could happen.

"That witch Sofya called," she said.

It wasn't such a great calamity after all. Okay, no one in our community really liked Sofya, but they sure did respect her. With her posh, luxurious lifestyle, founts of money that never ran dry, sordid connections, the parties she threw which everyone was always dying to be invited to, and her endless plastic surgery operations, Sofya was a true legend among us. The fact that she despised and constantly humiliated everyone was the reason why no one liked her.

"I see," I said, to prompt her.

She continued, sobbing.

"I thought she was calling me. I kindly asked her how she was doing and everything. Well, of course, she didn't know she was calling me. She thought she was calling you. She ordered me to hand the phone to you immediately. And because I didn't understand what she meant exactly, she said to me, 'I don't have any business to address with you, you slut.'"

There it was, that fatal word. The word "slut" had left Ponpon devastated. Even having to repeat it made her wail.

"Sweetie, *ayol*, don't you know that you're not? Why care about what she says? Plus, you know Sofya. She speaks without thinking."

The whining, wailing hysterical breakdown on the other end continued.

"But . . . but . . . if that's what she thinks of me, without thinking . . . Sss-lut . . . *Ayol*, you wouldn't even say that in a fight. What did I ever do to her? What ill have I ever done her?

She had clearly given it a lot of thought before calling me. There was no point in raking up the past and reminding her of all the things they had done to each other, both openly and secretly. It was common knowledge among the girls that there had been a three-way power struggle happening for some time—among Sofya, Ponpon, and me! Kindhearted Ponpon is sweet, people love her. Whereas they fear and dread Sofya. They dread what might befall them if they don't do as she says. As for me, the youngest candidate vying for power, I attribute my own position within this triangle to my status as a club owner. The girls do always compliment me on my intelligence and tell me how much they admire my success as a sleuth and as a businessperson. I am friends with

Ponpon. But not with Sofya. Despite Sofya's mischievous minions, most of the girls are on our side and the joining of my and Ponpon's forces has always proven victorious.

At present, we were even. And even if Sofya were to forge ahead a point, we'd always get even.

"And lots and lots of other calls . . . *Ayolcuğum*, you have so many people calling you. I don't get this many calls in a week. I swear, I feel like your secretary. Do you have a pen and paper? The list is long, and some of the messages are cryptic, so only you'll understand them . . . I'm ready when you are."

Sofya wanted me to contact her. It was an emergency. She had called twice, and called Ponpon a slut twice.

My boss, the moneylender Alı, was also expecting my call.

Kemal Barutçu, a.k.a. Jihad2000, had left the cryptic message, "When?" Never in this lifetime.

Andelip Turhan had said that I was in her cards and that she needed to see me.

Gül—my ticket to see the handsome Bahadır—had asked me to call when I had the time.

"Okay? You got that all written down?"

I answered in the affirmative.

"Listen here, *ayolcuğum*, is Andelip Turhan that famous tarot reader? The one that goes around dressed all weird?"

When I last saw her she was wearing a man's briefs over her head instead of a beret, I wanted to tell her; but I didn't.

"Yes."

"Then I'm certainly coming with you when you go to see her. I've been wanting to go for ages. You know how keen I am on fortune-telling."

Everyone knew how Ponpon wandered from one fortune-teller to the next. And not just those in Istanbul; she'd jump on the plane and go to Antalya for a day, to visit the fortune-teller Hülya for a single reading, or call Meto in Trabzon for a session over the phone.

"Fine," I said.

I had a long day ahead of me with Hüseyin. It would be a good idea to start planning. I didn't want to sit at home with him all day and rot in front of the television switching from this DVD to that channel and vice versa.

I was going to pop into the office sometime during the day. And I thought it would be amusing for Hüseyin.

I called Sofya straight after breakfast. Of course the answering machine came on. "Please tell me who you are and why you are calling, so I can decide whether or not to pick up the phone and speak to you. Thank you," it said. The nerve!

She picked up the phone just as I was saying my name.

"I've been expecting your call," she said scoldingly.

"Well, here I am," I replied. "Long time no see. How have you been?"

The truth was, our last encounter had been far from lovely.

"Fabulous! As always!"

The word "understatement" did not exist in the vocabulary of Sofya, that marvelous specimen of femininity.

"What's up with you forwarding your phone calls to Ponpon's? What adorable bonding . . . Yuck!"

I really didn't have the energy for a second dose; this time listening to Sofya complaining about Ponpon.

"You called me?" I said, in my most professional, in other words dull and numb, tone of voice.

One should never reveal any soft spots to Sofya. She'd nail you in the Achilles the first chance she got.

"There are people who want to see you."

If she was intending to pimp me out again, she was in for a disappointment. She couldn't use me the same way she did most of the girls; pimping them to celebrities at precious prices, getting them sucked into weird prostitution networks. I had fallen for that trick once in the past, and had learned my lesson. If there was anyone who fancied me since I'd appeared on TV and wanted to sleep with me, well, I had no intention whatsoever of reciprocating. No way would I tolerate being with someone whose understanding of sports was watching soccer on TV, who had saggy skin, a fat belly, a bald head, and greasy hands he'd move across my body, imagining himself to be the most attractive man on earth as his wheezing lungs breathed air all over me. I now chose my partners myself, according to my own taste. I never expect to find someone like John Pruitt, but I do prefer men who are clean-cut, smell fresh, and show concern for my feelings as well as their own pleasure. No matter the price she named, my answer was going to be no. Then again, what would be the harm in negotiating a sum? Just like there was a price for everyone, there was quite naturally one for me. I immediately began imagining astronomical sums and all the things I could do with the money.

"I don't do that anymore," I said. "It's been years . . ."

She let out an artificial hoot of laughter. How did she manage to be so pretentious?

"Don't be ridiculous!" she said, abruptly cutting her laughter short. "Who would want you when there are so many young chicks available? To think that they'd pay for it . . ."

She sure knew how to hit a gal where it hurts. And so I ceased counting dollars in my head and dreaming of the around the world tours I might embark upon.

"These people are important . . . I can't give you their names on the phone . . ."

Oh, how she loved being mysterious.

"So why do they want to see me?" I asked.

"You're after something, apparently . . . So Hasan said . . . They have some information for you . . ."

The wheel had started turning. Hasan had told everyone, the news had spread fast, and now some mysterious people wanted to share information with me. Seeing as they were somehow connected to Sofya, these very important people whose names were to be kept secret had to be the Mafia.

"They can call me . . ." I said. "Give them my number."

"*Ayol*, stop being so childish! These people don't order takeout on the phone. It has to be face-to-face . . ."

"So?"

"I've been told to arrange a rendezvous for you."

So she took orders too.

"I don't know if I can arrange it right away. These people are always busy. I'll let you know as soon as I set it up. Give me your mobile."

What would important people want with me? If the people in question were the types engaged in dark, sordid dealings, the types Sofya was prone to be involved with herself, then I'd really rather prefer to keep my distance. I didn't owe them anything, they didn't owe me anything. And I'd rather keep it that way, but I knew they had eyes and ears everywhere. Perhaps they did have information for me.

I still had to call Alı, Andelip, and Gül back. I was going to the office anyway. I'd call them later.

11.

"**Y**ou're not going to follow me around all day, are you?" I asked him. "That'll really suck, for the both of us."

Hüseyin was slouched in front of the television, zapping through channels.

"I don't mind," he said.

"What?"

"Sucking, I wouldn't mind. In fact, we could replace that *s* with an *f.*"

It was a stupid joke. He was the only one to laugh.

"What?" he said. "What else am I supposed to do? I'm only safe if I stay with you!"

He'd made breakfast but hadn't set about cleaning up. The kitchen where he'd made himself an omelet looked like it had been hit by a bomb. He'd used dozens of bowls, cups, and saucers to make a single omelet and then left them just sitting there.

Luckily, Satı was coming the next day. I can never stay at home when there's cleaning. Not only does the sound of the vacuum cleaner make my hair stand on end, but I get tense, feeling that Satı is following me around no matter where I hide.

We received a text message from our psycho on my mobile saying, "Don't mess around. I'm waiting for you," whereby he kindly reminded us of his existence. What did he expect me to do? Walk around in the streets with a magnifying glass in my hand like Sherlock Holmes? I hadn't yet found a single clue. Perhaps if Türkanş Hilmi brought me the CD tonight, I might have something. The television channels had already forgotten all about Süheyl, which was now yesterday's news. I had no hope of finding anything from that lead anyway. The police would handle it much more effectively using their own sources.

Hüseyin and I went to the office. He had promised to sit quietly no matter how bored he got. He was going to play games on the computer.

"We haven't seen you around for a while, sir," our secretary Figen greeted me. She eyed Hüseyin up and down, her gaze fixed on him; no shame at all! She was wondering what to make of us arriving together.

I confessed to save her the trouble.

"My chauffeur."

Hüseyin's eyes widened in objection.

"Open a game for him in a window. He's going to wait for me all day," I told her. God only knows what, as an experienced employee, she'd tell Hüseyin behind my back.

And with that, I barged into Alı's office.

He was playing games on his computer too.

He began showering me with compliments immediately. This meant there was something important, something I'd be expected to do as a favor that would remain unreturned. Alı would never think of complimenting someone without an ulterior motive.

"Come out with it, *ayol*," I said. "Seriously, I'm not in the mood."

"Okay, you go first, then," he said.

Offering to listen to me first was a sign that the request in question was going to be a difficult task.

In the hopes that he might change his mind about asking me for a favor if he knew the current situation I was in—so that I wouldn't have to have *that* on my hands too—I told him all about the threats, about Master Sermet's death, and finally, about Hüseyin.

"He's outside, playing games on the computer next to Figen," I said, giving him the latest update.

He shook his head thoughtfully.

He was musing on whether, given the circumstances, he still had the nerve to ask of me whatever it was he wanted.

"Come on, now it's your turn," I said. "What is it you want?"

"Well, it's really not that urgent, but it is important . . ."

The company Mare T. Docile, which we'd done work for recently, wanted their Web site updated. Free of charge.

It really wasn't such a big deal. If they were to send me all the documents, I could get it done in half a day.

"And to increase their Web site security."

Now, expecting that for free too was a big no-no. That was how we were planning to make the real money.

"But just think about it, these guys have sent a lot of work our way. We were able to get into the maritime transport sector thanks to their references."

He was right.

"Look, I'll do the job, but I need to postpone it for now. Let me go on their Web site and hack it a little first, so they realize why they need security, then they'll have to pay for it."

"No, man. Let's not do it that way this time. Let's do something clean for once."

Something was up with Alı. This dialogue would normally be reversed. He was the one obsessed with money. The yuppie lifestyle he led demanded it. He had to earn good money. "So what are you going to do for me in return?"

He looked into my eyes to gauge how serious I was. I was serious. He let out a forced laugh.

"Whatever you want," he said. "You name it and I promise to give it to you."

He thought that if he laughed it off, the promise he had just given would be invalidated.

"A week in Rio!" I said, without hesitation. That was the first thing I could think of. Being among cheerful, easygoing people; the sun, the ocean, the beaches filled with men with bodies that looked just like Greek and Roman statues . . . That would be enough to help me forget pretty much everything.

"That would cost a fortune!" he said immediately, switching on the calculator in his head.

"Not really," I said. "Plus, you just promised . . ."

As I went into my own office I asked Figen to make me a cup of Turkish coffee, without sugar. We had bought a new coffee machine that made superb Turkish coffee without fuss in less than two minutes.

"And you, you can get up and help yourself to whatever you want," I told Hüseyin. "There's fruit juice, Coke, and other stuff inside, in the kitchen."

"I'd like a cup of coffee too. With sugar, if that's okay," he told Figen, not missing a beat.

Figen turned to me, trying to understand if she should or shouldn't be serving him. Who was higher in rank? A driver or a secretary? But Hüseyin was a guest. I nodded my head yes. I was sure Figen felt humiliated. I'd call her to my office and explain the situation when I had the time.

My desk was buried under a mountain of mail. Magazines I was subscribed to, bills, advertisements . . . a gigantic mountain. I quickly separated out what could be thrown away. I put the magazines to one side. There was a card from my darling Nimet Hanoğlu. Her husband had first been accused of killing a gigolo and then was murdered himself. Nimet and I had met while trying to track down his murderer and had become fast friends. I had let her down, using work as an excuse, so that she ended up having to go by herself on the trip to Croatia that we had originally planned to take together. The postcard was a fairy-tale scene of a place called Primosten. It was a tear-shaped island in the Adriatic, with a narrow little road connecting it to the mainland. "Wish you were here," it said. "A pearl beach, marvelous seafood, juvenile lads, all of whom resemble the young Franco Nero, graceful girls the likes of Milla Jovovich. And at sunset, I play 'Stabat Mater' on a CD. It's a dream come true!" She knew I adored Franco Nero's youth; and our taste for Pergolesi's "Stabat Mater" was something we had in common.

There was one personal envelope. And inside, a single-line note. It was from my psycho!

In the middle of a huge blank page it said, "I know this place."

He had typed it up on a computer.

I quickly looked at the envelope. It had been posted from the post office in Taksim two days ago. I never knew the Turkish post could be so prompt.

I rushed outside, the envelope in my hand. I almost bumped straight into Figen, who was carrying my coffee.

"When did this arrive?" I asked.

My voice came out a bit too loud and tense.

Puzzled, Figen looked first at me, and then at the envelope. She placed the tray she was holding on my desk and said, "If you'll excuse me," as she pulled the envelope out of my hand; she then studied it, turning it over and over again.

"I don't know," she said. "The postman probably brought it."

I was expecting a much more helpful reply after all of that scrutinizing.

Having heard me, Alı had come out of his room and was trying to make sense of what was going on.

I took the letter to him.

"There you go!" I said. "He knows this place too."

Hüseyin and Alı buried their heads in the letter.

The only person who didn't understand what was going on, who had no clue about who it was that knew this place, and why their knowing caused such a fuss, was Figen.

"Who does?" she asked hesitantly.

The game Hüseyin had left unattended started beeping. He was dead.

"Someone tell Figen. I'm fed up with telling the same story over and over again," I said.

I was sure they were both eager to tell her.

I spent the whole day dealing with trivial matters. Not only was I incapable of getting anything done, but my thoughts were entirely preoccupied with the psycho. I wondered what he was like. Was he young or old? Was he an ignorant conservative, or a bully who had developed these skills later on in life? Or a commando who had become addicted to murder while he served in the military in southeastern Turkey? An ex–political militant? Or someone who simply suffered from dementia? No doubt he would turn out to be someone completely ordinary, someone I wouldn't stop to look at twice if I were to see him on the street.

Alı took us out for dinner, to an Italian restaurant that had just recently opened. He had tried the place before and had left satisfied. He chose our food for us. I didn't join in the wine, but he and Hüseyin had a bottle of red Antik Special Kav. Hüseyin's appetite was huge. I made do with nibbling at what was placed in front of me.

The club was quiet that evening. I think there was a national soccer match. We had very few customers on such nights, when everyone turned into pro soccer fanatics. Even among the girls there are plenty who are keen on soccer and who follow the league closely. They never miss a match—and, incredibly, the only moment they're interested in isn't the end of the game when soccer players take their tops off to display their muscular naked bodies all sweaty and shining.

Hüseyin, who by now felt quite at home, was even more relaxed thanks to the wine he had drunk. He drank less at the club. I'd seen him helping Şükrü behind the bar at one point. He was learning how to mix cocktails. Judging by their laughter and giggles, they seemed to be getting along just fine.

I sulked all night. I didn't even dance. I was bloated from the Virgin Marys I had gulped down one after the other.

I had hoped Officer Türkanş would show up at the club, but he didn't. And thus, neither did the CD he said I had burned. I'd have to call Selçuk the next day.

12.

Hüseyin, who had gotten plenty of sleep the night before, woke up at the crack of dawn. I hated getting out of bed without having gotten enough sleep, walking around like a zombie all day with bags under my eyes. I shouted from where I lay.

"Either sit quietly until noon or go back to sleep! No television, no music!"

He responded with a noisy flush of the toilet. There you have it, we were already getting a little too close for comfort!

He was holding me responsible for the voluntary imprisonment he himself had chosen, and kept calculating the loss he would incur by serving only me until the psycho killer got caught. Because he was afraid to go out on his own, our security guard Cüneyt had had to accompany him home the previous night to pick up his toothbrush, shaving kit, and some clean clothes.

Okay, he hadn't turned the television or radio on, but the racket he was making in the kitchen pretty much made up for it. Whatever it was he was looking for, he kept opening and closing each and every kitchen cupboard door. He shook the utensils drawer at least twice. Finally there was silence, followed by the creaking of my bedroom door. My thick curtains were drawn, my room was dark. He whispered, as if speaking in a low tone would be less likely to disturb my sleep.

"Where's the sugar?"

"There is none!" I said. "Whatever you're having, have it without sugar! And don't wake me . . ."

He murmured to himself as he shut the door. I pretended not to notice.

I wanted a stylish dream to carry me away, freeing me, even if only briefly, from this game of stress and suspense that I had been placed smack-bang in the middle of, from the nightmare of people being hunted down. I would like both my porn idol, Colt Studios superstar John Pruitt, and Audrey Hepburn to play the leading roles together. Well, all right, should Audrey not be available, I could take over her role. In one of her costumes from *My Fair Lady*, say the one she was wearing in the ballroom scene or at the Ascot Racecourse. There was no need for Rex Harrison. We could do without him. John Pruitt and I would be enough to make this a masterpiece. We could meet in the lush green countryside, on a bright sunny day. Or on a looong beach where tiny gentle waves licked the shore, swoosh, swoosh . . .

I was just getting into the groove, ready to doze off into this romantic and pornographic dream I had commissioned, when there was a second knock on the door. I was about to lose my temper now.

He was holding a piece of paper in his hand. And his face looked shattered.

"My mother gave me this when I was packing my stuff the other day. I just remembered and took a look. The bastard has been to my house. He gave this to her . . ."

So long, John Pruitt! The searing pain that surged through my head at that moment had nothing to do with the way I suddenly sprang up in bed.

"Give it here."

It was a single-page note, typed up on a computer and printed on legal-size paper.

I read it four times while Hüseyin pulled open the curtains.
It was short enough, anyway.

> Hello Hüseyin Talip Kozalak,
> It was pretty easy finding your home.
> Where are you going to run to?
> There's nowhere to hide.
> Wait for me.
> I'm watching you.

It was short, simple, and effective. It made one's blood run cold.
There was no name, signature, or pseudonym. Nor a date or time.
And on the envelope was only Hüseyin's name, and two red
stamps, one that read "Confidential" and the other "Urgent." It had
been delivered by hand. Hüseyin looked even more terrified in the
light.

"If he's found my apartment, he wouldn't go do anything to my
parents, would he?"

"I'm the one he wants," I said, hoping to console him.

I admitted to myself that we were up against a real psycho who
was temperamental and unpredictable and that, should he feel like
it, might well target Hüseyin's mom, dad, his whole extended family. In fact, he could even blow up the whole neighborhood if he felt
like it.

"What do we do now?"

I didn't know. My head felt like a balloon. And it hurt.

"I've barely woken up. I'll think of something in a minute," I
said, as I walked to the shower.

"Shall I tell them?"

"No!" I shouted as I turned on the water. "Not yet."

There was no point in making people who had no knowledge
of what was going on panic. Here, solely as a result of panic, was

Hüseyin, living in my home with refugee status. I had neither room nor patience for more refugees.

And I couldn't even open my eyes properly.

With this little sleep, I was certain to spend the rest of the day feeling an utter mess.

I wanted a spark of inspiration, or a comprehensive revelation to come to me in the shower.

Neither did.

When I came out of the shower, Hüseyin was kneeling down in the corridor, weeping and wailing over the threatening message he held in his hand.

"Don't panic! Don't panic!" I said, kneeling down next to him and trying to shake him out of his state.

He was acting like a stupid kid. Fear wouldn't get us anywhere. The best thing we could do was to stay calm.

He wiped his eyes with the back of his fists. His eyes were red.

"I'm just upset . . . That's why . . ." he said, pushing my arm away.

His manhood had been severely wounded in the last twenty-four hours. There was no need to be strong for me right now. He was right to be afraid, frustrated, and to cry. God knows what I would have done if I were him.

"My mom's alone at home, my dad's alone at the shop . . . If something were to happen to them . . . My mom opens the door to everyone without even asking who it is. Anyone can go in the shop . . . He's just an ironmonger. If the bastard were to pick up an adze and hit him over the head . . . that would be it!"

He cried as if these scenarios that had come to his mind had already come to pass. Tears were streaming down his cheeks.

"Calm down!" I said, raising my voice.

He opened his eyes wide and looked at me, as if he were seeing me for the first time in his life.

"Let's first get a grip on what's going on," I said, trying to be as calm as I possibly could. "Maybe this letter is a clue. Your mom might remember who brought it . . . If she could describe him, we'd know who we're looking for."

He kept on staring at me, sniffling. His eyes were blank. They looked lighter in color from all his crying. They shone.

"But first I need a cup of coffee!"

"But—"

I placed my hand over his mouth without waiting for him to finish. My hand was smeared in saliva and tears.

"We've waited long enough already, another hour won't matter," I said. "Plus, he's after me. He has nothing against you, or your parents. Capiche?"

I wiped my hand on my bathrobe. I would have to remind Satı to wash it.

As a matter of fact, it really wasn't clear who or what the psycho was after. He did whatever he felt like doing.

13

Hüseyin lived in the back part of Çağlayan. With a view of the
Golden Horn. It looked onto what was left of the legendary Sad-
abad District, that fairy-tale citadel of history books. The apartment was in a multistory building, and even though it was fairly
new, it already looked worn down because of the low-quality construction materials used to build it. Two rows consisting of six
nine-story blocks, identical except for their different colors.

There were plenty of parking spaces, since there weren't very
many cars around. Kids were playing soccer in the parking lot. As
part of so-called environmental planning, four young pine trees half
my height had been jammed into the tiny space between the blocks.

The Kozalaks' apartment was on the seventh floor of Block C.
There were four apartments on every floor.

Before we left my place, Hüseyin had strictly cautioned me to
behave properly and take great care not to reveal the "situation" to
his mother. The "situation," it seemed, was me!

"Careful with your arms and hands. And don't say *ayol*."

He had decided on what I should wear, choosing jeans, a tat-
tered cotton tracksuit top I only wore to bed when alone on cold
nights, and trainers. I wasn't even allowed to put on lip balm.

"The more ragged you look, the better. Men in our neighborhood shave once every three days."

He always had a nice smooth, close shave, reeked of deodorant, and splattered himself with aftershave lotion.

"They wouldn't suspect me. I don't bounce and wriggle when I walk."

I could be a wild stallion when need be. Once, when he had gotten a little too feisty while hitting on me, I pulled an aikido number and knocked some sense into him, right in the middle of the street. He was so embarrassed he couldn't bring himself to come to the taxi stand for days. So this was what he thought of me. Once everything was sorted out, and Hüseyin had calmed down and become his usual self again, I'd make him pay for this.

Mrs. Kozalak was a little shorter and slimmer than her son Hüseyin. Otherwise, she was the spitting image of her son. The same facial features, the same eyes . . . She was a cheerful, radiant woman. One of those people who are perfectly content to settle for the simple pleasures in life. So long as her son and husband enjoyed their supper, there was no fighting at home and no hard feelings with the neighbors, they had enough money to get them through the week, and she didn't have to dig into her wedding chest and sacrifice a gold bracelet because business was bad, and if, to top it all off, her favorite program was on that night, she'd be as happy as a cricket in midsummer.

She gave Hüseyin a loving cuddle. Her son had been absent from his bed for two nights, yet she caressed him with such longing, it was as if he'd just gotten back from a trip to Timbuktu.

She forced me to kiss her hand and place it on my forehead as tradition dictated. Since I was visiting her sweet nest, with flowerpots outside every window, I had to abide by its rules.

Her damp hands, which she dried on her skirt as she opened the door, had a culinary smell to them; so did the whole apartment—a smell of aromatic vegetables, herbs, all sorts of spices, onions, and garlic, which had seeped into the walls over the years. In homes like this, there was always sure to be a pot boiling on the stove. Either jam was being prepared for the coming season, or chickpeas or beans were being boiled, or bone marrow broth was brewing . . .

Following Hüseyin's example, I took off my shoes. If I had known, I would have worn loafers, which are easier to take off and put back on, instead of laced trainers.

His mother was one of those people who loved treating her guests, who couldn't sleep at night if she hadn't filled up their tummies until they burst.

We'd barely made it through the door before she started with the offerings: "Let me make you some *mantı* dumplings. They'll be ready in a jiffy . . ."

That's why she was so skinny. She never stopped, not for a second. She jumped about like a flea.

Once we had successfully managed to bypass the *mantı*, having joined forces to do so, she promptly moved on to the next item on offer: *gözlemes*. She'd roll them out in seconds. She had a gas-fired *saj*; it would be ready in less than five minutes. In other words, Mrs. Kozalak had no intention of leaving the kitchen.

"And I'll froth up some *ayran* to go with it. Ice-cold!"

I'd only had coffee before leaving home. The woman wouldn't stop talking about food, and I was beginning to feel hungry.

"No, thank you," I said. "I'm really full already."

After all, we were there for a totally different reason.

But then Hüseyin tempted both his mother and my stomach: "My mom's *gözlemes* are really something . . ."

"Whenever the neighbor ladies and I have our get-togethers, they always specially request my *gözlemes*," she chimed in. "Before they come over, they tell me, 'Mrs. Kozalak, just make *gözlemes* for us, nothing else.' That's how famous and delicious my *gözlemes* are."

Mrs. Kozalak wasn't the type of woman to send the neighbor ladies and their shrieking children off after having offered them merely one single dish. She'd be racked with guilt if she hadn't spent two days in the kitchen prior to their visit, making cakes, biscuits, *poğaças*, and *böreks*.

"I have both potato filling and *lor* cheese filling ready . . . Which would you prefer? Hüseyin likes his with potatoes. Shall I make you one of each, son?"

Hüseyin was miming behind his mother, trying to tell me something I couldn't understand.

"Okay," I said, without knowing what I had agreed to.

"While I roll out the dough, Hüseyin can run to the corner shop and buy some fresh yogurt. Right, son?"

Hüseyin was petrified by the idea of having to go outside, to the shop and back, on his own. He turned pale.

"We don't want *ayran*, Mom. We'll have tea instead," he said.

"No, no, no, son. I just promised our guest I'd froth some up . . ."

And I was the guest who had been promised *ayran*. I felt the need to intervene to keep the matter from getting out of hand.

"I don't want *ayran* either!"

Mrs. Kozalak stood motionless, as if betrayed, and then turned to look first at her son, and then at me. We had ruined the menu she had concocted in her head. She narrowed her eyes.

"But that's how it's served . . ." she said, in a final effort. "*I'll* have some, even if *you* don't."

I looked at Hüseyin. He was looking at me helplessly.

"Look, Mrs. Kozalak," I said. "We're actually here because of a very important matter. It's a long, quite complicated story, but suffice it to say that there has been a misunderstanding, and things might get unpleasant if we don't resolve it. Do you remember the person who delivered the envelope for you to give to Hüseyin the other day? We need to find that person."

I had managed to explain everything in one breath, without flashing any life-threatening signals or giving anything away. I was proud of myself.

Mrs. Kozalak paused. Of course, it took her some time to stop thinking about the topic of food and focus on the question I had asked.

"It was Melek," she said.

"Who's Melek?" I said.

I looked at Hüseyin out of the corner of my eye, wondering if he knew Melek.

"The little girl who lives downstairs. She's a good girl, God bless her. And her mother is such a lovely lady. She dresses her as clean as a penny every day; irons her uniform, plaits her hair tightly, with a starched white ribbon *this big* in her hair . . . But she's terribly ugly, that girl! If she doesn't change by the time she grows up, she'll never find herself a husband," Mrs. Kozalak continued.

The hilarity! I could have collapsed right then and there with laughter.

I would have to memorize the whole thing, verbatim, and repeat it to Ponpon. She'd laugh for days, and do imitations for everyone.

Instead of coming to the door himself, our psycho had had the little girl make his delivery for him. It was a clever trick, but kids have sharp memories. And ugly girls have especially sharp memories when it comes to men. If he had squeezed in a smile with his request, Melek would already be fantasizing about finding him when she grew up and making him her catch.

"Where does she live?" I asked. "We might as well go and speak to her while you're making the *gözlemes* . . ."

The fact that she would be reunited with her kitchen, the idea of feeding her son and his slovenly looking friend, made Kevser Kozalak's eyes light up.

"Number seventeen," she said. "Fifth floor. But she's probably at school now . . ."

Right, little girls did go to school.

"She'll be back in the afternoon," she added. "Her granny would probably be at home. She smokes by the window all day. Her mom and dad both work . . ."

"What school does she go to?" I asked.

"Well, now, that I wouldn't know," she answered. "It's a primary school, that's all I know . . ."

I quickly abandoned the bright idea of going to Melek's school and interrogating her during playtime. If someone were to see or hear, they'd think we were pedophiles and probably try to stone us to death.

"Go on, you boys watch some TV. There are some good shows on this time of the day. I'll whip up the *gözlemes.*"

At that time of day, the only things on TV are cooking programs. That's what she must have meant by "good shows."

Hüseyin and I sat opposite each other, tense and nervous. Television was a good idea; it broke the silence. Cooking program or not.

We were going to have to wait for the *gözlemes* anyway.

Mrs. Kozalak stuck her head out of her kitchen, her sacred sanctuary, and asked, "Would you like chili in your potato mix, son?"

"I'd love it," I answered.

Appetizing smells were already coming from the kitchen.

My mobile rang.

That marvelous and mysterious specimen of womanhood Sofya was telling me to turn on the news. "I'll call you back later."

And she hung up.

I grabbed the remote out of Hüseyin's hand and switched to a news channel. The news Sofya was talking about was written at the bottom of the screen: "Hit man who shot Süheyl Arkın has been arrested." The stock exchange news was on the main screen, so this bit of news was just a strip of words at the bottom, without any images. I quickly tried the other channels. They didn't mention it on Süheyl's channel, not even in the updates running at the bottom of the screen.

Both Hüseyin and I felt an overwhelming sense of relief. So our psycho had been caught!

The *gözlemes* really were delicious. With their crispy outsides and the spicy potato mix inside, they simply melted in your mouth. Like all good housewives, Kevser Kozalak had used plenty of butter, in complete disregard of such inconveniences as cholesterol, lipid levels, and atherosclerosis.

Thanking her just once hadn't sufficed. At every bite again and again she asked, "How'd you find it, son? You like it? Shall I make you another one? Is it cooked enough? Well, I had to rush it . . ." all the while expecting further compliments.

Sofya called again before I had started eating my second *gözleme*. "Hello," I said with some difficulty as I chewed a huge bite.

"Bon appétit," she said, as if I were up to no good just then. "You're to be at Aziz Bey Restaurant at three p.m. today."

I swallowed what was in my mouth even though I hadn't yet finished chewing it, and said, "But they've got him."

"Don't be such a child!" she said. This was her favorite expression of belittlement. "He's just a hit man . . . Don't forget, Aziz Bey Restaurant at three p.m. They'll explain it to you."

That was it.

At Aziz Bey Restaurant, some shady people were probably going to deliver some surprising explanations. And then I would have to be filled with gratitude toward Sofya. If I had been in a more appropriate setting, I would have called her back, but I couldn't just then, not with the queen of the kitchen circling about.

What was I going to say to Hüseyin? The dimwit was over the

moon thinking he was safe now. Once his tummy got full, he'd get horny and even try to feel me up on the way back. Well, would I prefer telling him the truth and being stuck with him again? But what if the guy who'd been caught really was just a hit man, and the psycho loitering the streets did away with Hüseyin in the meantime? How would I cope with my guilty conscience if that happened? I'd have to go on the Hajj, make vows, and, if worse came to the worst, go bathe in the filthy waters of the River Ganges for months to cleanse myself.

When Mrs. Kozalak went into the kitchen to refill our tea glasses, I took the opportunity to get Hüseyin up to speed.

He spat out the bite in his mouth without chewing it. And then he pushed away the *gözleme* plate, with half the *gözleme* still on it.

14.

*A*ziz Bey Restaurant, one of Istanbul's oldest, ranks right up there with such long-standing establishments as Pandeli in the Egyptian Bazaar, Borsa in Sirkeci, and Hacı Salih and Rejans in Beyoğlu. It hasn't been long since they closed down their century-old venue in Karaköy and moved to the business district of Fourth Levent. I was rather fond of their old place. It was dignified, with high, awe-inspiring ceilings. As soon as you set foot through the door, staring at you from the opposite wall, its frame revamped again and again over the years to keep up with the fashion trends of each passing era, had been a gigantic, hand-colored portrait of the founder, the apparently cross-eyed Aziz Bey, replete with Charlie Chaplin mustache.

The place was famous for its Ottoman cuisine. Their olive-oil dishes were especially spectacular. All the waiters were as old as fossils and worldly wise. They'd speak in low tones, suggesting dishes to those they knew, while regulars went so far as to leave their selection entirely to them.

In their new location, it was out with the old and in with the new. And I'm not only talking about the décor, but also the entire waitstaff, whose retirement ages had long since come and gone. Furnishings consisted primarily of light cherrywood and unpolished steel, which lent the place a cold atmosphere. The jars of food that used to be lined up around the walls of the restaurant, and which helped to whet clients' appetites, had been removed, and now only samples were displayed next to the cash register for those who might wish to purchase them. Jam had been added to the repertoire, with colorful ribbons tied around the lids to make them look extra adorable. So, if you ask me, the magic was gone.

Normally three o'clock would be a dead hour for a restaurant. Even those who were late for lunch would be gone by then, and even the earliest of early birds would not have arrived for dinner yet. And so, naturally, the steel-studded door was closed.

We knocked.

It opened right away.

Just as the busboy was getting ready to say, *We're closed*, two men in navy suits suddenly appeared at his side. Typical mafioso bodyguard apparel. But it was obvious that neither of them was the person we were expecting. Their arms stood slightly elevated, distanced from their bodies, as if their armpits were inflicted with heat rash.

"Burçak Veral?" said the one who appeared to be the smarter of the two.

"That's me."

"Please come in."

I was expected. I must truly be getting famous, I thought. Hüseyin didn't even warrant a glance.

They stepped aside, letting us through.

It was as cold as I remembered it to be. Opal glass screens, unpolished steel, and pale cherrywood; completely wrong according to feng shui. The color red, the symbol of abundance in restaurants, was nowhere to be seen.

"Excuse me," said one of the bodyguards, making it evident he was more senior. He motioned with his hands that he'd have to search us.

He searched our bodies, touching us from tip to toe, to make sure we weren't carrying guns or anything.

"Please leave your mobile phones with us."

They were taking all conceivable precautions to make sure we weren't wired or recording anything. But if I had had any such intention, I would have brought the tiny gadgets I had bought from the Queensway Spy Shop in London. And no one would have been the wiser. I even had eyeglass frames with a built-in camera.

The person of importance was sitting at a table by himself, at the opposite end of the restaurant. Once we got close, he motioned with his hand for us to take a seat. I was sure I didn't know him. But unlike the Mafia fathers in my mind's eye, he resembled an old male model. He was smartly dressed. He wore a gray suit, obviously Italian and expensive from the cut and just screaming name brand, a high-collar blue shirt with white stripes, and a sky-blue tie. And a handkerchief in his jacket pocket. He was slim enough to qualify as skinny. People who are skinny always give me the impression that they must be short-tempered. Nowhere to be found was the jewelry associated with "godfathers." He wasn't even wearing a Rolex, but rather an elegant lizard-strap Cartier.

He didn't stand up.

I reached out to shake his hand.

"I'm Burçak Veral," I said. "And this is Hüseyin Kozalak."

"Good," was his only response.

I would have expected him to introduce himself.

I found his lack of modesty appropriate, given his "godfather" status.

"Let's talk in private," he said, signaling to Hüseyin, who was getting ready to sit down, that he should leave.

"He can sit and wait with my men."

His men were sitting at a table close to the entrance, a glass of

Coke in front of each, watching their surroundings with blank eyes.

"Okay, Hüseyin," I said. "You wait with them."

I could sense he felt bitter, but there was nothing I could do.

"He can eat his fill if he's hungry."

The skinny godfather was making it clear that he was boss. But it was strange the way he was telling me what he was supposed to be telling Hüseyin, as if Hüseyin weren't even there, as if he were invisible.

We were now left alone.

"I've already ordered food," he said. "Would you like anything?"

I was stuffed to the gills with *gözlemes*. Even the thought of food was too much.

"One Turkish coffee, no sugar," I told the chief waiter who had approached the table. "And a mineral water."

I couldn't wait to get down to business. The godfather didn't appear to be in any rush whatsoever.

He took a sip from his water and then licked his thin lips.

He took a business card out of his pocket. Holding it between his index and middle fingers, he gave it an artistic twirl before extending it to me.

"Cemil Kazancı, Textile Manufacturer." And there was a phone number. That was it. It was one of the plainest business cards I had ever seen.

Men like this always did import-export, or were in the textile business. None of these cards would read doctor, architect, or engineer.

"Pleased to meet you," I said.

The man had a solemn air about him, the kind that comes with arrogance.

A bowl of mixed-season salad was delivered to the table. The salad looked delicious even though I was full. Arugula leaves, mint, and lamb's ears topped with pickled beets, cherry tomatoes, thick slices of green and yellow bell peppers, and finally pieces of walnut sprinkled on top.

"Now . . ." he said, ruining the marvelous appearance of the salad with his fork. He was pushing the walnuts to one side. "It's actually rather complicated . . ."

Instead of finishing his sentence, he put a piece of beet pickle and pepper in his mouth. He started chewing with his mouth open. I hate this. In fact, I despise it. Each time he opened and closed his mouth I could see his food getting crushed. I tried to look the other way.

"This mister from the television show . . ."

He made noises as he chewed. No wonder he dined alone.

"Süheyl Arkın," I said, as if I'd score a point for answering question number one.

"Please, no names."

He must have thought he belonged to the Russian Mafia, so paranoid was he. "Well, in a couple of the programs he hosted, he showed things he shouldn't have shown."

That was Süheyl's job. To go digging wherever there was dirt.

Now he was chewing a mouthful of arugula and parsley. A piece of parsley got stuck on his front tooth.

"It was a detail only eyes that knew would catch."

He paused again when the waiter approached.

My mineral water and his main course, *hünkar beğendi*, had arrived.

He pushed the salad away, indicating that he was done with it. He had ruined that darling of a salad. He began separating the fat on the meat, with the delicacy of a surgeon.

"But you see, after that show, the wheel started turning. A series of events; you could never guess . . ."

He tossed a tender, trimmed lump of meat into his mouth and began chewing, leaving nothing to the imagination, his inner mouth activities once again on display for all the world to see. The parsley leaf was still in place.

"There were some goods that shouldn't have been there where he was shooting. With labels on them. It was dangerous enough, for those who saw."

Certainly he wouldn't loudly chomp on the *beğendi* that he was about to put in his mouth? After all, it was already in purée form.

"First we gave him a polite warning . . ."

God only knows what they had done.

No, the *beğendi* he did whirl around in his mouth, from side to side. Yuck.

"He didn't listen."

He took a sip of water to help it go down.

"He broadcasted it again on purpose . . ."

He set about operating on the lamb again. There it was, that awful sound of the knife screeching against the plate—oh, how it grated on my nerves!

"The rules of our world are crystal clear."

I knew.

"This time we warned him in a way he would clearly understand."

He put another newly trimmed piece in his mouth.

"But he's seriously wounded. To my knowledge, warning bullets are generally aimed at the leg."

He laughed. I saw everything he had in his mouth.

"It turns out the boy was clumsy. He got nervous and missed the target. By sheer accident."

So what did it have to do with me? Why was I here? I already knew this much from the news report.

"The TV guy being shot has nothing to do with the threat you received. It's just a coincidence."

He was squashing the *beğendi* with his fork. As if he were searching for something inside it.

"So what about me?" I asked.

"You?" he said, looking at me as if he were setting eyes on me for the very first time.

"Where do I stand in this distasteful coincidence? What's it got to do with me?"

He put the *beğendi* that hung from his fork into his mouth, as if he couldn't possibly talk with his mouth empty.

"You are the reason why the police have taken an exaggerated interest in the matter."

My coffee finally arrived.

"Through your connections the matter has turned into a complicated mess. They're digging unnecessarily deep. We're now connected too. Our boy was bound to get caught after their investigation."

I always knew the police were into shady double-dealing, but I wasn't used to it being expressed so openly. I now understood why he was so cautious about voice recorders. Selçuk getting involved upon my request, and the way the investigation was consequently being followed by those higher up in command, had served to make the case more urgent. No wonder they were incredibly disturbed by their man being caught.

"Now . . ."

I silently begged for him to finish what he was saying without putting more food in his mouth. The look I gave him had the desired effect. His fork remained suspended in midair.

"What we ask of you . . ."

Aaaand the fork reached his mouth.

". . . in the hope that you won't turn us down . . ."

"I'll try," I said, lowering my head to stare at my coffee.

"Don't avert your eyes. It makes you seem insecure," he said, bestowing upon me a few crumbs of his infinite wisdom on the topic of body language and psychology.

"Right," I said, looking him straight in the eye. "Your request?"

"Have a word with your connection. Have them stop meddling. The boy has already confessed and surrendered."

"That's even better," I said. "He'll plea bargain and get a reduced sentence."

"They said you had a strange sense of humor. But we're serious."

His gaze was as cold as ice. If what they called charisma meant making people tremble with just one look, then this man definitely had it.

"Somewhere down the line, we'll be of help to you too. I gave you my card. You've got my private number."

I had already understood when it was handed to me what a great privilege it was to possess this card.

Now was the time for negotiation, if I played my cards right.

"I'm the one who's stuck with the psycho that made the threatening call," I told him. "He's claimed responsibility for shooting Süheyl Arkın and killing Sermet Kılıç."

He put his knife and fork down on the table, making a loud clatter.

"I thought we agreed, no names."

"Sorry, *ayol*," I said. The *"ayol"* had slipped out of my mouth out of sheer nervousness.

"Your psycho is lying," he said, taking his knife and fork and placing them across his plate, which was still only half empty. So that's as much as he ate. No wonder he was so skinny.

"But he's continuing to threaten me," I said, leaning toward him over the table. He quickly pulled back.

"We'll see what we can do," he said.

That was the best answer possible.

"You've made a promise," I said. "I could remain silent until you help me."

His tongue, which had discovered the parsley leaf on his tooth, kept moving around underneath his upper lip. When his tongue failed to do the trick, he stuck his finger in his mouth and swiped the parsley leaf off his tooth. And then he wiped his finger on a tissue, nice and clean.

"This is a pointless negotiation," he said. "It has nothing to do with our case."

"You said you'd see what you could do."

He reached out to pick up his glass and took another sip of water. He was thinking.

"I could assign you a bodyguard."

The solution he had offered was not appealing. I had already grown tired of Hüseyin, and now the last thing I needed was a bodyguard following me around like my shadow.

"That's no solution . . ." I said.

"So what is it you want, then?"

I could sense that he was getting angry.

The waiter was bringing him a dish of sunchokes cooked in olive oil. It would be a good idea if I left before he started eating. I was already beginning to feel sick.

As I stood up, I waved his business card curtly in the air.

"I'll call you when I think of something."

15.

I summarized the situation for Hüseyin, who was dying of curiosity, without going into too much detail. I only told him as much as he needed to know. It's never a good idea to know too much when involved in sordid affairs like this. If you do, one slip of the tongue and you could end up in big trouble.

I had to think of something quick, decide what I would ask Cemil Kazancı for and let him know. My delay gave me some power, but unwanted events for them could lead to undesired trouble for me. Right now they owed me. The tables, however, could turn at any moment.

I didn't know how much influence I could exercise over Selçuk, but if the wheel had already started turning, and if they really had obtained important clues, then it was going to be impossible to stop the police. Still, I was going to have to give it a shot.

But later. We had other business to attend to right now: like visiting Melek, who wore a large snow-white ribbon in her hair, but was horribly ugly nonetheless!

I had switched my cell phone off before handing it over to the bodyguards, and as soon as I turned it back on, I received a text message from that oh-so-familiar number.

"Switch your phone on, or else . . ." It was official, now confirmed by both the police and the Mafia: my psycho had not carried through with his threat. He was a liar and a coward. So much for his power to threaten me; he was scary no more. He could call me when he felt like it. I had a couple of things to say to him too.

Hüseyin was totally confused.

"So now there's two of them, right?" he asked. "And the one who was caught is the one who's not after me."

The phone rang and I grabbed it, thinking it was the liar psycho, but it wasn't. It was Ponpon. I answered.

"*Ayolcuğum*, something reeeally strange is going on," she said.

"Like what?"

"I received an envelope. Through the post. But it's got your name on it."

"What? What do you mean? In my name but to your address?"

"That's right, cream puff."

This expression was new.

"Who from?"

"Now, that I don't know, *ayolcuğum*. It doesn't say on the envelope. I can tell from the stamp that it was posted from Taksim. But there's something tiny in the envelope. I can feel it. Something like a button."

"Open it and see," I said.

"Well, if there's something private in it, don't go moaning afterwards!"

"*Ayol*, Ponpon, what do I have to hide from you? Open it, I'm telling you."

"Okay, then I will. But don't think I just believed you. You hide lots from me. I know you do."

She deliberately held the envelope near the handset so that I could hear the tearing sound of paper clearly.

"What is it?"

"A rosette" she said. "And there's a note."

"What kind of rosette? What does it say in the note? Read it to me."

We were just pulling in to Hüseyin's parents' marvelous estate. There were more cars than there had been that morning, and a great many more children.

"I'm reading it . . . The note, I mean . . . 'I know this place too. You'll remember this.' That's it. No name, no signature, no addressee. Nothing. I mean, you end a letter with 'good day' or 'kind regards' or something. I'm telling you, these days, people's manners have gone to pot. They used to teach etiquette in school, back in the old days. Nowadays they don't give two hoots about it in school. The right education is really very important—"

A long tirade was clearly on its way if I didn't intervene immediately.

"I know," I told her. "What about the rosette? What's on it?"

"I'm checking, darling . . . But it's nothing I've ever seen before. It's black. Square. It looks like something new age and fashionable. You know, the type girls pin on their clothes here or there. I think the pin is broken. Let me check if it's in the envelope."

She put the phone aside, making a racket as she rustled the paper again.

Given the style in which the latest threat had been delivered, it appeared to be my psycho's doing. He was proving to me that he knew the addresses of my friends, that he could go straight to them if he wanted to. I was curious to find out what he had sent me, though, since he claimed I would remember it . . .

"Nope! The pin isn't in the envelope."

"Anything written on it, or an emblem?"

"There's nothing written on it. Just a random combination of letters and numbers. Come see for yourself."

The thing she was describing wasn't a rosette; it was a computer chip. Ponpon's relationship with technology is based entirely upon consumption. She buys some piece of modern equipment on a whim, and then promptly fidgets with it, in an attempt to actually use it, of course, until it's broken and ends up in the bin. She even complains about the number of buttons on a remote control. On numerous occasions she has called me over when she can't use something because it's "not working!" Most recently she was trying to watch a DVD without connecting cables to her DVD player. So you can imagine: she wouldn't recognize a chip if she saw one.

"I'll drop by soon," I said.

"And tell me your latest secret too when you arrive, so that you're no longer lying about not having anything to hide from me. It's obvious you're up to something secretive again."

Melek was playing hopscotch with the other neighborhood girls. Mrs. Kozalak's description of her neighbor's child had been perfect. I immediately recognized Melek among the other kids, even if she wasn't wearing a gigantic starched ribbon on her head.

She wouldn't know me, but she knew her Hüseyin Abi. She stopped playing, apologized to her friends in the manner of a grown-up woman, and walked over to us. Clearly we were the news of the day in the neighborhood.

"Hello, Hüseyin Abi," she said affectionately, straightening her clothes. "Mrs. Kozalak told me you needed to ask me some questions."

The way she stared at Hüseyin was not at all innocent. It bespoke the bawdy interest in men so blatantly apparent in girls her age. If Ponpon had been there, she'd have called her a "Lolita."

Before shaking my hand and introducing herself, she looked me up and down, studying me closely in an effort to discern just what I was made of. It was like she was taking an MRI. Her instincts must have been strong, for she quickly sensed what was going on. Until today, she had admired her Hüseyin Abi from afar, and now as she gave me my grade, she graded him too, for hanging out with me. I'd bet you anything we got big fat F's.

"Please, go ahead, *ağabeyciğim*, I'm listening."

Some kids are cute; I can tolerate them. *Some* are pretty; I can tolerate them too. But some, like this girl, who are wiseass know-it-alls plus every bit as ugly as Mrs. Kozalak said, well, they are tough to tolerate. She was like those kids in old-fashioned movies. A grown-up and poisoned midget was trapped in her child's body.

Hüseyin knelt down so as to be able to see Melek's face as he spoke to her. I was curious to know where he'd learned that. I was certain he didn't watch those daytime shows that explained the psychology of children.

"Somebody brought an envelope for me yesterday. And gave it to you to take upstairs. Do you remember, Melek, dear?"

"Of course I do, Hüseyin Ağabeyciğim."

"Can you describe him to us? What did he look like?"

She was definitely a top student in her class. One who tattled on those who talked and were noisy when the teacher wasn't around, and who, as soon as she got back to the classroom, told on anyone who had said rude words during playtime; one who did her homework to the letter and studied the following day's topics ahead of time, just to get in the teacher's good graces.

"Please give me a few minutes to think," she said.

Her thinking pose consisted of an index finger to the cheek and a sideways tilt of the head. She had also narrowed her eyes. I bet she'd rehearsed this look in front of her mirror.

"It was a young *abla*."

But our psycho was male!

Now I knelt down too, immediately.

"What did she look like?"

Although I had posed the question, she nevertheless directed her answer at Hüseyin. Clearly she was bent on paying absolutely no attention to me.

"Around twenty, I think. She looked like Ebru Gündeş before she got famous."

I didn't remember what Ebru Gündeş looked like before she became famous, but I figured she was a petite brunette with large eyes.

"She had long hair, down to here."

She motioned, indicating that it was a little longer than shoulder length.

"What did she say to you, dear?" I asked.

"I don't believe we've met," she said, very grandly, sizing me up again.

A good slap in the face would knock some respect into this girl, but we still had questions to ask, so I contained my annoyance.

"Oh . . . I'm Burçak," I said, holding out my hand.

"And I'm Melek," she said, bending her knee in a slight curtsy.

"And so we've met . . . What did she say to you?"

"What are you to Hüseyin Abi?"

"He's my friend," Hüseyin quickly responded, thus relieving me of the need to search for an answer.

"I've never seen him before," she said, looking skeptically at us both.

It was official, signed, and notarized: the girl was openly flirting with Hüseyin and was jealous of me. This must be what is called a woman's instinct.

"Now let me answer your question," she said. "We were playing here when that *abla* came on her bike."

"A bike?"

"Yes, *Un-cle* Burçak, a bike."

And she'd called me uncle, emphasizing each syllable. While it was true that the younger generations were certainly lacking in the tactfulness department, the case at hand went beyond that; this pint-sized runt, in a fit of jealousy, was openly treating me with an obnoxious attitude.

"She asked us if anyone knew Hüseyin Kozalak. I stepped forward. I told her Hüseyin Abi and I lived in the same apartment block. She told me she was in a hurry, and that she needed to make it to an exam. She kindly asked me to deliver the envelope to his home."

The bike, the exam . . . A girl, a student . . . What did all this mean?

"What kind of a bike was it, Melek? Can you tell us?" said Hüseyin, moving on to a more fruitful line of questioning.

Melek assumed her thinking pose again.

"Let's see . . . It wasn't really new. If I'm not mistaken, it had gears. And it was blue in color. But it wasn't a girl's bike. There was a yellow water bottle where you'd normally put the pump. You know, one of those with a nozzle."

"You're a right know-it-all, aren't you . . . ?" I said.

Placing her hand on her Hüseyin Abi's shoulder for support, she answered.

"I'm knowledgeable, not a know-it-all."

Any other time I would have ripped to pieces anyone who back-talked to me like this. But we needed her, so I controlled myself. Besides, the details she remembered, if true, were important. And the girl clearly did have a sharp eye.

I proceeded to pose a question that fell within my own particular area of interest: "Do you remember what she was wearing?"

"She was wearing jeans," she said, without thinking this time. "And a jean jacket. I don't remember if they were purple or red but she had shiny, colorful sneakers. Converse sneakers. My mom's going to buy me a pair this summer."

A voice inside told me to run and buy two pairs of Converse sneakers for her. The details she was giving us were worth it.

"Anything else?"

"She was wearing a helmet. Like a motorcyclist. Black. With flame stickers on it."

"You're a star, Melek," I said.

She really was. I mean, I wasn't saying it just to be polite; plus, I had found myself a little moved by her Converse story and I liked her shrewdness.

"I know," she said. "That's what everyone says."

"Thanks a lot, you've been a big help," said Hüseyin.

"Oh, I just remembered: on the side of her helmet was a shiny sticker. The size of a stamp but bright and gleaming."

Her attention was sharp, her memory spotless. She must have been aware of how ugly she was. We are unbelievably malicious as children. One of her peers at school, or in the neighborhood, who was mad and wanted to hurt her, would have told her. And so she had learned to make up for her ugliness, which would have been brought to her attention at a very young age, with her intelligence and ability to pay attention to detail. I don't believe that saying about how all beautiful people are dumb, but there is some truth to it. The beautiful don't need anything else to make others admire them. People just naturally do. And so they don't need to use their brains. Those who realize they aren't beautiful seek out, find, develop, and display other qualities in order to impress.

We thanked her.

"Let's take you to the amusement park or cinema one day," I said in all sincerity.

"I don't like the amusement park. It's always too noisy. But let me consider the cinema offer. I'll ask my father."

Where she had learned to speak like a highly intelligent, fully adult midget remained a mystery.

As we approached the car, Hüseyin cried out, "You can't be serious about inviting her to the cinema!"

"I truly am," I said. "Why not? If I can't make it, then the two of you can go. Can't you see? The girl is madly in love with you."

16

*N*ow we had the female accomplice to deal with. Based on the information we'd been given, she was probably a university student or something, roaming the very hilly city of Istanbul on a bike. Seeing as she had a helmet, this bike-riding business wasn't something she did just for pleasure. She had flames and a hologram sticker on her helmet. Those were our clues. Now all we had to do was find her.

First we need to visit to Ponpon to figure out what was on that chip.

Hüseyin knew very well where to go but was worried parking would be bad. He was right. Parking was always problematic in Nişantaşı and Teşvikiye. We were going to have to park in a multi-story parking garage and walk two streets down from Ponpon's apartment.

A strange intuition popped into my head that I couldn't keep to myself.

"Hüseyin," I said as we walked to Ponpon's, "it's you who knows where I go, what I do."

"Yes . . ."

"And you know where all the people I see live . . ."

"Yeeeah . . ."

"Look, you even found Ponpon's house without directions. And the office . . ."

"I've been driving you around for years," he said proudly. "I should know."

"And you've got a crush on me."

"Alas, unrequited . . ."

I stopped and looked at him, narrowing my eyes.

"You're not the psycho, are you?"

He was baffled.

"Just kidding," I said. "I was just thinking . . . You might have planned all this to wriggle your way into my place. If that were the case, you've been quite successful. We're glued to each other like Siamese twins. At this rate, we'll have to get used to each other. The letter was even delivered to your place."

"But the phone call!" he said. "I was with you when he called!"

"Oh, but you very well could have had a friend call for you!"

"I swear to God and the heavens above, I've done no such thing!"

"I don't have much faith in those who swear a lot," I said.

"Goddamn it!" he said, throwing the car keys onto the sidewalk in a rage. "You can't seriously believe that I could possibly murder another human being."

He was standing in the middle of the road, screaming his head off. As soon as they heard the word "murder," everyone in the vicinity snapped to attention. All ears perked up, eager to hear the rest.

"Slow down!" I said. "Everyone's staring at us."

"They can stare all they like! What? Do I look like a murderer to you? Look at me!"

I bent down and picked the car keys up off the sidewalk, grabbed Hüseyin by the arm, and started dragging him toward Ponpon. If he went on screaming like this, he'd get more than a simple scolding from me; he'd get the living shit beaten out of him.

"I wouldn't do it for anyone, not even you. You understand? I couldn't. I can't even stand the Festival of Sacrifice. The only thing I'm capable of killing is a fly. A fly! How could you . . . Me and murder, for God's sake, no!"

He was clearly having a bit of a breakdown.

I lowered my voice in an effort to get him to lower his tone.

"All right, all right! Calm down . . . Let's sit down and talk about this like two grown adults. It was just a thought."

Trying to seem innocent, I gave him my sweetest smile. It usually worked.

"You have to admit it was a crazy thought. You got me all worked up!"

I put a friendly hand on his shoulder and gave him a good shake.

"You're right. I'm sorry."

I placed a tiny kiss on his cheek to make peace and calm him down.

We began walking again—now not saying a word.

Outside the apartment building was a cardboard box waiting for the trash collectors. Inside it I spotted the boomerang I had bought for Ponpon and brought as a gift all the way from Australia. Magical words had been inscribed on the boomerang by the Aborigines, who believed that the time a boomerang spent in the air before returning to the thrower would become additional moments added to the thrower's life span. I'd gone to the trouble of schlepping it halfway around the world, and it was sheer ingratitude for Ponpon to chuck it during her spring cleaning.

I felt rotten.

I peeked into the box a bit more carefully to see what else she had thrown out. There was an undamaged coffee mug, a checkered patterned tin box, the old kitchen curtain, in a creased ball . . . Thankfully, nothing else that I had given her.

When Ponpon opened the door to find me standing in front of her, she stared as if in reproach.

"I can't believe my eyes!"

What was it that she couldn't believe? There I was, and she already knew Hüseyin. He had dropped her off at home several times after she'd been over for a visit.

"*Ayolcuğum*, just look at yourself! I wouldn't go to my next-door neighbor for a morning coffee dressed like that."

"Nice to see you too," I said, stepping in. "I'm in disguise."

"But you look dreadful . . ."

Clearly, she wanted to prolong the topic. I, on the other hand, was in no mood to discuss the attire I had donned for my visit to Hüseyin's. I was still feeling rotten about the boomerang.

"We didn't have much choice," I said.

"And you say you've got nothing to hide from me . . . You see! You've been unmasked, *ayolcuğum*. The you I know is always elegant, always classy. Even if you don't keep up with the latest fashion trends, you're always smart and attractive. But just look at you now! You look like an ironmonger at the Thursday Market."

One could only drop so many bricks in a single sentence. Hüseyin's father was an ironmonger. It didn't matter if he worked at the Thursday Market or not; I saw that the insult had stung Hüseyin. Of course, Ponpon couldn't have known this.

"I picked it out at his place," Hüseyin said sulkily. "My father is an ironmonger!

"Ohhh, no! *Ay*, I'm so sorry, darlings. I swear I didn't mean it like that. It's simply my silly rudeness! Ignore me. I sometimes speak without thinking, and then I make such faux pas. *Ay*, I'm so ashamed."

She really was. I was seeing Ponpon blush for the first time in a long time.

And now, to make amends, she'd drown Hüseyin in compliments, treat him to various delicacies, find a way to give him a gift, and so on and so forth. The thing she liked giving away as a present most was her own portrait. Signed and framed. With a sweet look on her face, or her lips puckered up in a kiss, all the lines on her face smoothed out, an ageless Ponpon in full makeup! The frames sometimes even come in silver, depending upon the importance of the person and the gravity of the occasion. She then expects her portrait to be displayed in the most privileged, honored corner of the recipient's home. How many Ponpon portraits could any one sensible person possibly have in her home?

But, unlike Ponpon, I didn't go chuck them in the bin for the whole world to see!

Ponpon immediately brought the note and the chip she'd been calling a rosette. We were now back on track.

The note had again been typed up on a computer, and printed right in the center of an A4 page, in large, classic Times New Roman font. I was sure there were no fingerprints on the envelope or the note itself. I put the note aside.

It was impossible to learn anything from the chip just by looking at it. I'd only figure what it was once I placed it inside a computer.

"This is a computer chip," I said, turning it over in my hand.

"Which means?" said Hüseyin.

"I don't know yet," I said. "We'll see once we've put it in a computer."

I wanted to go home as soon as possible to find out what was on the chip. I moved to get up.

"Nooo, you're not going anywhere!" said Ponpon. "You just got here. I won't have it, cream puff. You can't just get up and leave. Now, I'm going to give you each a rice pudding."

Ponpon had gone on and on about my clothes, had ridiculed Hüseyin and his family, even if it was unintentional, and had carelessly discarded the present I had brought her. I was on edge and impatient as it was.

"Don't call me cream puff!" I said.

"*Ayolcuğum*, what's wrong with me calling you cream puff? Cream puff, cream puff, cream puff! There!"

On the last "cream puff" she had stamped her feet like an obstinate child. She stuck out her bottom lip and crossed her arms. Her chin rose into the air imperiously.

She couldn't help but be hilarious! With the way she talked, the words she chose, her behavior and lifestyle, and her attitude toward life, Ponpon has always been the antidote to a rational and consequently boring life. And yet again she had managed to make me laugh and unwind.

Besides, she makes one scrumptious rice pudding. We decided to stay.

Foodwise, I was having one delicious day.

17

I t was a good thing I'd given my mobile phone number to only a select few. Now that I'd turned it on, the thing was ringing off the hook! It was as if every person who had my number had wasted no time in sharing it with everyone and his brother. Every time I picked it up thinking it might be our psycho, the name of someone already saved or an unfamiliar number appeared on the screen. I couldn't answer them all. I was now a famous person who was learning the hardships of fame! With a press of my thumb, I let them know I was unavailable.

I could hardly imagine the bombardment to which my home phone, or rather, my answering machine, had been subjected. After all, that number *was* common knowledge.

We got caught in the evening rush-hour traffic as we tried to make our way home from Nişantaşı.

As we idled, my mind was busy pondering what favor I could possibly ask my new Mafia connection Cemil Kazancı for. I had to think of something good. It had to serve my purposes and help me in my current plight.

I looked at my phone: some insistent unknown number was ringing me for the third time. I answered, ready to deliver a scolding to someone who had the wrong number.

It was Andelip Turhan, the tarot card reader.

"Sorry for disturbing you, but there's something I have to tell you, and it's something important to me . . ." she said. "And it should be to you too."

I had no choice but to listen.

"I see you in every tarot reading I do. It's not normal. The cards are trying to tell me something, but I don't get it. Why you? And there's someone with you. A man, not quite your lover. You're in a dangerous situation. Maybe it hasn't happened yet, but it will soon. Every time I flip your cards, I'm filled with anxiety. My chest feels heavy. As if . . ."

My Reiki master Gül had already told me that Andelip Turhan really was actually a medium with advanced precognition, and that she only used the tarot pack as a secondary means of confirming her visions. From what she was saying, it seemed that the woman who walked around with boxer shorts on her head was seeing or sensing the situation Hüseyin and I were in. As for her definition of my relationship with Hüseyin, that was particularly apt.

"The signals I'm getting aren't so strong from afar. I can't see clearly enough. It's always easier in the person's presence, when I can have physical contact. Please come to my place, and bring your boyfriend with you. I have to read your cards. I'm constantly preoccupied with the two of you. I'm incapable of reading anyone else's cards. I'm stuck. I can't stay like this. I can't sleep at night."

"It's a bit late to come over tonight," I responded resignedly.

I was planning to go straight home and investigate the chip. It was going to take time to fit it into the computer, put it through security tests, and open it. If the chip turned out to be problematic, if it required further auxiliary programs to run, then the whole endeavor really would be a challenge and could take all night.

"I'll be expecting you, no matter how late," she said. "I always stay up late anyway. Besides, I can't sleep in the state that I'm in. Like I told you, my mind is absolutely stuck on you two."

From the determination in her voice, I could tell that she was not going to accept no for an answer.

"But I can't say when."

"Well, then don't," she said. "Just call me to say you're coming. I'll be waiting."

As if the day hadn't been busy and exhausting enough already, there I was with yet another appointment lined up: a tarot reading with Andelip Turhan.

I told Hüseyin the good news.

"Turkey's most famous tarot specialist, the medium Andelip Turhan, is going to read your cards tonight."

He gave me a strange look, as if I were insane.

When the car behind us honked, Hüseyin shifted into first gear and turned his attention back to the road.

My mind wandered back to my new Mafia connection. What could I ask Cemil Kazancı for? Something befitting his power and connections . . .

At home, my answering machine was flashing away as I'd expected, but first I had to change my clothes. I'd started feeling like a proper ironmonger. Being an ironmonger wouldn't be as bad as Ponpon had implied, but one could hardly argue it would be an appropriate profession for Audrey Hepburn and me.

The best thing would be to peel off my disguise and go nude; however, there was Hüseyin. If I traipsed around the apartment nude, I'd not be able to help seducing him. But what could I wear? I didn't feel like wearing anything manly. I'd gone around dressed like that all day. My hand went for the baby-pink shorts; I slipped them on without thinking twice. Then I pulled on my white Bearded Barbie T-shirt; the neck and arms had been cut off using nail clippers, thus leaving them scraggly with strings dangling here and there—very à la mode.

It would have been good to have had a shower before getting down to work, but my curiosity overpowered my wish for cleanliness. Hüseyin waited impatiently, pacing up and down and getting in my way, excited as if he were about to witness something extraordinary for the very first time.

"Let's listen to the messages first," I said.

The phone rang before I had a chance to push the play button. I didn't want another surprise like Andelip Turhan. I decided not to answer it, for the time being, at least. I could always change my mind once I'd heard who it was.

As soon as I heard our psycho's now all too familiar, mechanically deep voice say, "I know you two are home. Answer the phone," I lifted up the handset.

"Well, well, well," I said, sounding light and unconcerned, but with an edge. "Look who's calling! If it isn't our psycho liar!"

He had to be expecting this. The news that the hit man who shot Süheyl Arkın had been caught was all over the news.

Still there was a moment's pause.

Hüseyin held his breath as he listened to the phone, which I had put on speaker. After all, this whole thing did involve him too.

"There's been a misunderstanding," said the voice.

"What kind of a misunderstanding, *ayol*? You said you did it, but it's been proven that it wasn't you who shot Süheyl Arkın. How could that be a misunderstanding? Next thing you know, we'll find out Master Sermet poisoned himself by accident. You're nothing but a lousy opportunist!"

"Hey, slow down!" he said.

"*You* slow down! It must have been very convenient for you to take responsibility for something you didn't do. You probably thought you'd be scarier. You poor, pitiful soul!"

I intended to push his buttons; he'd gotten on my nerves and it was payback time.

"Then you still haven't found the clues I left for you," he said menacingly, trying to grab the upper hand.

No, I'd found no clues.

"Take a good look around your home!" he said. "I'd expect you to be more perceptive."

I quickly scanned my surroundings. There was nothing out of the ordinary in sight.

"I'll give you until midnight. Then I'm going to call again. If you haven't made any progress, well, you'll have a surprise in store!"

And with that, he hung up.

This man's surprises always turned out less than enjoyable. I wasn't sure I wanted a new one.

That's when Hüseyin, his eyes filled with panic again, asked, "How does he know we're back home?"

Good question.

"He must be spying on us."

Hüseyin ran over to the window and looked out. He looked hopeful, as if he'd spot the psycho instantly. I walked over next to him. There was no one standing in the street spying on our apartment. In fact, there was no one at all. The view was one of cramped apartment buildings as far as the eye could see. The usual Cihangir view. There were as many windows with lights on as there were with lights out. A nestled Cihangir extended before us, with the chic district of Gümüşsuyu to the right, and farther on the cozy and bohemian neighborhood of Setüstü at its edge. Narrow streets, not one of which was straight, not one of which ran parallel to another, streets that curled like worms, and apartment buildings of staggered heights, all joined in the darkness of nighttime shadows. Anyone possessing one of those Korean-made telescopes sold at the underpass in Karaköy, or even a crappy pair of binoculars, could have been watching the house right now.

Startled by the idea of being watched by someone, I quickly closed the curtains.

I knew I was being ridiculous, but at least he wouldn't be able to see what was happening inside if he really was watching us.

"The bastard is a bona fide psycho!" said Hüseyin.

I sank into my sofa. It felt as if my body had suddenly become too heavy for me to carry.

I pressed the button on the answering machine.

The first three messages were followed by a series of hang-ups. Then, finally, Hasan, the maître d'.

"I'm sure I'm dialing the right number. What's with the message? What's going on? Why aren't you answering your mobile?"

It was obvious what he was getting at. My answering machine message had been changed. That's why callers had hung up, because they thought they had the wrong number. I stopped the messages and pressed the button to listen to my outgoing message.

The psycho's deep croaking voice began to speak.

"Hello, there's no point in leaving a message for the person you have called. He is too busy to deal with you."

That impertinent so-and-so! He had been in my home, invaded my private space, and as if that weren't enough, he'd gone and changed the message on my answering machine. Suddenly I felt terribly disheartened. A knot formed in my throat. I wanted to break things, beat someone up . . . And then sit down and cry. I was seized by the feeling that my house had been invaded. Every corner, from the carpets to the ceilings, had been sullied. How could I possibly sleep in my bed now? He had sat where I was sitting now, and had touched what I was touching. I felt nauseous. My eyes filled with tears. I realized that I had begun shaking with anger.

I picked up the handmade Belgian cushion from the sofa I was sitting on and dashed it against the floor. It did no good as an outlet for my rage, nor did it help me feel better. The cushion just sat there on the floor, in the middle of the carpet.

It was impossible for me to battle someone who was unseen

and unknown. How could one stand up against an unknown threat? How to prepare, how to take precautions? Great disasters often occur when we must confront the unknown.

I was deeply unhappy. My unhappiness was feeding my rage. Hüseyin stood before me, helpless; not knowing what to do, he stretched his arms out toward me, and then put them down again. He did this a couple of times before finally somehow gathering the courage to come sit down next to me and put his arm around my shoulder.

"We have to be strong," he said. "This is a battle of nerves. Don't give him what he wants."

He was consoling me in a calm tone I'd never have expected of him.

I smiled weakly.

He pulled me toward him and shook me in a friendly manner.

"Now, first change that message! Others might call."

He was right.

I went and washed my face and blew my runny nose so that my voice would sound normal. I changed my message to what it should be. My voice sounded dreadful on the first take. But on the third, it was reasonably acceptable.

I had so much to do. I couldn't decide what to do first. What was on the chip he had sent me? Why had he sent it? Getting to the bottom of all this was going to take time. If I were to sleep in my home that night, I'd have to search every nook and cranny to find out what he had dirtied, what he had touched, and what he had moved about. What if he had hidden something somewhere . . . ? That was too much; I couldn't sleep here, not with such suspicion eating away at me. The only solution, of course, was to go somewhere else to sleep. I could call in a domestic cleaning company the next day and have the whole place disinfected. This wasn't something my cleaning lady Satı could take care of on her own.

Mafioso Cemil Kazancı was expecting to hear from me on how he could pay me back. I had to call Selçuk and ask him to stop the police from digging too deep for the time being. Andelip Turhan was expecting us for a tarot reading. I needed to contact the dozens of people who were undoubtedly shocked by the psycho's message on my machine, and explain the situation to them all, starting with Hasan. I would start with everyone who'd made a "missed call" to my mobile. All of them were expecting an explanation too. The psycho had given us until midnight, and had promised a new surprise afterward. Given us until midnight to do what, though? It was one heavy burden he had given me to bear, and in order to free myself of it, I had to catch him. In other words, everyone, even my psycho, was expecting something from me.

The thought of everything I had to do depressed me. I let out a deep sigh. It didn't help.

18.

The task was nerve-racking.

I was trying the chip.

I had opened the computer case, backed up my data in case any problems arose, and put the chip in. The annoying thing about it was that its contents were completely identical to that of my own computer. First I thought it simply wasn't working, that there was something wrong and that I was seeing the inside of my own computer instead of the chip. I tried again, and that's when I became certain. All my data files were on this chip. I couldn't have done a better job copying my computer if I'd backed it up myself. The last file was dated three days ago, meaning the day the psycho's threats had started. But he'd been in the house today; and he'd accessed my computer three days ago. I had multiple security systems protecting against cyber-intruders, but had taken no precautions at all with my own computer. There was never anyone else in the apartment to use it but me, until now! All he had had to do was press the on button. My psycho had sat at my computer three days ago.

The piercing headache I had was completely psychological. Half of my head was throbbing. A voice inside was telling me to drop everything and run. Where to, however, I did not know. Anywhere. Wherever there was a flight to at this hour, using whichever visa was still valid on my passport . . . I had enough savings to keep me comfortably afloat for some time. The club could finance itself. Although he might be a bigmouthed gossiper, Hasan was reliable. Give him a higher percentage and he'd embrace the business as his own and carry on. And what if the club went bankrupt? I'd find a job as an illegal fugitive. Worst-case scenario, I could do drag shows at clubs. I'd already had a successful venture as such in Paris; if that didn't work, I'd have to activate my international network of friends. A few days as a guest with each, and I could be safely sheltered for years.

I could go stay in Rio with my author Mehmet Murat Somer for six months a year, pester him, and ask him not to write about me anymore. Perhaps all this was happening to me because of what he had written. And since he had become a bestselling author because of me, he should open his home to me.

I didn't care what happened to my apartment. If he really wanted to, my psycho could come and settle in, and enjoy it if he wanted.

I could always ask Cemil Kazancı to use his Mafia connections abroad to lend me a helping hand. If they really were as tough as they purported to be, they could even supply me with a fake passport and ID. I'd bet I could ask for financial support too.

Plus, I was an expert hacker, and that was a moneymaking profession anywhere in the world.

By the time I returned—if I ever did return—things would have settled down. If he wasn't locked up for murder in the first degree by then, my psycho might have already forgotten all about me anyway.

I was seriously considering all of these options.

Everyone has a breaking point, and I had hit mine. Sometimes decisions made without much thought, upon sheer instinct, can have fortunate outcomes too. Maybe I was at exactly such a moment.

I got up and opened the drawer where I kept my passport. I was going to check its expiration date and my visas. I could also go someplace where you didn't need a visa. Although flights at this time of night were few, I could still catch the Turkish Airlines flight to Bangkok. You didn't need a visa to get into Thailand.

My long-term USA visa and two-year UK visa were both still valid. But my goddamn passport expired in less than a month; I had forgotten to renew it. A great many countries didn't show much hospitality to citizens of the Republic of Turkey who had less than three months left on their passports.

My passport in my hand, I sank onto the floor, sobbing. My escape and survival plan had crumbled to bits, just like that. And so had I!

I was having a nervous breakdown. Tears were streaming down my cheeks like a waterfall. I couldn't stop them. I wasn't too sure I wanted to either. I was a miserable wretch.

I'd had enough, and just wanted for this all to be over, no matter what might come to pass.

I sat there with my eyes open while I stared emptily, not seeing anything, not hearing a single noise.

Hüseyin lifted me up, took me to the bathroom, and washed my face. I needed a little love and compassion, a little pampering. For days everyone had been expecting things from me, but no one cared about poor me.

I handed myself over to Hüseyin's strong, compassionate arms and passionate lips.

19.

So much for the "fasting." I had thrown out my self-discipline and all control. Sometimes things which lie outside the boundaries of logic can be of use to us, can show us the path to truth. Like good sex! Although I knew I'd regret it afterward, Hüseyin's performance was truly magnificent. His lustful and crafty fingers had aroused my body and brought me to my senses. My tension had been replaced by a sweet lethargy. And my mind, meanwhile, had been restored to pristine clarity.

There must be a rational and reasonable explanation for the current situation, I told myself. There had to be.

Still reclining on Hüseyin's warm chest as he masterfully strove to tempt me again, I started making calls on my mobile from bed.

First I called Cemil Kazancı's very private number.

"Who is this?" he answered curtly.

I asked him to put my apartment under surveillance, twenty-four hours a day—and for everyone going in and out to be recorded—until I told him to stop.

"Not something we generally do, but we'll take care of it," he said. "I'll send one of the boys over. He'll come and introduce himself to you first . . ."

That made sense. "Have you seen to our matter?"

"I'm calling him now," I told him.

Hüseyin had greatly improved his performance over time. He went at it gently, masterfully, with tiny touches.

"Let's slow down," I said, planting a kiss on his lips. "We haven't sorted anything out yet."

He sucked my tongue into his mouth in reply as he stroked my inner thigh.

Now it was time to call Selçuk.

"Can you listen in on mobile phone calls?" was my first question.

"Yes," he said. "One can get hold of the recordings when necessary."

This was bad news. I didn't want what I was going to say to be recorded. The paranoid Cemil Kazancı was no worse than me when it came to this. My landline was already being monitored, and had been for some time, because of maniacs like this latest one.

"What are we going to do?" I asked. "There's a problem I want to discuss with you. But not on the phone if the lines are bugged."

There was a short silence on the other end of the line. Hüseyin, thinking the conversation was over, quickly sprang back into action. I pushed him away.

"Look," said Selçuk, "if that's the case, since I haven't yet mastered the art of telepathic information exchange, we're left with only one choice—the classical method."

He meant meeting up.

"I'll pick you up outside your place in half an hour. We'll go for a short ride."

Seeing the effort Hüseyin was making, "Make it forty-five minutes," I said.

We agreed.

I didn't tell Hüseyin I was going alone until we had finished.

I should have known I wouldn't have time to take a shower, but then Selçuk was an old pal, so I didn't feel I had to look my best. I quieted Hüseyin's objections to staying at home alone by telling him to lock the door and to sit and wait in the windowless storage room. He laughed. Sex had done him good too.

"I'll be back in half an hour, tops," I said, and gave him a kiss.

Selçuk was pulling up to the curb as I rushed down. He had come in his wife Ayla's Renault instead of his official car.

I explained the situation to him frankly. I wasn't going to hide anything from Selçuk. I hated people who weren't straightforward, and doing the same myself really wasn't my style. Half surprised, half curious, he listened until the very end of my story without interrupting me. The name Cemil Kazancı wasn't new to him.

"Only until this psycho gets caught," I said. "You can do what you want after that."

"Do you realize what you're asking me to do?"

"Yes," I said. "I know perfectly well . . ."

We fell silent for a while.

"It isn't as simple as he's made it out to be. The Drug Trafficking desk is involved, Organized Crimes, even Interpol. It's an old, rooted network. No one, let alone me, can intervene once the wheels have been set into motion."

"Well, have they? Have the wheels been set into motion?"

Again, a brief silence.

"I don't know," he said, shrugging his shoulders.

"So?" I said. "What do we do now?"

"I'm taking you back home."

He didn't say he would, but I was sure that he was going to try. His best and more. I knew his style.

Instead of sitting in the windowless storage room while I was out, Hüseyin, whose primary concern at the moment was filling his hungry stomach, had begun boiling pasta.

"Look what I found, darling," he said, grinning from ear to ear.

Now that we had slept together, I had suddenly become "darling."

When Satı had come to do the cleaning, she'd left me a note fixed to the fridge with a magnet. We had both missed it because we hadn't gone in the kitchen since we'd come home. And I had totally forgotten that today was Satı's cleaning day.

"Of course. She was at my place all morning."

The note read: "Mr. Veral, the telephone people came. They fixed the problem with the phone. We've run out of Omo detergent. And there's very little surface cleaner left. Thank you. Satı."

It always took them more than a week to show up when one actually needed a repair, so it was hardly likely that they'd have turned up just like that for routine maintenance.

"So they came into the house disguised as telephone technicians," said Hüseyin, laughing. "I don't know why we didn't think of it earlier!"

He was acting as if it were totally normal for people to turn up dressed as telephone technicians. Satı must have thought the same thing and let the psycho in. If she hadn't watched them—and clearly she hadn't—then we could easily deduce that our psycho had toured the house at his leisure, under cover of checking the cables.

The note said telephone people. People? So there were more than one. He couldn't have been accompanied by the girl with the bicycle. Girls never become telephone repair technicians in Turkey. So he must have a third collaborator. I must be up against an entire gang.

But his coming over today disguised as a technician didn't explain how he'd copied my desktop three days ago.

"What shall I put in the pasta? Tuna, or tomato and feta cheese? I can't find anything else in the fridge."

Hüseyin clearly didn't take after his mama when it came to creativity in the kitchen.

"Whatever you'd like," I said. I was going to call Satı.

"Yes, that's right," said Satı, groaning at every syllable—her way of letting me know how utterly exhausted she was. "The telephone people came. Two men. Youngish. One didn't speak at all. They went straight to the back room to check the cables. It was taking them a long time, so I just continued with my own work. I had all that ironing to do. Broke my back, I'm telling you."

"Describe them to me," I said.

"I told you, they were young. One had longer hair. The way they let it grow these days. I hear they allow it in public offices too. Scrawny, they were. I didn't stare 'cause I didn't want to give them the wrong idea."

"What about their height, their coloring?"

"Typical men, I'm telling you," she said. "They were taller than me, but not short or tall. Medium . . ."

"Look, Satı, dear," I said. "This is serious. You'd better jog that memory of yours."

Little Melek had given us a perfect, detailed description.

"Oh, now, don't you get heavy-handed with me," she said. "I told you, I don't remember. I'm a married lady. What business do I have looking at men I don't know? *Maşallah*, I have my own mister, as fit as a fiddle. If he were to find out, he'd go berserk. What would he think of me if I were to sit here on the phone with you going on and on about two telephone repairmen? He doesn't want me to work for you anyway. And there's always so much to do at your place. I swear, I have half a mind to never come back to that place of yours again."

That was her ultimate threat. To leave me, not to come back ever again. She used the same threat every time I gave her a little "constructive criticism." She had said the same thing when I cautioned her to be more careful after she washed my two cashmere sweaters in the washing machine, reducing them to the size of baby clothes, and burned my La Perla lace G-string trying to iron it. It was a tiny little G-string; it hardly needed ironing.

"It's up to you," I said furiously, recalling all her past accidents. "Don't come if you don't want to. In fact, don't come at all, *ayol*! I don't want you to, not anymore."

I didn't even begin to catalog all of the things she had dropped and broken over the years. Thanks to her, I made routine, tri-monthly visits to the Paşabahçe glassware shop.

"No, no, you've got the wrong idea. I didn't mean—"

"Look here, Satı," I said. "Please don't come again . . . I'm tired of your threats."

Certainly I would be able to find a cleaner who did less damage than Satı.

"You've got it all wrong," she said. "That's not what I said. I'm happy working for you. I said my mister was complaining, but I cut him down to size. I'm the one who makes a living here. I ought to have the say around here. But what's he do? He idles about at the coffeehouse all day, waiting for work to fall at his feet, and then comes home to boss me and the little ones around. I ain't taking that, nuh-uh."

Now I was listening to her own personal version of a feminist attitude.

"I can come tomorrow if you like. I'm free. I'll finish off what's left. I'll give every inch a good scrub. You don't have to pay me. Better than being home, sniffing that man's stinky feet . . ."

I gave in.

Hüseyin had made the pasta with tuna.

20.

It was best we get ready and go see my eccentric tarot card reader Andelip Turhan before it got too late. Yes, our psycho had given us until midnight, but I wasn't about to stay at home all that time in a paranoid state of mind, madly searching for secret traces he might have left behind. Then again, what else could I do but be paranoid? He had entered my house (twice!), and was watching me. *Veni* and *vidi* had been accomplished, but *vici*—not yet. I wasn't going to let him. No way!

This time Hüseyin and I showered together. We dried each other's backs. We whistled and shaved side by side.

"Have you started working out?" I asked him.

He'd built up some muscle since I'd last seen his naked body up close.

"You like?" he responded, smiling at me in the mirror.

He had slyly struck a pose when he noticed I was looking at his body, sucking his tummy in and opening his arms slightly to the side to reveal his lats.

"Nice," I said, as I carried on shaving.

"I sit at the wheel all day. I noticed my belly was starting to show . . . *Hüseyin, man*, I said to myself, *the only solution is to get yourself a gym membership*. It's been eight months. I go three days a week, in the evenings, regularly. I'm not looking too shabby now, am I?"

Everyone enjoys being admired.

The first unpleasant surprise was in my underwear drawer. All my bras had been cut up into shreds. When Hüseyin heard me cursing up a storm, he rushed in to see what was wrong, and didn't ask a single question when he saw the lacy shreds in my hands.

"Goddamn bastard," he hissed through clenched teeth.

Oh, well, I'd just have to go braless until I had a chance to buy new ones the next day. I could go without breasts. Audrey didn't have breasts her whole life. The singer Nükhet Duru was as flat as a board until she got new apple-shaped ones. I never was after Jayne Mansfield–style rocket tits, or grand ones like Dolly Parton's or Nigar Uluerer's, anyway. Elegant fullness always seemed sexy enough for me.

I got dressed quickly, still mumbling to myself. What a barbaric method he had chosen. Not even psychos in movies did things like slashing underwear anymore. Hüseyin put his clean clothes on too. We were both dressed in black, from tip to toe.

"Men in Black," I said cheekily.

Of course I wasn't expecting him to understand or remember the film. He wasn't one to go to the movies much, as he was always driving his cab, trying to make a living.

"You mean the agents that chase those aliens . . ." he said, surprising me. "What was his name? The black guy with the cute face. You know, the one who's a singer as well . . . He has video clips too."

He really did know him.

"Will Smith," I said.

"That's the one," he said, snapping his fingers.

Andelip Turhan lived in one of those tiny apartments in Levent that banks had built to give as prizes. Before the government relinquished its control over interest on deposits, banks lured new customers by having drawings to give out presents to their depositors. My aunt who was a banker used to tell us all about the lotteries whenever she was recalling her career. She'd then go on about how Istanbul used to be. Back then, apparently Levent and Etiler weren't in vogue like they are now. No one fancied living there. The only people who lived in the area were a few antisocial and artsy types, a category into which my aunt lumped anyone and everyone who, to her, gave off an air of strangeness, and to which homosexuals too naturally belonged.

As soon as Andelip Turhan opened the door, a dense cloud of incense came wafting out. A different stick must have been burning in every corner of the itsy-bitsy flat.

I had warned Hüseyin beforehand about Andelip's weird taste in fashion, but not even I was expecting this. She was wearing a long navy kimono that brushed the floor. Compared to Ponpon's kimonos, which were embroidered on the front and back, Andelip's rather plain kimono might even be said to qualify as perfectly acceptable. But instead of a sash she was wearing a lace garter belt around her waist. Over the kimono! And as if this weren't enough, she had attached tiny handkerchiefs of different colors to the belt's stocking clasps. She had four on each leg. She had pulled back her curly hair using a cord made by tying the same color combination of handkerchiefs to each other. With a different ring on each finger and countless bracelets on her wrists, the woman looked like a walking Christmas tree.

She put on a little show for us, twirling twice right where she stood, so that her stocking clasps and the handkerchiefs attached to them lifted into the air and seemed to take flight.

"Cute, isn't it?" she asked.

"Very," I said, thinking the look on my face wouldn't give me away.

I'd always wondered who could possibly wear those clothes by wild designers like Vivienne Westwood—I didn't need to anymore.

"Darling, wearing special clothes is an essential part of tarot rituals. Clothes that you wear *only* during tarot readings. And mine is this garter belt and colorful handkerchiefs that help balance energy. Why else would I be dressed like this? Right, sweetie?"

The scent wafting from the apartment combined with the view before him was clearly making Hüseyin have second thoughts. I had to grab him by the arm and shove him inside as I introduced him to Andelip.

"Yes, this is him," said Andelip, adding, "I recognize his aura," as she stroked the confused and wary Hüseyin's face.

Just two more steps and we were in the middle of the apartment.

"Please excuse me, this place is a mess. My thoughts are so preoccupied with you two I couldn't even tidy up. I see you in each and every reading. This isn't normal at all. Then again, what is? Right, sweetie?"

The overfamiliar "sweetie" was directed at me. She wouldn't address Hüseyin, whom she had only just met, as sweetie. I swallowed my irritation.

The mess she was talking about wasn't a mess made over two or three days. It seemed there wasn't a single closet in the entire apartment. Everything was just lying about. The TV was on. A muted Kevin Spacey film was playing.

"I was watching a film while I waited for you."

She fished the remote control out of the mess with the kind of expertise that only comes with practice, and paused the DVD.

"I've seen it God knows how many times already. I know it by heart."

We looked for somewhere to perch. Alas, the huge divan by the window and the two armchairs next to it were buried under heaps of junk. Accessorizing the divan was a mountain of magazines, newspapers, clothes rolled up in balls so that you couldn't tell what was what, bits and bobs all tangled up, and at the summit, an orange. Now, that's what I call a still life.

"Please, sit down," she said.

She must have thought her place was the lobby of the large and spacious Hilton, with its rows of empty seats and aisles you could walk down for miles. When I reached out to move the thing I thought was a blanket from the armchair next to me, I realized it was a jacket made from a blanket.

Andelip held her arm out.

"I'll take that."

It would take an eternity if we went about removing the things on the armchair one by one. She threw the jacket onto the divan, and then, shoving a few things aside, made room for one buttock, while the other squashed against the precarious mountain of magazines and balled-up clothing.

Mimicking the host is a general rule of good manners. I pushed aside the pile on the armchair to make enough room for me to keep my balance, and seated myself.

Hüseyin stared at the humongous mess around him, not knowing what to do.

"Good thing you turned up," said Andelip. "I'm receiving strong signals already."

The smell of incense was strong enough to burn the back of one's throat. I coughed.

"Is it the incense?" she asked. "Or is that a cough of skepticism?"

When she asked me to follow her into the kitchen, I thought she wanted me to help serve the treats she had prepared for us. I was wrong.

She took a whirl on the spot and gave flight again to her colorful handkerchiefs. Her spin cornered me by the refrigerator.

"He is a pleasant and clean-cut man. But isn't he a bit young for you?" she asked.

She had suddenly triggered all my conscious and unconscious defense mechanisms.

"We don't have that sort of an attachment."

She stared right into my eyes, as if by boring into them she would succeed in seeing the truth of which she was convinced.

She tapped my chest with her finger.

"Actually, that's what I want too . . . Someone who's not going to question me about what, where, how, and from whom I learned what I know."

I had no intention of asking such a thing. Just because she was going to tell our fortune didn't mean that I had to know all of Andelip's bedroom secrets and how she developed her mysterious skills. If, however, this intimate moment we were having was meant to prod me to share my secrets—well, she had best not get her hopes up.

"I really am sick and tired of every man I'm with asking me where I learned the tricks I know, who I've slept with before, what I've tried, how I became such an expert . . ."

I think she was flattering herself—I wasn't biting at her need to share her secrets with me. I had no desire to know her area of expertise.

"Someone plain and simple like this one could do me good . . . You understand what I mean, don't you, sweetie?"

"Of course," I said, to cut her short and keep her from prying any further.

"Men always ask," she continued. "The young ones ask because they're curious to learn, the old ones because they fear I might be more experienced than them. But you've got the best . . ."

What she meant by "the best" was of course a mystery to me.

The table where she would do the reading was located on a veranda that had been enclosed after construction, and which she preferred to call her "office." The entire space was enveloped in dark red velvet curtains. The massive walnut table was covered, as per tradition, with a black silk tablecloth, and on the table, in a chest with a velvet inner lining, wrapped again in a black head-scarf, the tarot pack awaited us. She had placed an egg-shaped bloodstone, which she said increases clairvoyance, on one end, and on the other a natural unworked lapis lazuli, which she said en-hanced psychic activity.

When Hüseyin, curious, reached out to touch the lapis, which glittered eerily in the light of the burning candles, Andelip stopped him.

"Crystals," she said, "they're unbelievably powerful . . . But please don't touch. They're filled with my energy . . ."

Hüseyin, who was trying to figure out what sort of sorcery, witchcraft, or exorcism he was caught up in, quickly pulled his hand away and seated himself in the chair that Andelip had pointed to.

"The cards are actually more active after midnight, but when we're dealing with signals as strong as these, it doesn't really matter."

She studied Hüseyin, scrutinizing him carefully, before we got started. She narrowed her eyes and stared, opened them wide and stared, closed them tight, lifted her chin, and stared. And then, fi-nally, she announced the result of her examination.

"You need to be cleansed, dear. I'll do that for you another day."

A puzzled look fell over Hüseyin's face. His eyes asked what exactly needed cleansing; did cleansing mean "doing away with someone," like it did in Turkish slang? If so, how would it be per-formed? His confused expression said, *I don't quite understand what I'm supposed to understand.* Yes, I could read all of that simply from the look on his face.

"She means your energy," I said, trying to keep it as brief as possible. "You know how everything in the universe has its own energy . . ."

"You mean aura," said Hüseyin, surprising me for the second time that day. He must have taken a crash course in general knowledge since we'd last slept together.

"Yes," I said, smiling a smile of satisfaction, "aura. Andelip can see people's auras."

"Not always," Andelip corrected me. "Only if I concentrate properly. Or if the person in question is strong."

Just as Hüseyin was about to puff up thinking his aura was being complimented, "Burçak's energy is extremely powerful. That's why we definitely want him in our Reiki sessions," explained Andelip. "I think that's why I got stuck on him today . . . His energy has an effect on me. It has an effect on my cards."

Andelip closed her eyes, then opened her right palm and waved it about, as if searching for something in the empty space between us.

"He doesn't know it, but his energy is tremendous. It reaches all the way to here, look . . ."

She was pointing to the empty space approximately seventy centimeters away from me.

"Sweethearts. We'd best begin. My head is throbbing."

With utmost reverence she reached out to the pack of cards in front of her and unfolded the black silk in which the cards were meticulously wrapped.

"In normal sessions I use a mythic tarot deck because it's more posh and intellectual, but yours is a different situation. I've chosen the Rider-Waite deck, which has become one with me over the years. As a matter of fact, I wasn't the one doing the choosing. I put all the decks in front of me and waited, thinking it was going to be Celtic tarot. But, lucky you, it was my favorite deck that spoke to me instead."

Hüseyin's eyes continued to widen in disbelief. He stretched out his leg underneath the table and gently kicked me.

"I'll do the ten-card Celtic cross spread. We won't open the last card if you don't want to . . ."

As Andelip looked at the cards that she turned over one by one, she groped for a strand of her curly hair, pulled on it, took it between her lips, and began slowly chewing. Once she'd finished sucking one strand, she'd find a different one from a different area, and the process would begin all over again.

The lovers card was reversed; the moon and wheel of fortune were right side up.

"Someone who is madly in love," she said, tapping the lovers card with her index finger.

It was impossible to miss the smile spreading across Hüseyin's face.

"At the same time, a warning against enemies. You have a dangerous admirer," she said, placing her hand on the moon card. "It's as if he's walking toward the dark. The dark . . . It is impossible for him to escape . . . He's delusional.

"As for the wheel of fortune . . . The most difficult card to interpret. Events beyond their own power . . . Marking the end of an era . . . New, inescapable events await you . . . Things that are beyond control . . . Could be good or bad . . . But it's usually not auspicious when paired with the five of swords and moon card. Close . . . Very close . . . Someone very close to you . . ."

The hanged man was also reversed. Andelip tapped it with her index finger a couple of times as she chewed on a particularly thick bundle of hair. She lifted her eyes from the cards and seemed to stare into infinity over my shoulder.

"A loss . . . Warning against a loss . . . Inability to see the truth . . . Oh, I don't know! Three of swords, warning . . . Warning!

Warning! It keeps appearing . . . Prepare for something undesirable . . ."

I gulped. I was short of breath, as if someone had placed a heavy stone on my chest. Hüseyin had finally stopped trying to play footsie with me; his cheeks aflame, he stared at the card in the middle without blinking an eye, watching Andelip's ringed finger as if hypnotized.

"The devil card . . . Reversed . . . Disastrous inclinations! Uncontrollable powers . . . Actions for which explanations are denied . . . Fear! Damage of unprecedented proportions . . ."

I held my breath and listened. Just when we had reached the most vital point, we jumped from our seats at the sound of car horns rising from the street. The silence of the tarot ritual had been broken. The noise grew louder all of a sudden, even though we were at the back of the building. People were screaming and shouting. The doorbell rang.

Andelip went to the door with an annoyed look on her face.

We could hear her talking to a man who was clearly nervous, but we couldn't make out his words.

She called inside.

"If the taxicab outside is yours, apparently it's on fire."

Shocked, Hüseyin didn't respond at first.

"It's ours!" I said, jumping up from my seat.

By the time I reached the garden gate with Hüseyin in tow, flames had already enveloped the entire hood. Out of solidarity, two other taxi drivers were trying to put it out with fire extinguishers. There was dense smoke and a burning smell. I stopped and turned around. There was Hüseyin, kneeling on the ground, his head buried in his hands, watching with disbelief as his livelihood went up in flames.

I glanced at my watch. It was past midnight.

"Son of a bitch!" I said angrily from between clenched teeth.

21.

*T*he car wasn't insured.

"They don't insure taxis," explained Hüseyin. "Because we're in traffic all day . . . The only thing that's worth money on this is the registration plate. But it's gone!"

The other two taxi drivers, whom we had thanked, had left, as well as the curious crowd of onlookers, and we stood in front of the burned car, the blanket of foam turning into white stains. If I hadn't known better, I never would have believed that this had been a yellow cab just half an hour ago.

"The bastard must have doused it in gas or petrol or something!" he said.

We stood there as if hoping that, if we waited long enough, the taxi would return to its previous state.

It was a starry night.

A sweet breeze caressed my skin. It was a quiet street, not very busy. No passersby. The lights in the building opposite were already out.

Even the street dogs that multiply in this season and roam the streets in packs at this time of night were nowhere to be seen.

How quiet it was.

We stood there with the stars above us.

Did Andelip's prophecies have to come true so quickly? Loss, events beyond our control, darkness, the wheel of fortune, five of swords, the reversed hanged man and reversed devil.

"What now?" I asked calmly.

Hüseyin looked me straight in the face. I wanted to avert my eyes but didn't. I didn't know what to do, how and with what expression to look at him. What was he looking for in my eyes? What feeling? I raised my eyebrows and tightened my lips, only to repeat my question.

Hüseyin huffed and puffed noisily, looking up at the stars in the sky. He was chewing on his bottom lip. Then his head sank down. With the tip of his shoe he spread a blob of the fire extinguisher foam splattered in front of him onto the pavement. And then he slowly lifted his head, looked into my eyes, and answered with a crooked smile.

"We've got to go and report it to the police. Then I'll borrow some money, or take out a loan from the bank, get my dad to back me up, get my mom to hand over a couple of gold bracelets, and I'll buy a new one."

I wanted to hug him, whisper words of consolation, tell him I loved him even though I wasn't in love. I did neither.

We stood there motionless, until Andelip called us in. "I've made you a special mix of herbal tea."

There was an ounce of the famous weed in the special herbal mix. Its smell had mixed with that of the incense, but it was still distinctive when I brought the cup closer to my nose.

"Just a pinch," said Andelip, grinning. "The rest is linden, fennel, a little hibiscus, and chamomile. Just to relax you before going to sleep . . . It isn't that powerful when brewed . . . And it's not addictive. Not one bit! I know because I've been having cups and cups before going to bed for years. If it were addictive I would have grown addicted to it by now. Isn't that right, sweetie? I know what I'm talking about. One hundred percent natural."

She giggled as if we were partners in crime.

She'd been drinking cups and cups for years and it wasn't addictive.

I pulled my mobile from the pocket of my jacket, which I had left on top of Andelip's crowded armchair. The expected message had arrived.

"There! I kept my promise. This is only the beginning . . ." he had written. The message had been sent eight minutes after midnight. He was both punctual and violent.

How many "beginnings" did this make already? I was dealing with a psycho who couldn't count. He had said the same thing after Master Sermet, and after Süheyl Arkın, whom he hadn't even shot himself . . .

We finished our natural herbal tea and got up to leave.

"Gül was looking for you. Did she find you?" asked Andelip.

"I got her message, but I haven't had a chance to call her back yet," I answered, with hardly a blush of embarrassment.

I motioned toward the cards on the tarot table, the reading of which remained unfinished.

"Life recently . . . you know . . ."

"Oh, of course," she said, fiddling with the handkerchiefs hanging from the garter belt. "You're coming on Monday, aren't you? We're meeting at Cavit and Şirin's place."

She was referring to our routine Reiki meetings.

"If everything turns out all right . . ."

"He's such a cutie!" she whispered in my ear. "I really like him. He's upset now. Make him happy."

With a kinky wink she indicated just how I could make Hüseyin happy.

No, he's not my boyfriend, and he never will be, I wanted to say, but Hüseyin was right next to me. And he'd been through enough for one day as it was.

"And before I forget, he needs a serious aura cleansing. See that it gets done . . ."

I wanted to tell her to be careful, that the loathsome creature that was after me now knew where she lived too, that he was unpredictable, like she had said; a dark person lost in the dark, who used uncontrollable power. But I didn't. Who was I to warn someone who saw and knew everything so clearly? Certainly her cards, crystals, or clairvoyance would warn her if she were in danger. Still, the fact that my psycho now knew her address too weighed upon my mind.

Now our midnight roller-coaster ride of police, police station, reporting the event, Hüseyin's Breathalyzer test had begun. Only a little well-placed "donation" oiled the creaky machinery of the police department. It was an uphill battle because Hüseyin, like every driver, had left his registration tucked in the pocket of the sun visor and so it had gone up in flames together with the car. We had to get more generous with our "donations." Andelip's natural herbal tea had made us very relaxed. I silently submitted to insulting behavior I would have objected to on any other day, with a moronic grin plastered on my face the entire time. Judging by the uninterested looks on the faces of those I encountered, I hadn't yet done anything truly weird.

It had been not only a nerve-racking day, but a physically exhausting one too, and I'd woken up earlier than ever. And it hadn't yet ended; here I was among police officers, a profession which wasn't a particular favorite of mine, at the police station. I felt as if my tongue had swollen, a tingling sensation buzzed in my head, and I wanted to keep yawning big, gaping yawns.

Yes, I was simply drained, completely exhausted.

I stood waiting in the corridor, leaning against the wall while Hüseyin dashed from one room to the next trying to sort out his documents, sloppy every now and then only to borrow more money from me.

By the time we reached the club at nearly two o'clock in the morning, I had sobered up completely.

Our bodyguard Cüneyt instantly took notice of the fact that Hüseyin was emerging from a taxi he wasn't driving himself.

He grinned, displaying each and every one of his teeth.

"What's up, Hüseyin Abi? Have you sold the car and come to spend all the money?"

Followed by a flirtatious wink of the eye.

Neither I nor Hüseyin responded. Cüneyt, seeing the sullen look on my face and regretting his father joke, quickly pulled himself together and stood at attention as he held the door open for us.

I wasn't in the mood for the club. I didn't know why I had come. It must have been habit.

DJ Osman was at it as usual, playing that electronic trance music I despise. Before even saying hello to anyone, I signaled for him to switch to a decent melody, which he did immediately. Those who had been swaying mindlessly in the middle of the dance floor, carried away by a trance rhythm capable of rearranging my internal organs, suddenly stopped, confused. He now played one of the Brazilian CDs left to us by Suzy Bumbum Ricardo, whom we had presented as "The Girl from Ipanema," as in the famous song; it was Djavan's "Milagreiro," which Osman had grown especially fond of. It didn't put anyone in the mood to dance and the floor quickly emptied. It was a rather melancholic, mournful tune. To change the track again, though, would be too jarring. I let it play, a melody of hurt; it was a chance for people to sit down, have a few drinks, and make the club some money.

Hasan, who had noticed I was sulking from the moment we walked in, preferred to wave from a distance rather than come near me and risk treading on a mine. He was sitting with a girl whose face I couldn't see because her back was turned to me. Who-

ever it was, she was gaudy as could be and was wearing a Mireille
Mathieu wig you could tell was fake from miles away. I always tell
the girls not to come dressed so gaudily, that they look like they're
wearing their mother's hand-me-downs when they do.

Şükrü slipped a Virgin Mary into my hand at the speed of light.
He knew from experience that he would be scolded if he kept me
waiting, and that he'd be in for a real lashing if he did so at a time
like this, with me sulking the way I was.

"What can I get you, *abi*?" he asked Hüseyin.

First Cüneyt at the door, and now Şükrü, who was a full-grown
man. Addressing Hüseyin as *"abi"* could mean only one thing: a
sign of respect for my "partner."

"Ayol, you're over forty. How can Hüseyin ever be your *abi*?"
I said.

"It's a sign of respect," he said, with a saucy grin on his face.

Right, that was it. Hasan was in deep shit.

I looked over to where he was sitting and wiggled my finger at
him in warning. But instead of Hasan, the gaudy chick sitting opposite him turned to look at me. She opened her mouth halfway as
if for a dental inspection, thinking she was presenting a winning
smile. Then she waved at me. Her makeup was monstrous. The
fake eyelashes, the lavish coating of blue eye shadow, whore-red
lips, and, as if all that weren't enough, she had applied glitter to her
cheeks and neck. The face looked familiar, but, no, it couldn't be!
That horrific imitation of a transvestite could not possibly be Chief
Police Inspector Hilmi.

I went over to her, forging a path through the crowd that had
now returned to the dance floor.

"Hello," she said, straightening the artificial hair on her temples.

"What an incredible transformation," I said. "I can hardly believe my eyes. What a surprise . . ."

Thus did I avoid making comments that included adjectives like "good," "beautiful," "nice," or, more truthfully, "horrific."

She reached out and placed her hand on Hasan's.

"Hasan helped me out," she said proudly.

So it was Hasan who had done this to her. This was his understanding of fun; he had turned the man into a laughingstock. Meanwhile, she had no idea what was going on and was quite happy and content with herself. I was sure she thought she looked like that goddess of pop star beauty, Türkan Şoray.

"It hasn't been easy, but I have another surprise for you."

So *this*, this state of hers, was intended as a surprise for me. She handed me the second surprise—the CD I was supposed to have recorded, found in Master Sermet's home.

"That's not the original," he said, in his deep officer voice. "We copied it."

"Then the source code is going to be from your computer, isn't it?"

"Well, I wouldn't know that. But the contents are *exactly* the same."

These last two sentences were said in a confusing mix of identities: half serious officer tone, half in the voice of a transvestite on the verge of reaching a fake orgasm.

Overcome with enthusiasm at the sight of a girl he hadn't tried before, Gazanfer had come to the table. Hasan didn't miss his chance.

"Let me introduce you two. Gazanfer Abi, this is Türkanş. Türkanş—"

The smile on Gazanfer's face froze when he heard the name.

"Pardon me, I didn't quite catch that," he said, doing his best to remain polite. Thinking he had misunderstood, he leaned in closer to Hasan to hear better.

"What kind of a name is that?" I almost heard him say, as I walked away with the copy of the CD in my hand.

I wasn't going to stay until closing time. I was exhausted.

We collapsed onto the bed. I didn't object to Hüseyin sleeping next to me, though neither he nor I had the mental or the physical energy for another round.

22.

 his time I was the one to wake up first. I was sweaty, needed to pee, and had a headache. Half of Hüseyin was on top of me. Taking great care not to wake him, I pushed his arm and leg off of me and got out of bed.

A new day was starting.

It was a bright, sunny day, just as the starry sky the night before had heralded. Colors were clear and bright, the Bosporus, of which I could see a nib in the distance, was sapphire blue. I opened the windows wide to get some fresh air.

I took two Advils for my headache and made myself some strong coffee. A shower and I'd be ready for the day.

I sat in front of the window and, as I drank my coffee with a view of the roofs of Cihangir out my window, planned my day. I had to make Satı, who had promised to come today to make amends, clean the whole house. Then I had to look into the CD. I couldn't sit at home all day and wait for the bodyguard Cemil Kazancı was going to send. I hoped he'd call me soon and let me know when to expect my "protection."

I heard someone pass by on a bike. I looked out the window anxiously: it was only a man out with his dog. One lazy dog walker, though: he got to ride his bike while the beautiful golden retriever had to run alongside him. Not every cyclist in the city was going to be my psycho's female collaborator. Still, the sight of someone riding a bike was enough to put me on edge. My psycho was achieving his goal, and turning me into a complete neurotic. He had destroyed that "inner peace" of which he had been so jealous.

The arabesque song "So Long, My Peace of Mind" played in my head. It was now time to take a shower and investigate the CD Türkanş had brought.

Just as I was about to exit the shower, Hüseyin walked into the bathroom, scratching his messy hair.

"Morning, babe," he said, in his husky morning voice.

He was getting too carried away with this boyfriend business.

"Don't come out. I'll join you in a minute," he said, starting to piss.

"I've finished," I said, drying myself off. "Besides, we've got a lot to do."

I left him alone with his early morning enthusiasm. Discussing and clarifying our current situation, we quickly added to today's to-do list.

The CD found in my aikido Master Sermet Kılıç's apartment, which was supposed to have been recorded on my computer, was an ordinary mixed-music CD. I examined it carefully to see if there were any hidden files or other encoded data. Nope, nada. Twenty-four tracks had been recorded. The playing time was seventy-eight minutes and thirteen seconds. There was no way I had burned it: the music choice was nothing like the type of music I'd listen to. A bunch of string instruments playing minor rhythms and a woefully dismal melody. I listened to the songs one by one. Maybe something would turn up in between tracks.

While I listened, I examined my face in the hallway mirror. My face seemed to have aged a good three years from so much exhaustion, and stress, and lack of sleep. I immediately applied a skin-freshening beauty mask made from extracts of seaweed harvested from the depths of the ocean. The tiny jar cost a fortune but it was worth it.

Hüseyin paced up and down the apartment grumbling to himself. While preparing breakfast he called everyone he knew, starting with his father, to inform them about his taxi being set on fire. The phone was constantly busy.

I was still sitting in my bathrobe, a towel wrapped around my head, the green mask starting to dry on my face, when the doorbell rang.

"Can you get the door?" I called to Hüseyin.

A second later he was standing in front of me.

"Someone's asking for you," he said.

Of course a person at the door would be asking for me. This was my place.

"Who is it?" I asked.

"I don't know, I didn't ask."

I untied the waistband on my bathrobe, tied it again tightly, and made my way to the living room.

Hüseyin hadn't let the visitor in but had left him at the front door.

"Yes," I said, in my most green-skinned alien state. "I'm Burçak Veral."

Before me stood a man with a huge chin, huge nose, and a flimsy mustache in between.

"The boss sent me," he said. "Mr. Kazancı."

The name was explanatory enough.

It was strange that the Mafia should send a guy who looked like a hawker from an outdoor bazaar to watch over my house. I was expecting someone more flashy, muscular, with shoulders, tall, clean-shaven, and, most importantly, younger; someone like the lifeguards in the TV series *The Guard*.

My "protection" was about fifty, feeble-looking, and short. He had combed back his plentiful hair. His forehead was wide, his cheeks sunken. He had large hands. For me, he was disappointment on all counts.

"I'm Yılmaz," he said, holding the front of his jacket. "Yılmaz Karataş."

"Okay," I said, tightening my bathrobe waistband some more.

"I've been asked to watch your apartment."

"Yes."

I glared at him.

"I'm a retired sergeant," he said, as if sensing my disappointment. "From the intelligence agency."

That was good news, at least.

"Where would you like me to wait?"

"What do you mean?" I said.

I wasn't about to choose where he'd sit and wait.

"I could stand outside the apartment building or sit in my car across the street," he said, shedding light upon the issue at hand. "It's a '98 gray Toyota."

Indicating the bag on the floor by his feet, which resembled a miniature suitcase, "I've come prepared," he said. "I've brought my portable stool, my music, and crossword puzzles with me."

He smiled a reassuring smile. He had big teeth that were black in between. The fourth or fifth tooth on the right was missing. You could see it when he smiled.

"Don't you worry, sir," he said. "Not even a fly will enter without me knowing. It's not a busy street anyway. I'll take a good look at everyone who passes by this street. But what are we going to tell the building residents?"

"I don't know," I said. "What can we say?"

"We'll think of something," he said, nodding his head. "If you need anything, I'll be downstairs. I wouldn't want to disturb you any further. I can see you're doing your skin care."

I apologized for the mask on my face. There was no need for me to be rude to the man just because he had disappointed me in the looks department.

When he reached the top of the stairs, he turned around and asked another question.

"Excuse me, may I disturb you if I need to go? Or would you rather I used the caretaker's lodgings?"

This hadn't occurred to me, but of course he could use the toilet.

"And to eat, please do come up to eat," I said. "Tea will be ready any minute."

"Please don't go to any trouble," he said, motioning toward his bag again. "I've got my thermos and sandwiches with me."

"I didn't think much of him at first, but he actually seems a rather skillful man, unassuming but observant," I said to Hüseyin.

"I wouldn't know."

As if I would. As if I'd always lived with bodyguards, under surveillance.

"We need to go to the drivers' union," he said. "I don't know what needs to be done, but there must be a procedure for a taxi being set on fire, a way to use the license plate on another car."

I told Hüseyin that I had other plans.

"If we finish early, we can go see a couple of cars. I've told the guys about it, they're going to let me know if they find something suitable."

It seemed the time had come for me to address that delicate topic of us. I ran the risk of hurting him, but it had to be done.

"You know what—" I began.

But I was interrupted by the sudden sound of people talking in the next room.

We both noticed it at the same time.

We looked at each other, trying to figure out what was going on.

I stood up and went into the study. I had completely forgotten about the CD, which had been playing softly in the background. Now it was playing the sound of groans, and a conversation interspersed with gasps and screams. One of the voices belonged to my ex, the opera background singer Aykut. And the other person making the erotic noises must have been me. I went red all the way to the roots of my hair. My lovemaking with Aykut had been recorded. We were listening to it. My blood froze. I knew my mouth was open in shock.

Someone had recorded the noises in my bedroom! In my bedroom!

I rushed to stop the CD.

I didn't know what to think.

"Who was that?"

At first I didn't understand what he meant.

"Who was the man you were making love with?" repeated Hüseyin.

I would rather he hadn't heard it. But the noises we were making were not easily ignored. We were literally screaming and shouting.

"An old someone," I said. "It was months ago."

That was true. I hadn't seen him for months. He had dreams of becoming a pop star. He was making an album. It wasn't out yet.

"He must have been pretty good, judging by the noises you're making," Hüseyin said sulkily.

That was true too. Aykut was a stallion. There was no stopping him. And it seemed Hüseyin was jealous.

"You're jealous . . ." I said in amazement.

His head hanging low, he straightened the tassels on the edge of the carpet with his bare feet. His feet were nice and smooth too, just like his hands.

"So?" he said. "Only stupid and ugly people don't have jealous lovers. And you're not ugly or stupid."

He lifted his head and looked at me. There was a bright, hopeful expression on his face.

"But I'm not in love with you," I said, just like that.

I couldn't possibly have known how many different versions of this conversation he had already played out in his head, but it seemed he had prepared himself for such a reply.

"You can get used to me if you want to," he said. "I'm a good person. I'll try to make you happy. Okay, I might not be as good as him in bed, but tell me what you want, and I'll do it. I can do anything."

A man's pride rarely permitted such declarations. Yet there was Hüseyin, willingly pouring his heart out, holding nothing back.

His goodwill was heart-wrenching.

"That's not the point," I said, trying to smile.

I could feel my face grimacing in lieu of a smile.

"What, then?" he said. "I'm not cultured, sophisticated, smart, or flashy enough for you, is that it? You're ashamed of me because I'm a taxi driver. Is that it? I saw yesterday how difficult you find it to introduce me to other people. You didn't know what to say."

He was right. I really didn't know how to describe or introduce him.

"Why didn't you say I was your lover? Or your boyfriend? I wouldn't have been ashamed."

Yeah, right, as if you weren't the one telling me what to wear when we were going to see your mom. Don't be ashamed around her next time, I thought of saying.

"What about your family?" I said to cut it short.

"Oh . . . You mean when we were going to my mom's . . ."

"Yep, that's exactly what I mean . . ."

He scratched his nose.

"I don't know," he said. "I hadn't thought of it like that. But you might be right. They need to know too. They might not understand at first, but they'll probably get used to it. However long it takes . . ."

This conversation would have been so much easier if he hadn't been so understanding. He was leaning against my desk. I didn't move. His gaze had entrapped me.

"You're too good for me," I said, gulping. "But I want you to know that everything you said has made me very proud. Really. Thank you."

I couldn't have given a more professional talk.

"You don't want a relationship," he said, going back to where he'd left off, as if I hadn't said anything.

He had fixed his eyes on mine, waiting, ready to make meaning out of a single blink, a single twitch.

His Adam's apple moved up and down when he swallowed. He held his shoulders upright.

We just waited. For something to happen, for someone to come, come and interfere. We needed a savior, someone other than the two of us.

Time had frozen like it always does in scenes like this.

Someone had to do something.

"I can't come with you," I said quietly. "To the union or the . . ."

"I understand," he said.

His voice was deeper and huskier than ever.

He turned around and walked out of the room.

Hüseyin arranged to meet with one of his friends from the taxi stand to sort out the bureaucratic to-do list together. He thought he'd already had his turn as the target of the psycho's wrath with his car being burned. Forgetting his fear of the psycho for a while, he let the realities of everyday life take over.

"Can I come back when I've finished?" he said.

What could I say? I simply nodded.

He placed a kiss on my cheek before he left.

Now I was going to sit down and listen to this CD with the pornographic recordings, from start to finish. I had listened to the first track, I knew that one already, so I skipped it. I knew the next one too. This was the group Emerson, Lake & Palmer, which I sometimes listened to myself. There were noises in the background I couldn't make out that kept surfacing and then disappearing. It was hard to understand while listening like this. I put my earbuds in. Yes, there sure were other noises in the background. In the next, and the next track too. And then in the fifth, the noises got louder and clearer. This was Handel's *Water Music*. And I could hear my own telephone conversation over it. It sent shivers down my spine. I was giving one of the girls advice. Next track. It was Handel again. This time it was the Alcina opera series and there were water sounds in the foreground. The shower! My shower! I was trying to sing along with the aria.

My apartment was bugged! The psycho had been recording and listening in on my apartment for months. My bedroom, my living room, my bathroom . . . it was everywhere. I looked around in panic, as if I were going to turn around and immediately see the listening device. I wanted to find it, rip it apart, and throw it away. I was sure that I was being being watched too.

My back went ice-cold. My hair stood on end.

Everything I said in the house was being listened to.

I remembered that audio recordings do not count as valid evidence in court, which was a relief as I recalled the million illegal things I'd talked about in my apartment, the latest being the Cemil Kazancı business.

I couldn't speak a word at home anymore. I couldn't call anyone.

I listened to the whole CD. It was simply scandalous. Everything was on it. He'd done the sampling, queued a bit of this and a bit of that, and then created this CD. Everything that had happened in the privacy of my home.

I had to search for the listening devices. But where were they? And what were they? The more technology advanced, the smaller the little bugs had gotten. The latest photocell technology ones resembled stamp-sized tinfoil. No wires, no batteries. As long as they absorbed a little daylight every now and then, they could function flawlessly for years.

When had they bugged me? My relationship with Aykut had ended months ago. So that trick the previous day with the telephone technicians, or something of a similar sort, had happened at least once before. Satı, as I'd learned, wouldn't volunteer anything unless she was asked. They must have come the previous day to replace a bug that had malfunctioned. Why was I the target? What did he want?

He'd hacked my Web site. And my computer. He knew where I went and who I was seeing. He was both watching and listening in on my home. What kind of a pest, what sort of a lunatic, was I up against?

Again, I thought longingly of escape plans, leaving everything behind and fleeing. But I had forgotten to extend my goddamn passport.

I hadn't thought of it in my first sudden fit of depression, but I could call Selçuk and have my passport extended the same day. All I'd have to do was pack up my things.

I would be able to escape Hüseyin and his hopeless love for me. And the psycho. It would be like a long, never-ending holiday. I could get lost in places where no one knew me, where people expected nothing from me.

After dreaming up such radical fantasies of escape, it became easier to generate more reasonable solutions. I could move to a hotel or stay with someone for a while. Ponpon's home was a castle I could seek refuge in any day. But, alas, my psycho knew that place too, and thus it would mean putting Ponpon in danger.

Although he would complain, I could be a guest at Alı's place for a while. But it would be a blow to his machismo in the eyes of his neighbors, and in the area where he lived, *that* was equivalent to death.

I could move into Genteel Gönül's, where I was sure the psycho would never think of looking for me. Then again, I had spoken to Gönül on the phone quite often. He'd find me if our conversations had been recorded, so I'd end up pulling Gönül down with me as well.

He had turned me into a poisonous plant. Whoever came near me was in danger.

A hotel was the wisest option.

When Satı arrived I tried acting normal, as if nothing had happened. After all, I was being spied on. I packed a tiny bag, offering no explanations, only taking the essentials. I could buy new clothes, underwear, makeup equipment, and a toothbrush later.

Before leaving the building, I told Yılmaz, who had pitched a camp at the entrance of the apartment building and was solving crosswords busily, about the girl with the bicycle, whom he should watch out for. I gave him all the details about her supplied by know-it-all Melek. And I left a little note for him to pass on to Hüseyin when Hüseyin came back.

Yılmaz didn't ask a single question, or even give me a quizzical look. He was like one of those people who had long ago solved the mystery of life.

23.

*N*ext stop, the Blue Sky Hotel in Taksim. I knew the manager. He'd give me a deep discount.

I went up to my room and, after making the phone calls I needed to make without my psycho listening in, I headed straight to an Internet café. I had a lot to do.

As a precaution in case my Internet user IDs were also being traced, I created a new e-mail account.

I sent an urgent request for help to the Web-Guerrillas group, where good and evil hackers from all walks of life gathered. "Someone is accessing and using my computer, what should I do?" I asked. Suggestions would pour in before the end of the day.

Then I sent Jihad2000 a separate, private message. Of course, I took advantage of the opportunity to tell him just how much he had let me down. I explained at length that the situation was much more serious than he'd made it seem, that I really needed help, that if we were still friends now was the time for him to prove it, and exactly what it was I expected him to do. I was sure he'd be at his computer even in his sleep.

Sure enough, while I was still looking at a few Web sites, a short and simple reply from Jihad2000 arrived: "Okay." One thing down.

Once I had finished, I went to the brasserie at the Marmara Hotel. I ordered myself a ritz salad and a mineral water. Considering all of the food I had consumed over the previous couple of days, I'd best watch what I was eating.

I was now ready to turn on my mobile, which had been switched off since the night before. I was ready to hear from my psycho again.

As I sipped my mineral water and waited for my salad, a series of text messages, *his* text messages, were delivered to my in-box. He was raging. Each message got more and more angry.

Just when my salad arrived at the table, my phone rang. It came from yet another pay-as-you-go number.

"Like the recordings?" he asked in his croaking voice.

Of course, if he was listening in on my house, he knew I'd listened to the disc.

"Interesting," I said.

"You're just too *cool* for your own good, now, aren't you? Interesting? Hah! They're exquisite! Absolute perfection!"

"You're a lousy piece of shit," I said in a low voice. "It was pathetic of you to cut up my bras."

"You don't need them, you're a man."

"I get to decide what I wear," I said. "Setting the car on fire was unnecessary too. Hüseyin hasn't done anything to you."

"Now you're defending him just because he screwed you twice. Was it really worth being fucked? Did it give you inner peace, him fucking you like that, huh?"

Oh, so we were getting vulgar. I was ready to talk dirty.

"I'm sure your cock is tiny. I bet you can't even get it up."

Accusations of sexual inadequacy due to an itty-bitty malfunctioning wiener are enough to send a knife through the heart of any man. As a man myself, that much at least I knew for sure.

There was the silence I expected.

"You're wrong," he said.

"Your silence tells me that I'm not. Or maybe you were taking a look. So is it still in place?"

"Tonight," he said, in his thoroughly pissed off psycho voice, "Hüseyin dies!"

That had gotten him worked up; I could switch off my mobile now.

When I finished my salad I went upstairs to the lobby. There were phones on the side wall. I dialed Jihad2000's number.

"So?" I asked as soon as he picked up.

"Right," he said. "I was able to pick up the base station he's calling through. It's in your neighborhood."

"No shit! I know that already, *ayol*. The man is spying on my home. Of course he'd be calling from the same neighborhood."

"I'm not the CIA or Mossad. Don't overrate me. Mine is just an amateur home system. This is the best I can do. I can't give you an exact location."

It was impossible to miss the bitterness in his voice.

"Sorry," I said. "That's not what I meant. Thank you. By the way, how are you?"

"Compared to you, I'm good. I take on the jobs you lot turn your noses up at. Luckily I'm not stuck with another psycho like you."

With that, he reminded me of a previous stalker, in what had been another unpleasant scenario. Jihad2000 and I had first met thanks to similar threatening messages, written by none other than Jihad2000 himself.

"Let's not go down that road," he said when I reminded him. "It was an aggression rooted in suppression. I've overcome it, thanks to you."

It was kind of him to credit me.

"I'm seeing Pamir in a while," he said. "Going to her place . . . For the first time. Seeing as there's no hope with you . . ."

I wished him a wonderful time. I couldn't expect everyone to live a monk's life just because I was being sucked into a whirlpool of terror.

But I had urgent plans to make.

24.

When Hüseyin arrived, I was lying on my bed in the hotel room, reading a book. I had tried watching television to relax my mind, and when I couldn't find anything of interest to me, I'd gone out to buy a pay-as-you-go SIM card and a book. As the book's description promised, it would leave the reader breathless. Before I knew it, I'd already breezed through a third of it. It was just what I needed.

"I don't understand what's going on," he said. "But when Yılmaz handed me your note, I came as quickly as I could. Why are we staying at a hotel?" he continued, sitting down on the edge of the bed.

I put the book down and turned sideways. Placing my elbow on the bed, I rested my head in my hand. I smiled as adorably as Audrey would have.

"You first," I said. "How was your day? Did you sort everything out?"

First he took off his shoes, then his socks, and then he stretched his legs out on to the bed.

"Tiring," he said, exhaling a long sigh. "I'm not used to running around . . . I always sit at the wheel . . ."

He told me that he'd sorted out quite a lot. He'd even found a car he liked.

If he could get the money together, it could be running in four or five days, and he could get back to work.

"How much do you need?"

He was lying next to me, staring at the ceiling, twitching his tired toes.

"I can't ask you for money," he said. "I just can't."

I laughed. Him and his pride.

"I didn't say I was going to give it to you. I just asked how much you needed."

"A lot," he said, his eyes still fixed on the ceiling. "I mean, for me it is."

Of course I had to lend him money. What had happened to him was all my fault. But I had to find a way to overcome the tension generated by his manly pride.

"I'll lend it to you," I said. "You can pay me back whenever. You know I've got money."

"I can tell because we're staying at a hotel," he said with a laugh.

"I'm serious," I said, to convince him.

He turned his gaze from the ceiling to me.

I could tell he was weighing our relationship. If he owed me money he would be the one in debt to the relationship. I knew he didn't want this. While he thought of himself as lower than me on a number of levels, him owing me money too could jeopardize the relationship even more. On the other hand, he needed the money. If he got money from a pawnbroker or a bank he'd have to pay it back with interest.

"It's better if I handle it myself," he said calmly. "It looks like it's going to work out. If it doesn't, I'll let you know."

"I could give it to you, rather than you taking out a loan from the bank."

"We'll see," he said. "If I can't . . ."

I didn't mention that the psycho was planning to kill him to-night. What could he do if he did know?

Here we were lying side by side, a polite tension between us. He didn't have the energy for sex, and I had no inclination for it. If Andelip Turhan's mediumistic eyes were to see us like this, she'd probably say, *The tension between you is palpable.* Whereas Vildan Karaca, the feng shui master, would try to melt it away with all sorts of different crystals.

"Come on, let's go see the girls and have your aura cleansed," I said. "We have nothing else to do until nine o'clock."

"What are we doing at nine?"

"I don't know," I replied. "Pamir called and said she has a sur-prise for us. She and Jihad2000 must have found something. We're going to meet them at my place."

25.

By the time it was almost nine, Hüseyin's aura had been cleansed and we had both filled our stomachs. Bursting with powerful energy, we were ready for Pamir's surprise.

We hailed a passing taxi, to Hüseyin's sad chagrin.

I had already begun to sense something strange was happening as we drew closer to my place. There were far too many taxis lined up near the pavement, and far too much activity, unusual for our narrow little street.

There were our girls, gathered in a crowd in front of my apartment building. They appeared greater in number than they really were due to the size of the narrow street, barely enough for two cars to pass each other.

The watchman Yılmaz Karataş was standing behind the glass door of the building, his hands on his waist, observing the girls with a concerned look on his face, trying to figure out what was going on.

What was happening? Had the girls decided to gang up to protect me?

There was a commotion in the group when they noticed I had arrived.

I saluted them all as I stepped out of the cab. I felt like a king saluting his people, a queen saluting her subjects.

All the girls and some other people from the club were there waiting. Hasan and Pamir stood side by side outside the building door. What was Hasan doing here? What could those two possibly have conjured up? It seemed Pamir had gotten carried away playing the dominatrix in Jihad2000's arms and gone over the top. The crowd, thirsty for an outburst, was the product of Pamir's extreme shrewdness and Hasan's gossip network. Whatever it was they had in mind, it was sure to be a shocking surprise.

Pamir stepped forward as soon as she saw me. She was like a dignified general waiting for a command.

Murmurs rose from the group.

"How's it going, *abla*?" Pamir said with a proud look on her face before kissing me.

"What's going on, *ayol*?" I asked, without seeing any need to hide my confusion.

"Just you wait," she said, giving me a smart-ass wink.

She raised her hand for silence. "In a moment, I'm going to make a statement and explain everything," she said. "But please, give me a minute."

The response was a mingling of discontented grumbles and mumbles of curiosity.

"Sir, who are all these . . . these . . . ?" said Yılmaz, standing behind the apartment door, his eyes wide in astonishment.

I turned around to look at the crowd again. He was right in not knowing what to call them. The girls were each as colorful as could be; big and tall, they stood like Amazons ready for battle. The diversity in clothes, makeup, and wigs was truly indescribable.

"Transvestites," I said. "My friends."

One could tell from the look on his face that he didn't approve of the girls and that this gathering was not to his liking. "*Maşallah*, there are so many of them," he said, smiling halfheartedly. There was that missing tooth again.

Pamir pushed me into the building. Hasan followed, and we almost knocked Yılmaz Karataş over. As he stepped back, peeking at the notes he was holding in his hand, he recounted in a single breath everything that had happened during the day, who went in and out of the building, and everyone who had passed by. My eyes lit up when I heard the word "bicycle."

"We're going to catch your psycho on the job, *abla*," Pamir began, her eyes shining with excitement as she explained. "We know he's here. The bastard is hiding somewhere in these two streets."

It was a genius plan, if you asked her. My mind boggled at her organizational skills.

"I've sent news to all our girls and all the taxi drivers that know Hüseyin. They're on their way . . ."

Are you mad? I wanted to ask her, but not a single word escaped my mouth. My eyes were wide with astonishment; I simply listened. Hasan nodded at everything she said, and Yılmaz Karataş, who was clearly struggling to grasp what was going on, kept asking questions that were left unanswered.

"Just like in the eighties! We must take action!" She beamed bravely.

Yes, "take action" was an often used phrase. In the past, "take action" meant a gang of girls would gather to cause scenes and raise a ruckus in revenge on behalf of another girl believed to have been wronged. It could mean house raids, flushing towels down toilets, making messes (fecal and otherwise), shattering windows, breaking and ruining every fragile item in a home, tearing apart pillows, mattresses, armchairs, leaving not a single electronic item undamaged, cutting clothes up into a thousand pieces, in other words, inflicting the maximum amount of damage possible. The victim or victims would be those who hadn't paid a girl what she was owed, who had tricked one of the girls or treated her badly. There were those who raided police homes if they felt they'd been wronged. Once, even the boyfriend of one of the girls, who'd been living with her for four years, was dealt his share of a "take action" for refusing to pay for her cosmetic surgery expenses.

"Remember," said Pamir, "how many neighborhoods we raided during the resistance! There's no better time than now. Go on, take action!"

She was right, but it was different in those days. What we did back then was our way of taking a stance against those who'd provoked us. Whenever a couple of narrow-minded neighborhood inhabitants went about collecting signatures, trying to persuade others to join one of those "Away With the Transvestites" campaigns, the girls would attack, breaking doors and windows, entering and wrecking homes. Due to the hefty tips they received from the girls, and because they sold goods to them at inflated prices, local business owners were perfectly content to have them as neighborhood residents and so would have no part in these campaigns. As for those local business owners who did dare to oppose them, the girls would loot their stores and make a huge mess of their shops.

When the local campaigns succeeded, the transvestites would be packed onto trains and sent into exile. As if anyone actually believed that in Eskişehir, the city they were sent to, they would magically adopt the two-faced norms of the middle class and its heterosexual lifestyle. While there may have been some who truly believed such results would occur, their hopes would soon be dashed: the girls would promptly catch the next train back to Istanbul. The "Take Action" campaigns had helped to stop these misplaced raids and evictions. Now, even though my common sense objected, a piece of that old transvestite bravery and recklessness was whispering, *What if . . .*

Knowing that I was so dearly loved and protected and seeing that people would go to the ends of the earth for me filled my heart with pride. Nothing can beat pride. It heals you. A feeling of warmth spread throughout my body as I looked over to the crowd, quelling the restlessness in my mind.

Out of the corner of my eye I could see drivers pulling up in their taxis and joining the crowd. This was getting out of hand. Pamir's *perfect* plan was working.

At nine o'clock sharp we took our places in front of the door.

Pamir let out a sharp whistle. The murmuring ceased and all heads turned to face us. I made a rough count: there were more than forty people.

Though I couldn't see them, I was pretty certain residents of the apartment building were peering out of their windows too—especially the cat lover, retired Hümeyra, who lived on the ground floor, and my nosy downstairs neighbor Wimpy Ferdı—watching so as not to miss a thing. I could clearly see that residents of the entire building opposite were already at their windows.

A gathering of dozens of transvestites and local taxi drivers at this time of night in our little street probably wasn't making my neighbors feel relaxed. But they looked on, dying of curiosity. Something scandalous had landed right at their doorstep. They didn't want to miss a detail. Their minds were already spinning as they thought how they would recount the entire incident for those who had missed out, embellishing and exaggerating and twisting it all around into something absolutely extraordinary!

"First of all, I'd like to thank you all for gathering here and not letting me down," said Pamir in her thunderous voice. "As some of you might already know, Burçak is in danger. A psycho is stalking her. Threatening her. Breaking into her home. Spying on her and listening in on her. And that's not all. Whatever it is he wants, he takes out his anger onto those close to her, onto Hüseyin, Hasan, all of you, everyone that knows and is connected to her. We are under threat. You are all under threat! This man is a murderer! He has killed someone! Poisoned him . . . shot another! He set fire to Hüseyin's car . . . He sends out threat after threat to the club . . ."

Pamir, whose outrage increased with every sentence, was like a politician delivering a speech at a public rally. She was counting on the taxi drivers to act in solidarity in support of Hüseyin, and for the girls to do the same for me. It was important. She was appealing to their consciences, their minds, and their fears.

She recounted a slightly embellished version of what I had told Jihad2000 and he in turn had told her.

"This man is not alone. He has one male, one female collaborator. The girl rides a bike . . ."

"Why don't you give us the full description?" she turned to me and said. "You know better than me."

Now she was pushing me onto center stage. I stepped forward, unwillingly yet with that same recklessness brought on by their support of me. I shared Melek's description with them, re-creating the unknown accomplice in front of their eyes with my words. All eyes watched me curiously while heads nodded in approval.

"They have access to advanced technological devices," I added.

Of course, most of them weren't going to understand what I meant, so I went into detail and explained what bugging and recording devices looked like, what kinds of devices they'd needed in order to spy on me.

The crowd was getting bigger. Newcomers were trying to find out from the others what was going on.

"And here!" said Pamir, jumping at the opportunity presented by my brief pause. "In this neighborhood! In this street . . . he could be watching us right now . . ."

Heads immediately went into motion; eyes scanned their surroundings. Some of the neighbors began to look anxious.

"People are starting to look anxious," I whispered into Pamir's ear.

"Good, *ayol!*" she said. "The psycho killer is among them. They should stop hiding him! They should feel guilty for not having turned him in yet!"

She was right, I was sure of it: the psycho was among them. It was going to take time for them to digest what Pamir had said. I quickly scanned their faces. As their unease got louder, I raised my hands to silence them.

"What I ask of you—"

It would be best if no one did anything rash, I thought, but Pamir had something different in mind.

She grabbed me by the arm, pushed me back, and stepped forward again.

"Look!" she said. "What we're going to do is simple . . ."

Next she explained that we were going to search the neighborhood, by knocking on every door. In groups of twos or threes, starting at the building where I lived. We would then widen the circle. She repeated what we were looking for: a blue bike, a helmet with flame stickers and a hologram on it, red or purple Converse shoes, multichannel receivers likely connected to an ordinary computer, and, quite possibly, a sound mixer and an editing bay.

"I know these items won't be that easy to find, but if we find them all in once place, we may find our psycho."

She pulled out the cell phone tower area map Jihad2000 had drawn, and clearly outlined the borders of the area we'd be searching. Technology was such a wonderful thing. Jihad2000 had discovered which cell tower functioned in what street, and the apartment building number where each cell tower changed.

Someone was knocking on a window behind me. I turned to look. It was Hümeyra, motioning for me to come over.

"Yes?" I said, lowering my voice.

"Dear, they stole my bag on the street the other day. Thieves. From our neighborhood. In broad daylight. My black leather bag. It has brass ring handles. If you're doing such a thorough search, could you keep an eye open for my bag? Maybe you'll come across it. I don't care about the money, but my grandchildren's pictures and my marriage certificate were in it . . ."

I didn't know what to say.

Those at the front who overheard had already started giggling.

"Okay," said Hüseyin, standing next to me. "We'll keep an eye out for it, ma'am."

"It's black," repeated the old doddering dear. "With brass rings . . ." She proceeded to hold her hands out indicating the bag's size.

"All right, ma'am, we get it," said Hüseyin.

"Thank you, son," she said, and closed her window.

Our crowd was ready for action.

"Hold on a minute," called Hasan. "Don't get started just yet . . ."

It was natural for Hasan to want to say a couple more things, now that he'd found a ready crowd of listeners. He'd never miss the chance to take charge. Sure, our posse was ready to take action, but not all of the local residents would be so ready and willing to open up their doors to them and have their homes searched. Thus there were going to be doors that would remain closed.

"We're going to give you these maps," he said, waving the photocopies in the air, "so you can mark which apartments you've searched, which ones didn't answer, and which ones didn't let you in! Street by street . . ."

Clearly they had put a lot of work into this.

"If they don't let us in, then they must have something to hide," rang out a voice that was clearly prepared to riot.

"We'll force our way in, then!" said another.

"No-no-no-no . . . Friends," I said, feeling the need to intervene. "We will not use force . . . Just explain the situation and ask nicely. That's all. If they don't let you in, they don't let you in."

"But mark those apartments," said Hasan, "so we know who they are."

"What if we made them swear on the Koran that they weren't hiding the psycho?"

This question had to be from one of the girls. It was obvious from the tone and the naïveté. Many people did not take such oaths seriously these days. What made her think that people here would?

"That will never work, *ayol!*" said Pamir, trying not to laugh. On the one hand, we had Hümeyra, who wanted us to return her stolen bag, and on the other, our girls, who would be perfectly satisfied by an "honest to God oath" . . . It wasn't going to be easy to catch our psycho, but if we were relentless, perhaps we could pull it off.

"Does anyone else have any questions?"

The girls and some of the drivers were clearly ready to cause a commotion.

"Now, please, let's get into search groups," said Hasan, with all the authority of a military commander. "Twos or threes . . . Then everyone can take one of these sheets and each unit can start searching its own area!"

We were ready to embark upon our desperate operation.

The start signal had been given.

26.

*J*ust as Hasan finished, two police cars and one police van with blue and red police lights flashing on their roofs arrived. They closed off both ends of the street.

Our tiny little street was turning into a circus.

"All right, everyone, come on, clear out," they began, the words blaring through the vehicle megaphones. "C'mon, now, clear out!"

They were more than ready to charge at us.

The girls weren't afraid of the police; to the contrary, they were capable of standing up to them, even openly defying them. But the taxi drivers weren't like that. The drivers shrank back immediately.

Someone had called the police.

It could have been a neighborhood inhabitant who was alarmed at what was going on outside her window, or even our psycho himself.

Clearly the police didn't want to miss this opportunity. They always saw transvestites as trouble (from whom they were nevertheless plenty eager to demand free sex whenever they caught us alone in a quiet corner), and now those same transvestites had fallen into their clutches en masse; they were ready to play it rough. We were ready to give it right back to them.

I remembered what Hakan Gülseven, a journalist I admired, had once written: "Doubtless the wheels will continue to turn this way until the security forces realize it is their duty to save people's necks, not break them."

I was the cause of all this. It would have been unfair for Pamir or Hasan to be blamed just because they were the organizers.

I stepped forward.

I would accept all responsibility as the leader of this gang, on the condition that no one else was taken into custody. They invited me to the police station in an extremely polite manner I found difficult to fathom.

Even though Pamir tried to intervene—"No way, *abla*, you won't go alone!"—I was having none of it.

"Stay out of this," I said. "This has nothing to do with you."

This motley crew crowding the small street was her doing, it was true, but I was the one who had let it go on. I could have stopped it. I hadn't. So I had become responsible.

Hüseyin, who didn't want to leave me on my own, and Hasan, who couldn't bear to miss a single moment of this adventure, were determined to come with me. A driver whose face I recognized but whose name I didn't know stepped forward heroically to support Hüseyin.

When Pamir almost ignited an uprising to stop them from taking me away, I had to calm the girls down.

"Thank you," I said. "But there's no need. You all have things to do, families to go to . . . We'll handle it."

Our visit to the police station was perfectly civil—both on our part, and on those of the police officer gentlemen. They offered us tea. We sat in the chief's office, opposite the chief. He looked at me and muttered something or other every now and then; unsure of what to do, I looked at him and played silent piano sonatas on his table with my fingers.

We were waiting but didn't know for what.

About an hour later, my friend and police contact Selçuk Tayanç arrived. He'd been informed of what had happened. The station staff stood at attention to greet him. The chief left us his office so we could speak in private.

Selçuk waited until the door was shut.

"Are you out of your mind?"

He was angry. Really angry. I know him when he's like this . . . and how to handle him when he's in a mood like this. After all, we spent our entire childhood together.

"You create panic in the neighborhood. Start a human hunt to find the psycho killer. You were practically inciting a public riot!"

He was exaggerating, but I wouldn't have my say until he'd calmed down.

"I can't believe it! And there I was, thinking you a perfectly smart and rational human being . . . Now look what you've done! Typical transvestite behavior! I don't know where you get these crazy ideas. If I didn't know you . . ."

It was no use trying to explain myself when he was so angry. He roared and thundered.

"How could you? Calling an entire neighborhood to arms . . . A gang of transvestites convening in the middle of the street! Taxi drivers joining them . . . Who are you, to plan such a search? What were you going to do if you found him? Lynch him? Beat him to death? . . . You couldn't have stopped them . . . Like in a murderous riot! No wonder a neighbor called the police."

He finally sat down. Not at the chief's desk, but in the chair opposite me. He pulled out a pack of Marlboro 100's and tossed it onto the coffee table (which really could have used a new coat of varnish) between us.

"I quit, you know, but then I started back up again because of you! I smoked two on my way here."

"I'm sorry," I said.

Well, if it really was my fault he'd started smoking again, then what else could I say?

"But please, stop scolding me as if I were a child."

"But what you did was childish. You have to admit it."

He reached out and took a cigarette from the pack. He placed it between his lips and lit it with the plastic red lighter he was holding in his hand. He dragged on the cigarette, held the smoke in his lungs for a while, and then exhaled. In his actions I saw the passionate behavior commonly exhibited by nicotine addicts who had started again after quitting. He inhaled the smoke with immense pleasure, held the cigarette in his hand cautiously so as not to waste a single breath of it—like a lover fulfilling his hunger for a beloved he had remained separated from for a long time.

"Look, Burçak," he said, stretching his arm out toward me without letting go of the cigarette caught between his fingers. "What you've done . . . it isn't right."

"I know," I said calmly. "But it was the best idea we could come up with. We had even localized it. We might have even found him if your lot hadn't turned up."

It made no difference how much of what I said he did or did not believe. I had to put up a defense, no matter what. I had done this, allowed it to happen, and I had no intention of making excuses. He knew how stubborn I could be.

"Please don't start again! What did I just say? . . . Only the police have the right to conduct searches . . . It's not up to you. If you've localized him to a certain area, let us take care of the rest . . ."

Selçuk was getting old too. His body was still toned, but I noticed a few white hairs on his temples. And the contours of his face were not what they used to be.

"If you think you can fool me by saying that, well, you're

wrong," I said. "The police need a zillion documents to get a search warrant. There's a whole load of procedures. I read all about it, I know."

I really had read the new laws line by line. I did it so that I could protect the club from the officers who were new to the area and didn't know me, and came to the club claiming they were there to search us, but who were really just asking for protection money. I knew they couldn't walk in whenever they felt like it, and no way could they search us.

I was right. And Selçuk knew it. Instead of answering me, he took a puff from his cigarette.

"If you really know so well what we can and can't do, don't call me every time you get yourself into a mess! I just left my family's dinner table to come here."

"I really do apologize," I said.

The lines of his dimples were getting deeper. Those tiny holes, once attractive when he smiled, now looked like deep scars. He really was getting old.

"I'm not telling you so that you apologize," he said, lowering his voice and smiling to soften the effect of having lashed out at me a second ago. "I wouldn't have come if I didn't want to. But I did. Didn't I? Just leave this to me, that's all I ask."

I must be getting old too. Selçuk was two years older than me. Did two years make that much of a difference? Were my cheeks starting to sag too?

"I'm the one who's in danger," I said. "I get threats every second, my home is bugged with listening devices, someone has access to my computer and can do whatever he wants on it. He sends letters everywhere addressed to me. And other people are in danger too. Sermet Kılıç was murdered. Hüseyin's car was set on fire. You want me to go on?"

He listened to me, his mouth firmly closed, his eyebrows

raised. I noticed when he fiddled with his hair that it was getting thin, even though he wasn't losing it entirely. He had combed it back, carefully, like he always did.

His angry glare was chilling. I couldn't bring myself to continue.

It was Jihad2000 who had triggered the whole thing. He had called the psycho from his own pay-as-you-go SIM again and again, and dialed from my number every now and then too, waiting for him to pick up. Of course he hadn't picked up, but instead called my number to make new threats, which Jihad2000 had redirected to his own computer. This was enough to determine which cell towers he was calling through. He was in my neighborhood. Once Jihad2000 shared all of his findings with Pamir, Pamir had called Hasan, and the plan of action was made. Even though I wanted to believe that they had acted with all good intentions, I couldn't help being mad at them both. They were both in for a stern lecture, once my anger had cooled off.

And if our psycho had any brains at all, he wouldn't be sticking around after all that had happened.

Selçuk dropped the three of us off at the club on his way back home. Our invitation to join us for a drink was kindly turned down. I owed him, yet again.

27.

$\mathcal{A}$ll of the girls, led by Pamir, were waiting for us, brimming with curiosity. There was a small cry of joy when they saw we had made it back safe and sound. Yes, the neighborhood raid had fallen through, the psycho hadn't been found, their appetite for lynching had been left unsated, but still, they said, they had enjoyed themselves. As if this were some kind of game.

The marvelous plan had come to naught, I had made yet another visit to the police station, and I had been scolded by Selçuk. What's more, the psycho was still loose. I didn't have the energy to join in the girls' laughter, or recount the psycho's threats, make fun of him, and entertain them. The night in our world was still young, and I realized that his threat to get Hüseyin must still be valid.

Hasan got back to work, and Hüseyin went behind the bar to join Şükrü the bartender, where he could have some peace without being pestered by anybody. The two of them got along well enough.

I summoned DJ Osman. He knew from Hasan that I was pissed off; he wiped that saucy smile off his face and walked over to me.

"I want a peaceful night," I said. "Play soft, sweet music. No Brazilian CDs . . . And don't go trying to squeeze in any other pieces that will annoy me either."

I knew how he was. Now that I'd said this, he'd start by playing all the pathetic, tearful songs he could find, and then switch to techno, trance, and hip-hop because the customers were asking for it.

"Not going to happen," I said. "We will not be taking those kinds of requests from customers, not tonight."

My testiness had proven quite useful; in one go Osman had understood what I didn't want. He remained unsure, however, as to what exactly I *did* want.

"So what should I play?" he asked.

"You're the one who's the DJ, darling. I can't choose for you."

He gave me a hesitant, worried look, as if to say that he knew I'd object to every piece of music he'd play, and then all hell would break loose.

"You tell me what to play, ma'am . . ."

Even if I were to tell him two songs, the third was again going to be a problem. Or he'd keep coming to me all night asking if that was okay, or whether he should play this, and so forth. That, or he'd just play whatever he felt like playing and drive me mad.

Thankfully, I was rescued by the arrival of Belinda D. and her husband Naim. They liked dropping by the club. And I liked them. Belinda D. had recently made a habit of popping in on her way home from DJ'ing gigs at high-society clubs and private parties.

"Belinda, my lamb," I said, pointing at Osman, "please tell this man what to play. Something calm and quiet that won't put us all to sleep. No one would know better than you."

Vivacious as ever, Belinda burst out into a hearty laugh, making her large breasts bounce up and down.

"Don't you worry, my sweet *bon filet*," she said, pinching my cheek.

The *"bon filet"* in this sentence had to be me. No one had called me *bon filet* before. Or was I putting on weight? Perhaps my cheeks were getting chubby?

"I have a spectacular album with me," she said. "It's new . . . not even out yet. They sent it to me to be previewed. It's fabulous!"

She turned to her husband, who stood behind her, smiling.

"Hand over the CD case!"

Quite naturally, the financial advisor husband was responsible for schlepping the CDs to and from gigs.

She went on praising the new album as she shuffled through the CDs trying to find it.

"He's a new guy . . . with a ravishing voice. What they call a baritone tenor . . . He's good-looking too . . . He's going to be massive, you'll see, everyone will be talking about him . . . He's going to steamroll right over those pathetic, wishy-washy, second-rate acts that dare to call themselves singers!"

She had finally found what she was looking for. She passed the coverless CD to Osman.

"Be sure to give it back when you're finished, though," she warned him.

I led them to the table reserved for our most respectable customers. I told Hasan to take their drink orders. Meanwhile, Osman had turned down the lights, and once the dim light on the dance floor was reduced to nearly complete darkness, he started to play the CD. It was a familiar tune. Yes, it was "Hijo de la Luna," originally made famous by Montserrat Caballé, who had sung it in celebration of International Women's Day, but which then found its way onto the albums of all sorts of different singers, from the shrieking soprano Sarah Brightman to María Dolores Pradera, whose voice absolutely mesmerized me, and the pristinely voiced Mario Frangoulis, that handsome young man of classical music. This new singer was singing in Turkish. He had a beautiful and familiar voice.

"Who is this, *ayol*?" I asked. "What a beautiful voice. It sounds very familiar."

Belinda D. let out another hoot of laughter. She wasn't one to hold back or feign embarrassment if she got a little loud. Her laughter was vibrant and carefree.

"Oh, of course you know him . . . Aykut Batur! You know, the backup singer at the opera!"

I did. In fact, it was only this morning I had listened to the pirated copy of a special duet we had done together. I shuddered. I didn't know if it was the song or the past that made me shudder.

"Did you see Süheyl after what happened?" she asked.

"I went to the hospital but it was too crowded, I couldn't get into his room."

"Well, *I* have seen him," she said, boasting. "He's as fit as a fiddle, *maşallah*! But he was terrified! He still is, if you ask me . . ."

The man had every right to be.

She burst into a fit of laughter once again. Belinda D. was one of those people whose joy could be contagious. I was gradually beginning to lighten up myself.

Aykut's album really was magnificent.

I had started laughing at the stories Belinda D. told one after the other. There were five celebrity names in every sentence she spoke. She had a hilarious story about everyone. And she made herself laugh most of all. The stories were never ending. There was the one about the long-established singer who'd been calling her every hour for a week begging for an endorsement for her new album, and all the latest on who'd had plastic surgery in which part of the body, and who was getting it on with whom in the world of pop music . . . If I'd been my usual self, I would have retained everything she said, each story a jewel to be recounted later. But, as it was, I simply laughed and forgot them instantly.

Şükrü, who approached us to refresh our drinks, encouraged by the cheerful look on my face, told me he'd like to speak to me *in private*, when I had a minute.

"Right away," I said.

I am always sensitive when it comes to the plight of my workers.

We made our way upstairs, him ahead, me following.

He began talking, rubbing his hands together as he spoke.

"Boss, I know you've got a lot to deal with these days."

"Go ahead Şükrü, dear," I said. "I always have time to listen."

I myself was shocked at how reasonable I sounded. Or was Şükrü popping Prozac pills into my Virgin Marys?

"There's someone," he said, looking down.

Based on the intro, I was betting he had the hots for an under-age boy again. That was the problem with Şükrü. Whenever he found a young, skinny, girlish boy with slightly long hair, he instantly fell for him. He would become mad with desire, absolutely smitten, talk about the amorous object of his affections for days, take pictures, send gifts . . .

"Who is it this time?" I asked. "Which high school did you meet him in front of?"

He gave me a reproachful look.

"This one's not like that," he answered. "He's a college graduate. He's got a job too. He's really smart."

Now, that was a radical change for sure. The boy had to be over twenty, at least. I was sure Şükrü had pointed out the boy's intelligence in order to win my approval.

"We met at a pub."

Fine. People at that age were free to go to a pub for a pint and flirt with each other if they wished.

"That's nice," I said, waiting for him to spit out the rest. He certainly hadn't insisted on speaking with me *in private* just so he could tell me this.

"He admires you," he said.

"Well, isn't that sweet," I said, instantly loosening up.

Why and how he had become my admirer was not important in the least. He could have seen me from a distance, walking down the street. Never mind the why or wherefore, being admired is always, *always* good for the soul.

"He wants to meet you, but he's too chicken . . ."

Now, what on earth did that mean? I knew people said I was stuck-up, arrogant, cool, and sometimes even insolent, but these weren't reasons for people to fear me!

"Why, *ayol*?" I asked.

"He met you once before but you brushed him off . . ."

"Well, darling, I can't sit and listen to the life story of every Tom, Dick, and Harry I encounter, or talk to them for hours about the films I like, the singers I adore, the memories I have of certain songs and whatnot, can I? It must have been bad timing."

There are types like that: all they do is chitchat all day long, recounting this, sharing that . . . Just fifteen, twenty minutes into an initial conversation and all of a sudden it's, *Oh, let's be chums*, or even worse, *Let's be the best of chums*. I simply have no patience for this.

"But he really admires you," he said, his eyes narrowing in their sockets. "You'd be impressed if you spoke to him."

If he was as skinny as a stick, no shoulders, had long hair, and looked like a girl, I was sure to have brushed him off. If I wanted to be with girls and women, I would. I don't fancy effeminate men.

"Why, *ayol*?" I said.

"He wants to meet you."

The Şükrü I knew wouldn't talk about stuff like this so openly. Not unless he was piss drunk. And he didn't look drunk.

"Your boyfriend," I said, "wants to be with me. And you . . . are fixing us up?"

This was strange.

"Not like that," he said. "It's not sex that he wants. He wants to meet you, talk to you, tell you about himself. He's got something he wants to ask you, a request of you. He says he'll end our relationship if I don't set this up. My relationship is at stake . . ."

What did he mean, he only wanted to talk? And what to make of this "request"?

"That's ridiculous, *ayol*. How pathetic is that! If he loves you . . . What sort of a relationship do the two you have anyway?"

"That's the whole point! He doesn't love me, *I* love him. I'd do anything not to lose him. Please, just this once . . ."

"Ay, don't be ridiculous, Şükrü." I was getting angry.

"Still, if you were to meet him and see . . . He's a smart, intelligent guy. Maybe you'd get along?"

I started to laugh, purely out of frustration. Just a few moments earlier, downstairs with Belinda D., I'd finally managed to unwind, and now here I was, once again as tense as could be. Frankly, this new admirer business was really getting on my nerves.

"Forget it!" I said, standing up to indicate to him that the conversation was over. "Act a bit professional. Learn to separate your work from your private life!"

It was hard for the words that had just escaped my mouth to sound believable, since not even I found them convincing.

Dump Truck Beyza caught me at the top of the stairs.

"*Abla*, for God's sake, make that Osman play more lively stuff. That wailing fiddle's about to put me to sleep. And I've got a customer, you know. I need to get out there on the dance floor and work my magic!"

Aykut's CD had finished, and because Osman was too scared to play anything else, he'd started playing it again, from the beginning. I signaled at him as I walked passed the DJ cabin. He'd switch on the spotlights and start playing something more animated in a moment.

I had already started napping in the taxi on our way back to the hotel when Hüseyin, whose shoulder I'd rested my head against, awoke me by bringing up that annoying topic again.

"Şükrü's twink is an admirer of yours, apparently," he said.

"Oh, please, don't you start too," I said, without lifting my head. I really didn't have the energy.

"He was at the bar tonight, you must have seen him," he said.

I couldn't possibly notice every person who came in. Besides, it had been darker than usual, as per my orders.

"So, is he a looker?" I asked, just to make conversation.

"He's . . . ordinary . . . I think he's someone from our neighborhood . . . You'd recognize him if you saw him."

I was terribly drowsy.

28.

We were planning on going straight to sleep, wrapped in a platonic embrace, like brother and sister. We were both tired.

I was just about to fall asleep when Hüseyin began to show signs of distress, tossing and turning in bed.

"I feel sick to my stomach," he said.

It was psychological. Psychosomatic symptoms were different in all of us. I, for example, would get piercing headaches often when I was under stress.

"Let me do Reiki on you," I said, placing my hands on his solar plexus chakra. I could feel it sucking up energy immediately. My hands instantly began heating up. His body was ice-cold, but he was sweating.

Hüseyin couldn't bear it any longer; he got up and rushed to the bathroom. I could hear him retching his poor guts out.

I lit the bedside lamp and sat up in bed. I couldn't just turn around and go back to sleep when the man was in such an awful state.

"It must have been something I ate," I heard him say over the sound of running water.

He made his way back into the bedroom, and I could see that his forehead was covered in beads of sweat.

We had eaten the same food. There was nothing wrong with me.

"What did you drink?" I asked.

"Coke," he said.

He hurried back to the bathroom.

I got out of bed and walked over to his side. He was sitting on the floor, his head over the toilet bowl. He looked pale, but was quickly turning green. His condition appeared far from normal.

"It's blood . . ." he said, choking.

In a panic, I drew closer to see. It was true: he was literally puking blood.

We had to get to the hospital. The night porter at the reception desk helped me carry Hüseyin. We ruined the carpets in the elevator. We jumped into a cab and went straight to the emergency room.

Hüseyin had been poisoned. It wasn't food poisoning; it was pesticides. Deadly pesticides. If we hadn't made it to the hospital in time, it would have been fatal. His stomach was pumped and he was put on a drip.

By the time I went outside to get some fresh air and to regain my composure, the sun was already up. Our psycho had done exactly what he'd said he would and tried to finish Hüseyin off before the night was through.

But who had given Hüseyin the poison, and when?

He had been with me at the club all night. Besides, pesticides took effect right away. He couldn't have been given them earlier.

I went into the patisserie opposite the hospital and ordered a cup of coffee. The smell of freshly baked *poğaça* and *çörek* whetted my appetite. So I ordered a cheese *poğaça*. I hadn't slept a wink. I needed caffeine. And I was hungry as a wolf. I sank my teeth into the *poğaça*. It was as soft as a sponge. It melted in my mouth. I post-

poned any thoughts of maintaining my figure, and thus the guilt I
would feel for consuming so much fat, until later on. I considered
ordering another one, but quickly came to my senses. *Don't overdo
it*, I told myself.

I tried to re-create the night before in my head, like a movie.
We'd had dinner, then gathered in the street for the neighborhood
search operation. Then there was the police station, the tea at the
station . . . Sure, the tea was awful, but the police station wasn't
exactly the best place to poison someone. And besides, we'd all
drunk the same tea. Hüseyin had been outside while I was talking
with Selçuk. But Hasan had been with him. Maybe they'd eaten or
drunk something while waiting for me.

I'd call Hasan and find out once I'd finished my coffee.

Then we were at the club. He was behind the bar, next to
Şükrü, I was next to Belinda D. Then I'd had the lights turned
down. There was always so much traffic at the bar, people standing there and having their drinks, or walking up to order new
ones. Hüseyin must have made small talk with them. There was
no way Şükrü could have put poison in his Coke. He's too much of
a coward to even think about such things, let alone do them. Afterward, I had gone upstairs with Şükrü, leaving Hüseyin alone at the
bar. I didn't remember seeing Hüseyin after I came down. I hadn't
paid attention to what he was doing until we left the bar together.

Someone who came to the bar must have put poison in his
Coke.

Our psycho or one of his accomplices had been within arm's
reach of us tonight, had infiltrated our castle, put poison in Hüseyin's Coke under our very noses, and fled. *Well, bravo*, I said to myself. Our security system was marvelous! We behaved as if there
were some kind of protective shield that was activated as soon as
we walked through the club's door, keeping us safe from all the
dangers of the outside world. The girls, the customers, me . . . we

were all so carefree. But there you have it, someone with such evil intentions was able to pass through the same protective shields, penetrate our shelter, and do as he pleased. How blind could we be? Was the outside world really not the remote place we believed it to be? In this vast city of Istanbul, could we not create a tiny little itsy-bitsy heaven for ourselves, one measuring just one hundred and sixty square meters?

29.

I had to go home. Hüseyin needed clean clothes. All his clothes were covered in puke and blood. They had given him a surgical smock to wear at the hospital; the rest of his body was naked. We were in such a rush we had even left his shoes at the hotel. I had called Hasan and asked him to stay by Hüseyin's side. He was still half asleep but came without complaining. He was aware of how serious the situation was. At times like this, Hasan was capable of turning off his amateur histrionics and becoming coolheaded and commonsensical. I hadn't asked for much, just for him to stay with Hüseyin while I left to sort out a few things. He could even fall asleep if he wished. Hüseyin had been sedated anyway; he was fast asleep. He clearly wasn't going to open his eyes for quite some time, and would need no special assistance.

I was the one still up, who hadn't slept and was completely exhausted. There was a ceaseless droning in my head. My eyes kept twitching. I could feel a muscle pulsing in my temple.

I had to inform Hüseyin's family, but I didn't know how. Their son had stayed out for two nights; on the first his car was set on fire, on the second he had been poisoned. It would be impossible for them to understand, to approach the matter logically and reasonably. They were going to hate me. As if it weren't enough that I had led their son down the wrong path into unnatural relationships, now I had brought all this destruction upon him. All the marvelous vampy femme fatales of cinema history would seem perfectly innocent compared to what his mother Kevser Kozalak would think of me.

I didn't know their home phone, and I could never work out where they lived. Someone at the taxi stand was bound to know their phone number. In my head I rehearsed what I would say. None of it would be glad tidings.

Yılmaz wasn't at his usual spot. Seeing as I wasn't around, it seemed he'd taken the opportunity to leave himself. I cursed him from the bottom of my heart.

Satı had visited, scrubbed, cleaned, and tidied every corner of the apartment as promised. She had left a new note for me on the refrigerator:

"Your home is as clean as a whistle. Have fun messing it up again. I don't see why you'd butcher your bras. You should have given them to me if you didn't want them."

I'd feel better if I took a shower.

I had enough time for that.

The doorbell rang before I could turn the water on.

I dragged my feet to the door.

My downstairs neighbor, the nosy Wimpy Ferdı, stood before me.

I could tell I wasn't looking good when he took a step back at the sight of me. He had that ever present annoying grin on his face.

"I apologize," I said, ashamed of how I must have looked. "I had a really terrible night. I'm tired and haven't slept at all. I was just about to take a shower."

"Ummm . . ." he said. "About last night . . ."

Of course he must have watched everything from his window. He wouldn't have missed it for the world. He was wearing a faded T-shirt that was damp with sweat and clung to his scrawny little body. His trousers, on the other hand, were as loose and baggy as ever.

"Please accept my apologies, we caused a bit of a racket," I said. "Especially when the police arrived . . ."

"Ummm . . . I mean . . . I wanted to . . . ummm . . . ask . . . if there was anything I could do."

Just because he was nosy didn't mean he wasn't stupid. He couldn't string a single sentence together.

"I was just wondering if . . ." he said, rolling the words around in his mouth.

"Wondering if what?" I said, trying to speed things along.

"You found the person you were looking for?"

Ayol, would I be in this state if we had found him? Roses would be blossoming on my cheeks, my energy would be sky-high. I simply grunted no.

"I'd like to help," he said, doing his best to drag this unbearable conversation out even further. "I have immense respect for you. Please don't hesitate to let me know if there's anything I can do. If you need to talk, you know, or anything."

"*Merci*," I said, indicating that that would never happen, not in a million years.

He wasn't the only man on earth yet.

I was getting ready to close the door when he grabbed it.

"Oh, yeah, and the gentleman downstairs. . . ." he said, holding the door open.

"Yılmaz," I said, yawning for real. "You mean Yılmaz Karataş?"

"He couldn't find you, so he knocked on my door this morning."

I was waiting for the rest of his story, but he kept trying to poke his head into my apartment. Apparently he was incapable of craning his neck and talking at the same time.

"And did he say anything?" I asked. "I was just about to go take a shower . . . I'm sort of in a hurry."

"I understand . . ." he said, staring blankly.

If he really truly did understand, he'd deliver Yılmaz's message and be gone.

"What did Yılmaz say?" I repeated, this time in a sharper tone.

"That he was going to take a shower, change his clothes, refresh his packed lunch box, and then be back."

What an important message! I would have worried all day long if I hadn't received it.

"Thank you," I said, pushing the door closed.

He stopped it with his hand again. The ink stains on his hands made him look even filthier than he really was.

"It was seven o'clock in the morning when he knocked . . ."

What was I supposed to do about that? The man had spent all night perched on the edge of a portable stool and knocked on my wimpy neighbor's door as soon as the day dawned.

"I apologize if he woke you," I said, making one final attempt. "I'm really in a hurry. My friend is in the hospital. I have to get back."

He must have had a tic. His mouth twitched to the right again.

"If you'd like me to come with you . . ."

I had always managed to maintain a respectable distance between my neighbors and myself and I had no intention of changing that policy today. I was not in the mood for building neighborly relations. Especially not with Ferdı.

"No, thank you," I said. "I'll handle it myself. Bye-bye."

And then I shut the door, tight.

I felt better after the shower. I'd grounded my negative energy in the process. I stayed under the water longer than usual. I sent him a message in the shower in case my psycho was recording. It was an offensive swear word. I repeated it several times in case he had missed it.

I quickly shaved. My reflection in the mirror looked awful. I had purple rings under my eyes. A nod of gratitude to my psycho for that! Thanks to him, I was on the verge of becoming a walking cadaver. I quickly stepped away from the mirror. I wasn't happy with how I looked. What good would it do me to study myself and fray my nerves even further? I'd have the opportunity to sleep at some point, and I'd look better after I'd done so. Then, after a good, thorough skin-care treatment, I'd be completely revived. *Thank God for cosmetics*, I said to myself.

Coffee and a shower had made me feel good, if only temporarily. Still, I took a vitamin pill, just in case—at least it would keep me on my feet.

I was planning on taking some clean underwear and clothes from Hüseyin's bag, but then I decided taking the whole thing made better sense. There was no point in leaving it at home.

The message light on the answering machine was flashing. I ignored it. My mobile was switched off too. I had no intention of chitchatting on the phone with anyone.

Sleep had already started descending upon me before I even left the house. I must resist it.

At the bottom of the stairs I bumped into Yılmaz, who was drinking his morning tea and reading his paper. As promised in the message, he was back and already seated on his portable stool.

"Morning, sir," he said.

"Good morning."

He had changed his clothes and put on something more comfortable, but he still had the tie and V-neck sweater.

"Is everything okay? Are you all right?"

Did he have to remind me that I looked like a hag? As if I didn't know already.

"I didn't sleep very well," I said.

"I just ran home and back myself. I left you a message. With number three."

"Yes, he told me," I said. "He said it was seven in the morning when you left."

I expected him to understand that seven o'clock was a bit early to be knocking on people's doors, but he just responded with a self-assured smile, displaying his missing tooth.

"I thought I'd go early and be back early, while no one was about."

That was enough chitchat. I moved toward the door.

"Taking a trip?" he asked, motioning at the huge sports bag I was carrying.

It would take too long to recount the details of *Hüseyin was poisoned and hospitalized last night*, and if I said I was going on a trip, well, that would only give rise to more questions requiring further explanation on my part.

"I'm off to the gym," I said, inspired by the shape of the bag I was holding.

"I've noted down everyone going in and out," he said, pulling out a folded piece of paper from the inside pocket of his jacket. "And the times . . ."

I really didn't want to listen to him reading all the way through his list right now.

"Let me," I said reaching out my hand. "I'll take a look myself."

My eyes were burning from lack of sleep. I took a quick glance. It was two pages long. His handwriting was neat. Clearly he had military discipline, after all. I slipped the note into the side pocket of the sports bag.

I jumped into the first taxi I could find and went straight back to the hospital.

30.

Hüseyin lay there with a drip in his wrist, a tube in his nose, and a tube in his mouth. His eyes were closed.

In the armchair by his side, Hasan had his eyes closed. He opened them the minute I walked in.

"They just came to check on him," he said quietly. "He's fine . . ."

How could he be? The guy's car had been burned, he'd been poisoned with pesticides, his stomach had been pumped, and now he was lying in the hospital with tubes sticking out all over his body.

"I'll wait," I said. "You can go now."

He looked at my face.

"I think you should go and rest a bit, seriously. You're pale. I don't want to get you down, but you look like a corpse. I'll stay here. He's not going to ask for anything anyway. Go and sleep for a couple of hours and then come back. You'll feel much better. He'll need you more when he wakes up anyway."

He was right.

"I can give you my keys if you like. You can go to my place."

My room at the Blue Sky Hotel, which I'd be paying for anyway, awaited me. I thanked him nevertheless.

"Call me if anything happens," I said, giving him my new pay-as-you-go SIM number. I didn't want to switch on the other one and hear the psycho's latest psycho babble.

"And whatever you do, don't let anyone in! I mean, except for people we know . . ." I added.

I thought for a minute; maybe someone we knew had poisoned him at the club yesterday.

"No!" I said. "No one! Whether we know them or not. Only me . . . If you want, we can have a 'No Visitors Allowed' sign put on the door."

The receptionist at the hotel had changed, but I still felt that I had to offer an explanation. We had dashed out, leaving a messy room and filthy elevator behind us.

"No pwoblem at all, sir," replied the girl, who spoke with a lisp. "Tings like tat happen. How is his healt? Tat's what matters most. Is he better?"

I thanked her for her concern and kindly requested that no phone calls whatsoever be put through to my room.

I had to make two phone calls before lying down on the bed: one to Ponpon, and one to Jihad2000. I would take care of Hüseyin's family when I woke up, when I had a calm, fresh mind.

If we didn't have daily contact, the ever panicky Ponpon would raise hell, alarm friends, then acquaintances, and finally the police to find out what had happened to me. Even if Pamir had recounted her own version of events of the previous night, Jihad2000 still must have been waiting to hear from me. It wasn't hard to guess that he was probably bursting with curiosity. I called him first. He listened to the latest updates without comment.

"It's unlikely he'd come after me," he said.

He was possibly right: if my psycho was tracking my Internet access from my computer, he would have located Jihad2000 ages ago.

"I think you shouldn't be so optimistic," I said. It would be best if he remained a bit anxious, especially considering that he was one of those responsible for the events of the previous night. "Keep your security tight these days. There's no guessing what he'll do next. No one is innocent in his eyes. I mean, look at Hüseyin!"

There was no sound for a while, which made me think the line had been cut.

"Hello? You there?"

"I'll talk to Pamir. Perhaps we should escape to Cyprus for a week or so."

It seemed they were becoming an item very fast; from hotel rendezvous and home visits, to holidaying together. It was a good thing that he had directed his interest away from me and toward Pamir, but not so good that he was now panicking and making escape plans.

"*Ayolcuğum*, where have you been?" Ponpon answered the phone. "I called your home number, but there was no answer. I think your answering machine isn't working either. I almost lost my mind."

I was in no mood for reproachful comments.

"There's nothing to lose your mind about. Here I am, on the other end of the line!" I said scoldingly. Hasan must have already told her about last night. He could easily go without food, drink, or sleep, but he'd break out in rashes if he didn't rush gossip about last night's events like this to interested parties as soon as possible.

"*Ayolcuğum*, what's wrong with you? Why this rage and fury? I was calling to thank you for the present you sent . . . But by the sound of your voice, you're fuming."

"What present?" I said. "I didn't send you any present."

"Oh, come on, *ayol*! It arrived early in the morning, before I even got out of bed. A young boy brought it. There's a card attached. The message is quite sweet."

I hadn't sent her a present or written her a card.

And since I hadn't, it had to be my psycho's latest deadly plan. He might have sent her a bomb. The Internet was full of descriptions of how to prepare homemade bombs.

"Ponpon, I didn't send it!" I said. "Don't open it!"

"But I already have . . ." she said, and by the sound of her voice I was certain she had puckered up her lips while doing so. "I was so happy to receive a present from you that I actually liked—it's the first time in years! You always buy me such weird stuff . . ."

She didn't refrain, even now, from needling me. It was her nature . . .

"I'm telling you again, *I did not send you a present*," I said loud and clear. "Still, will you tell me what I sent?"

"Well, if it wasn't you, then it's none of your business, *ayol!*"

I wasn't in the mood to deal with her coyness.

"Look, dear," I said, "it must be the doing of the psycho I told you about. It could be something dangerous. He poisoned Hüseyin last night. The boy is in the hospital. He almost died. We had his stomach pumped. Do you understand?"

That she would understand.

"You could have explained it to me without shouting," she responded resentfully. "What good will it do to frighten me? Do you want me to lock the doors and sit at home crying after I put down the phone? Then my eyes will get puffy, and I'll be a disgrace onstage tonight. Is that what you want? Please, I don't want to have anything to do with your psycho!"

"What has he sent?" I asked once again.

"A huge box of mixed chocolates from the Gezi patisserie!"

This couldn't possibly be the gift she had been expecting from me all her life. After all the things I had bought her, a box of chocolates had won out over all of them!

"They could be poisonous. He might be doing the same thing to you as he did to Hüseyin last night . . . Don't eat them, throw them away, all of them," I said.

"No way, *ayol*!" she said. "What a dreadful waste . . ."

I told her in repulsively vivid detail what would happen to her if she were poisoned. Finally, she understood, but she still couldn't bring herself to throw them out.

"I'll offer them to guests," she said, as if that were a solution.

"Don't be crazy, *ayol*. Are you going to poison your guests?"

"Why not?" she said, giggling. "Sometimes they get on my nerves. I'll offer them one at a time. Not enough to kill them . . . Just enough to give them a stomachache."

"Don't you dare!" I said. "Okay, don't throw it away. But don't eat it either."

We'd have it tested in a lab and find out what it was later, when we had time. If it was clean, which I didn't think it would be, she could sit down and gobble up the whole box.

Before hanging up, I had to ask one more question—or else I wouldn't be able to sleep, no matter how tired I was.

"Do you really think a box of chocolates is the best gift possible?"

"Of course, *ayolcuğum*. I already have everything I need, thank God. I can buy whatever I fancy anyway. I can't fit anything else into my wardrobes, they're already packed full. And I have no room at all for any more furniture . . . Besides, everyone likes chocolate . . ."

31.

It was afternoon by the time I woke up. I'd had no dreams, but then, I hadn't really slept either; I'd literally passed out. I opened the curtains. I lay in bed for a bit, stretching and yawning, then I called room service and ordered a cup of black coffee and headed for the shower. I'd be out by the time the coffee arrived.

Hasan was in the corridor when I arrived at the hospital. He was leaning against the wall near the room door, cleaning underneath his nails.

"They're giving him an enema," he said. "He didn't want me to stay. I came out so he wouldn't feel embarrassed. I've been waiting here."

Best that I wait outside too until the nurse came out.

"So, how is he?" I asked, not really expecting anything new.

"Same. He's getting better. Otherwise, pretty much the same. They've given him his medicine, a new drip, and stopped the oxygen . . . He just woke up."

"Has anyone called?"

"Nope," he said. "No one . . . I've been chatting with the nurse out of boredom. Found out who's staying in each room and what's wrong with them. Wanna know?"

No, I didn't.

I thanked Hasan and sent him home. There was no need for

both of us to be there. I told him I didn't know whether I'd show up at the club that night, but I'd call to let him know.

When the nurse had left, I went into the room.

Hüseyin lay there with an angelic expression on his face. He looked horribly thin. They had taken his catheter out. His face lit up when he saw me.

"Hello," he said, smiling. "Just look at what's happened to me . . ."

"Don't you worry," I said. "You're getting better already. Would you like anything to eat?" I asked. "I could order—"

"Not allowed," he said, twitching his nose.

It must have been doctor's orders to not let him eat in the state he was in. The truth was, I was hungry myself.

"I thought about it while you were gone," he began. "Perhaps this happened for a reason, to help us bond with each other. A twist of fate. I mean, look at us . . ."

It really wasn't the right time for lovers' talk. At least, for me it wasn't. Of course I had feelings for Hüseyin, but I didn't know how much of it was compassion, how much of it sympathy, and how much sexual attraction. The only thing I knew for sure was that I wasn't in love and I had no intention of analyzing it, or sitting and talking about it right then and there.

"Let's discuss that later," I said.

"Why? It's not like we have anything better to do. It's just the two of us . . ."

His mom and dad entered the room, interrupting a conversation that I had had no intention of pursuing.

Hüseyin's father, İsmail Kozalak, was perfectly logical and reasonable, just as he had been on the phone with me. He approached the matter with a resolute trust in God. As a result of his wife's feeding regimen, he was fat. He was the ideal family guy. His eyebrows, which hung low, lent a confused and sorrowful look to his face. The expression in his eyes was soft, gentle. He had a mustache, the middle of which was stained yellow from nicotine.

Mrs. Kozalak, on the other hand, was doing her best to stand strong; she sighed, biting her bottom lip every now and then, and wiping the tears from her eyes with the back of her hand. As soon as she walked into the room, she rushed over and sat down at her son's side. She could hardly bear not touching and embracing him, but she couldn't, for fear of hurting him. She kept wiping Hüseyin's forehead with wet wipes that she pulled out of her bag, and massaging his feet.

I felt like a stranger among them. My presence in the room was unnecessary, but I couldn't leave. I was so paranoid that someone might come in while I was away and attack Hüseyin again that I couldn't bring myself to move.

"Dad, you go," said Hüseyin. "You should be at the store."

"No, no, son. I won't hear none of that."

İsmail Kozalak seated himself in the other armchair and crossed his arms to show that he had no intention of leaving. He carried traces of all the affectionate father characters engraved in my memory from Turkish cinema. He had the sense of humor of Gazanfer Özcan, the strict but sweet disposition of Hulusi Kentmen, and the sensitivity of Münir Özkul.

"What's a dad for, if not to help his son through the rough patches? You know we're here for you, through thick and thin."

He turned to me for backup.

He looked funny, settled there in the armchair with his folded arms, chubby body, and drooping eyebrows.

"He's my son! Where am I supposed to be if not here, isn't that right?"

"Yes, yes, it is," I said, smiling.

Mrs. Kozalak finally stopped fighting back the tears. She didn't speak or move but just sat there crying as she held Hüseyin's hand, the one without the drip attached. Because I didn't cry, I searched my pockets for a tissue.

"Here, Auntie . . ." I said, moving closer to her.

I didn't know what to say next.

"Let her cry, son," said İsmail Kozalak from where he sat, in an authoritarian tone. "She'll feel better if she does . . ."

There was quite a bit of mischief hiding beneath İsmail Kozalak's paternal compassion. It may not have seemed that way from the way he was seated, but one could tell it from the sound of his voice and the look in his eyes.

"Let her cry; it'll do her good . . . It's better she cry than go eating herself and me up about it. Let her pour out the pain in her heart. She'll feel better . . . much better."

She was his wife. Who was I to intervene? I stepped back, the tissue still in my hand.

Mrs. Kozalak threw a glance at her husband, then reached out and snatched the tissue from my hand.

"What harm have I done to you, husband?" she said to him reproachfully. "Leave me be. So I'm crying, so what? Mine is a mother's heart. You wouldn't understand."

If I were to hear these sentences any other time, especially accompanied by the expression on Kevser Kozalak's face, I would have laughed my head off. A marriage that had turned into a habit over the years now clearly sustained itself on sweet little squabbles and tiffs. One picked on the other, and the other shot right back, with no intention of being outdone.

Perhaps there was something wrong with me: maybe there was nothing to laugh about. Or maybe what the writer Michael Cunningham had said about those who watched a lot of movies being better able to see the humor in everyday life applied to me too.

Mrs. Kozalak, who really was a very ladylike woman, had her final word. Slamming her hand against the bed, "I'll cry if I want to, what's it to you!" she wailed. She was like an obstinate child having a fit, and then she began sighing deeply. As far as performances go, it was really very good.

We then moved on to a phase of silence that only served to exacerbate my anxiety. Well, it wasn't complete silence: Mrs. Kozalak continued to sob and blow her nose at regular intervals.

"I'll be leaving, then," I said in a low voice. "There are a couple of things I need to sort out . . ."

In other words, I needed an excuse in order to leave; otherwise, I would be expected to stay.

"When will you be back?" asked Hüseyin.

I was going to have to ignore the love and hope in his eyes.

"Your mom and dad are here," I said as I left.

I know: it wasn't exactly an answer to his question.

32.

My apartment was under my psycho's control. My home, the place where I would normally seek refuge, was no longer my private space. I didn't want to go home. If I went to one of the girls' places, I'd be expected to explain for an hour all that had happened. What I needed was to gather my thoughts and think things through clearly.

I was hungry. Since I wasn't going to give birth to a robust, clever plan on an empty stomach, it seemed a good idea for me to get some food in there first.

It wasn't yet lunchtime and the Marmara Hotel café was close. Would dining at the same place two days in a row turn me into one of those obsessive-compulsive people who never break a habit and always live by the exact same routine? I had been very pleased with the salad I'd eaten the previous day, but today, though, I had no intention of settling for just a salad: I was starving.

Because it was in between mealtimes, there were seats free on the terrace. I sat watching passersby while eating a huge hamburger. I drank grapefruit juice, hoping it would burn the fat intake from the burger. To finish, I enjoyed a tasty vanilla-flavored filtered coffee.

Just as I was finishing my coffee, I saw our bartender Şükrü among the crowd of people waiting to cross at the traffic lights in the near distance. If he saw me, he'd rush over, take a seat, and go on and on for hours about how perfect his new boyfriend was. Wasn't every new lover like that? When they're new, we see their good qualities; once they're old, we see their defects. And then, as if having to listen to all that weren't enough, I knew I'd have to foot the bill because I was the boss. I leaned back so he wouldn't notice me. I wished I'd had a newspaper to hide behind.

He didn't even look my way. His back was turned and he was crossing the road. He was talking to the guy next to him. I could only see him from behind, but it must have been his new boyfriend, the lad with the longish hair; my admirer.

Now that I had filled my stomach, it was time to gather my thoughts. For this I could go and have a thorough, expensive complete skin-care treatment. I was tired of everyone, and I do mean *everyone*, saying I looked tired, or in other words, that I looked like shit. With masks, creams, massages, and a little solarium, my skin would be refreshed, and at least people would be able to look me in the face again. I didn't have an appointment, but if I went without one I'd either be handed over to the trusted hands of apprentices or they'd keep me waiting for ages.

Actually, I knew a few other things that made me feel better at times like this: sex and shopping. I didn't have the energy or the drive for sex. It was going to have to be shopping.

Fully aware of my expensive shopping habit, I knew I had to be careful to choose an appropriate place. If I went to Akmerkez, Nişantaşı, or Bağdat Avenue, where expensive brands and designer boutiques were found, the adventure was sure to cost me a fortune. If I didn't go clothes shopping but went around to bookshops and music stores instead, I would end up lugging home all sorts of rubbish, buying dozens of books thinking I'd read them someday, and different versions of the CDs I already owned at home, out of simple, silly curiosity. These books and CDs would wander from front shelves, to back shelves, to high, out-of-reach shelves, and then one day I would go to the trouble of sorting them, packing them in boxes, and sending them off to a secondhand shop. I'd get Satı to do the packing.

The second problem was that I had nowhere to take what I bought. Since I wasn't going home, was I going to carry the books and CDs back to the hotel?

The most reasonable thing to do was to go to Beyoğlu. Chances were I wouldn't spend too much there, so long as I didn't go into my favorite boutique, Vakko, that is. I had left home with no other clothes but the ones I was wearing. It wouldn't be a bad idea at all to get some new clothes to wear. It was, in fact, necessary that I do so.

I ignored the stingy voice inside me telling me to go home and change, that I had plenty of clothes in my wardrobe already. Why did that grating inner voice have to go and interfere, just when I was in the mood for some nice shopping? I would have to turn a deaf ear.

Going to the Terkos Alley first was a good idea. The stuff you could get down there—peanuts—all export surplus.

I picked up my pace. I had already passed Galatasaray.

"Burçak!" I heard a man's voice call out from behind me.

I turned around sharply.

Bahadır, my Reiki master Gül's lover, had just exited a bank on the left and was waving.

He couldn't possibly have known about my dream, but I suddenly blushed as if he had already read it from my face.

He came up and gave me a hug and a kiss. I couldn't recall having developed such a close friendship, but I had no objections to being kissed by Bahadır.

He was even better looking than I remembered. He looked

very smart in his suit, with his trenchcoat hanging over his arm. He was extremely sexy.

"What a nice surprise," he said. "What are you doing in this part of town?"

He looked even sexier when he smiled. His lips were well formed, his teeth were straight, and the look in his eyes was most certainly erotic.

"Wandering about, hoping to do some shopping," I said. "How about you?"

"I work here," he said, motioning in the direction of the Tünel. "I just came down to the bank for something. Good thing I did, because look: I bumped into you."

The man was giving off hormones like some kind of powerful radiation. He made me have sexual thoughts when sex was the farthest thing from my mind.

"Gül and I called you a bunch of times but we couldn't get through," he said. "And yesterday when you called, Gül was out. She had to visit her son's school. She called you when she got back but couldn't catch you. We suspected you'd grown weary of fame and changed your phone numbers."

I'd answer all these one by one.

"I'm constantly on the run these days. I simply haven't had a chance to call back. I was free for a bit yesterday. In fact, a friend of mine needed an aura cleansing. That's why I called. But then Cavit and Şirin helped us out. I haven't changed my numbers, but they need to stay switched off for a while. You know . . ."

I didn't know why I had winked at the end of that. Bahadır derived a meaning of some sort from it, though.

"Of course . . ." he said. "I understand."

If what he meant by "of course" were the shameless acts I sensed were behind his eyes and that he assumed were behind mine, then he'd gotten it wrong for sure! Well, okay, the look on Bahadır's face always brought shameless acts to my mind.

"The phone psycho," I said, to put things straight.

"Ohhh . . ."

"But I'm going to call as soon as I get the chance. I haven't forgotten."

"Come, let me buy you a drink," he said, placing his arm over my shoulder. "You look like you need one."

I should have gone to skin care instead of idling in the streets shopping! I would have wanted him to see me on one of my nicer, charming, attractive, elegant Audrey days. It was good he had reminded me of the state I was in. My sexual thoughts subsided out of shame for my appearance, but didn't disappear altogether. . . .

"I . . . ummm . . . I'd rather not today . . . because . . . I need to grab a couple of things and return right away . . . I mean, a friend of mine is in the hospital . . . I was going to buy him a . . ."

It was all because of him that I hemmed and hawed and failed to string a single proper sentence together, like some shy young thing on her very first date.

"It's okay!" he said. "There's no need for excuses. Let's walk together, then, if you're going down this way too."

There was no need for him to go flinging my excuse in my face like that.

We started walking.

He was talking about Gül, about the last concert they'd gone to together.

I stumbled twice. Not at all my style. I hate clumsy walkers.

"Take my arm if you like," he said.

My heart started pounding ferociously.

I was feeling a bit aroused.

Truth was, walking arm in arm with Bahadır was making me horny. I couldn't help it. My body was responding to the man. His charisma, his energy or aura, whatever it was, it was enough. I grew angry at myself. But then, recalling how long it had been since I'd last made love, I decided it was normal to feel horny after so much time, and especially given all that had happened. Good sex is the best way to dispel distasteful incidents from one's mind.

We passed the Terkos Alley and walked toward the Tünel, arm in arm.

I felt like I was in a romantic French film. I was walking arm in arm with someone as positively breathtaking as Catherine Deneuve, Sami Frey, or Laurent Terzieff.

Outside Markiz Patisserie, a cyclist rode past us, slaloming between pedestrians. He almost knocked Bahadır over.

Catherine Deneuve evaporated. I awoke from my rose-colored dream. Neither was the bike blue nor the rider a girl with flames on her helmet, but it was enough to remind me of my psycho.

My whole body tensed up. I stopped.

"I need to go," I said in a determined voice.

I knew that later I'd desperately regret having cut this scene so short, leaving Bahadır in the middle of the street like that.

"What is it?" he said.

He had noticed the change in me, that something wasn't right, but he couldn't put his finger on it. As a matter of fact, neither could I. It was just something, a feeling I got, that stood between me and my Prince Charming. My libido had plummeted to minus zero in a matter of seconds.

As we parted, I sent my regards to Gül, just to make sure this little adventure of ours would weigh heavily on both our consciences.

33.

I t was getting dark. As I walked briskly toward Tepebaşı to catch a taxi, I thought, *There has to be something I'm just not seeing, a detail I've missed.* But what?

My taxi driver was moaning and groaning, because not only was it a busy time of day in terms of traffic, but I was only going a short distance. I wasn't about to be outdone; I began grumbling even louder than him.

When we reached Taksim, a taxi overtook us and turned in the direction of Sıraselviler, and the people inside waved at us. When I paid no attention, they honked their horn.

"Sir, they're pointing at you," said the taxi driver, who'd finally shut up once I'd come out on top in our battle of moan and groan.

I looked. It was Şükrü, grinning from ear to ear and waving, and next to him was someone with long hair. I couldn't really make out much more than that in the darkness of the night. It must have been his new lover, the one who looked like a chick but wasn't. My admirer, that is. Having recalled that detail, my curiosity was piqued. I took a more careful look, but traffic had started flowing and we were soon on our separate ways. His silhouette seemed familiar. I might recognize him from the club, or the neighborhood, like Hüseyin had said—as he hadn't caught my attention before, though, clearly he was just an ordinary boy.

When I arrived outside my apartment building, I realized that Yılmaz wasn't behind the glass door. He had disappeared again. It seemed the man was a wee bit irresponsible, despite his military training. He was supposed to be watching the place, not me. Just because I wasn't about didn't mean he could scram at the first opportunity. I intended to reprimand him the next time I saw him.

I was at the bottom of the stairs when Hümeyra's door opened.

"Mr. Veral," she said.

If she was going to ask after the bag she had lost to thieves or something equally ridiculous, I wasn't in the mood.

"The *bey* who was waiting here," she said. "He's gone. But he left you a note. He said it's important."

It seemed Yılmaz enjoyed writing reports.

Leaving the door ajar, she went inside to bring the note. It had been neatly placed in an envelope, and the envelope firmly closed. It was addressed to me in careful, respectful handwriting.

"He used my toilet while you were away," Hümeyra complained. "But then I guess it is a human need, after all."

If she thought she'd have me running after stolen items such as her bag out of gratitude, she was gravely mistaken.

"You are very kind."

For delivering the note, and letting Yılmaz use her toilet.

"Now, he is one clean man, I'm telling you," she said, shutting her eyes. "He takes his shoes off outside. Washes his hands after he's done. I can hear the water running. But do you mind kindly telling him that the next time he uses the toilet . . ."

Now would come the details about how he didn't flush afterward, didn't lift the seat when he was peeing, drip-dropped all over the place . . . So what! All of that was true of the majority of the Turkish population anyway. We still lacked basic toilet training.

". . . . to put the toilet paper in the bin, not down the toilet? I'm worried the sewers might get blocked. When it's blocked, you know it floods my apartment. I was too embarrassed to tell him. If you could . . ."

She wasn't embarrassed to tell me.

"Of course, ma'am, I'll remind him," I responded as I began climbing the stairs.

She called after me.

"One more thing," she said.

I turned to look.

She smiled her sweetest smile and batted her eyelashes.

"My handbag. The one I told you about yesterday . . . with the brass handles . . ."

People either lost their senses as they got older, or developed obsessions. I wondered if all the obsessions I had were actually signs of aging.

There must have been thunder in my eyes, because she fell silent.

"I was going to ask if there's any news, if you've found it . . ."

She had asked. I had heard it with my own ears. I stared at her with thunder in my eyes, feeling very much like Zeus himself.

She retreated back into her apartment.

"Okay. I understand. You couldn't find it. Never mind . . ."

The first thing I did upon entering my apartment was call the hospital. I wasn't surprised at how quickly they found the room where Hüseyin was staying and connected. After all, we paid private hospitals loads of money, so of course they were going to do their jobs well. There is this thing called "quality of service." The hospital Hüseyin was staying in took great pride in its quality certificate, and they charged as much as a five-star hotel.

İsmail Kozalak answered the phone.

Hüseyin was okay. They had given him his medicine and he had gone back to sleep.

"Son," he said, "there's a note in the side pocket of Hüseyin's bag, addressed to you. Could it be something important?"

With nothing to do in a hospital room, İsmail Kozalak must have gone snooping around, putting to use his organizational skills as an ironmonger, and out of sheer boredom read whatever he had found. What he had found was Yılmaz Karataş's report from yesterday, which I had totally forgotten about: the list of people going in and out of the apartment.

"I'll take a look when I'm back," I said. "Don't throw it away."

"Your friends came to visit," he said. "They brought flowers and cologne; it was very kind of them. We had bought some already, but still . . ."

Who? Panic alarms went off in my head. No one knew Hüseyin was there except for Hasan and Ponpon. Hasan was at the hospital all morning, and must have been at home resting right now. The Ponpon I knew would never go visit.

"Who did you say came to visit?"

"Your friends," he said. "Şükrü and his friend."

What was Şükrü doing at the hospital? It had to be that blabbermouth Hasan. He'd just die if he didn't tell everyone the latest news. Good thing I warned him not to!

Şükrü I understood, fine, but who was his friend? Had he dragged the new boyfriend I'd just seen with him down to the hospital? Maybe he thought I'd be there too, and that I'd be more cooperative this time due to the setting, and he'd be able to introduce me to my shy admirer.

I went into the toilet with Yılmaz Karataş's note in my hand, and sat down.

He had written the time and date on the top of the page, and "TOP SECRET" in block capitals in the middle, and underlined it. He sure was weird.

"The wanted female with the bicycle visited the Veral apartment building, apartment three, at 2:27. She was wearing the helmet previously described. The same female had visited yesterday
without her bike, and gone upstairs. (Please see my report dated
yesterday.) I think I'm on the right track. Keeping the urgency of
the matter in mind, I shall have to leave my appointed location
without your permission and follow the bicycle."

I couldn't believe my eyes. I read it over from start to finish.
The bike had been here yesterday? Yılmaz was proving to be
pretty handy. It seemed he was going to pass this test with flying
colors, assuming none of those pesky bureaucratic obstacles got in
the way.

It is indeed a fact, not a myth, that time in the toilet enhances
brain functions. "Hurray!" I said to myself.

I went out to make my phone calls, given that the house was
still bugged.

First I called the hospital again. This time Hüseyin picked up.

"I knew it was you," he said.

I asked to speak to his father.

"I'm better," he said, as if I'd asked. "When are you coming? I
told my parents you'd be back. They're going to leave."

I asked to speak to his father again.

"The note we were just talking about," I said. "The one you
found in the bag. I'm going to ask you a couple of questions about
it, if that's okay?"

"I don't have my glasses with me," he said, embarrassed and
self-conscious about the fact that he'd gotten old and could no longer read without glasses. "I'll give it back to Hüseyin."

It was easier making myself understood to Hüseyin. He knew
what I was looking for.

Yes, the information I was looking for was in yesterday's note. I
had been stupid enough to miss it. At any rate, it meant only one

thing: the girl on the bicycle was directly collaborating with someone who lived in my apartment building. In apartment three.

"You're wonderful," I said cheerfully.

"I knew you'd realize that someday," he replied.

I really should have told him it wasn't him but the situation that was wonderful, or the retired sergeant from the intelligence service Yılmaz Karataş, who prepared such thorough reports; but he was in the hospital. He might be in need of a little love and compassion.

"When are you coming back?" he asked once again.

"When I'm done," I told him.

Now what I needed was backup. I wasn't going get the police involved. When Selçuk found out, he'd flip his lid and rip me a new one, but there were going to be no police. I was going to sort it out on my own, with my own special forces unit.

Cüneyt, the bodyguard, though a bit feeble in the mind, certainly liked to show off his muscles. He was, after all, a bodyguard by profession. *And now here is his chance, an opportunity to prove himself,* I thought. I phoned and told him to come straight over, no questions asked.

Then I contacted Tarık, whom Hasan had always described as good-looking, and who I knew to be Hüseyin's friend from the taxi stand. He seemed like a strong guy.

While I waited for them to arrive, I did some of the exercises I had been neglecting for days, to stretch myself and warm up a bit. I lifted my legs up one by one and put them against the wall. I realized as I was stretching them that my inner thighs had become stiff. In the corridor I tried two somersaults: the first touching the floor with my hands, the second in midair. I almost hit the wall and smashed my skull to pieces. I focused on the midair backward left-footed head kick I always found so challenging. It's good to be prepared.

Tarık arrived first. Hasan had such bad taste. Well, what would you expect from someone whose favorite actors were Daniel Auteuil and Gérard Depardieu? The guy wasn't good-looking. He just had that fresh-faced glow of youth. If he didn't look after himself, he was bound to start deteriorating before he hit thirty-five. I grabbed him by the arm and dragged him downstairs, motioning for him to keep quiet. The best place to talk, where we wouldn't be heard and where I could see Cüneyt when he arrived, was the entrance of the apartment building next door.

"It's about Hüseyin," I said.

"I thought so, *abi*," he said. "Traffic's jammed anyway. If I went out to work, it'd take half an hour just to get two blocks down the road; the money'd all be spent on fuel."

"Can you fight?"

He couldn't fathom what I meant, of course.

"Fight," I said. "Martial arts? . . . Punching? . . . Kicking? . . . Karate?"

"Sure thing, *abi*," he said. "Hüseyin's my blood brother; we'll do whatever it takes. What sort of a mate would I be if I didn't? Ain't nothing like that in my book, nuh-uh."

I hadn't been in his car many times or spoken more than two words to him, but this hooligan speaking style certainly didn't suit him, especially if he was Hüseyin's blood brother. Hüseyin was impeccably polite. Perhaps here before me stood the cause of the *kahvehane* jargon that Hüseyin occasionally employed, and which I absolutely detested.

I made a sudden attack to test his reflexes. With the kick he received to his back, he buckled up on the floor. The kick had actually been a very light one; I did not intend to hurt him at all.

"Fuck!" he said. "What's going on, man? You knocked the wind right out of me."

"Just testing," I said, trying not to laugh at the state of him. I held my hand out and helped him up.

"Don't leap to the front lines unless you have to," I said, winking an eye. "You're a bit stiff."

I didn't test Cüneyt when he arrived. I knew he went down at the second blow. Best to refrain from injuring my team members.

We were ready for operation number two.

34.

$\mathcal{A}$partment number three was right below me. In other words, it was Wimpy Ferdı's place.

With Cüneyt and Tarık right behind me, we rang the doorbell. If it didn't open, it would only take a kick and a shoulder to break it down.

It didn't. I pressed the bell again, this time keeping my finger on it longer. Wimpy Ferdı was always home to spy on me when I went in and out of the building, so where was he now? The door wasn't opening.

"Let's knock it down," I said.

I actually meant, *You guys knock it down.*

"I take full responsibility."

It wasn't so much my reputation on the block that concerned me, as the scolding I'd get from Selçuk if nothing came of breaking down the door. He'd have every right.

It only took two shoulder blows to open the door. Cüneyt and Tarık stepped aside so I could enter first. Apart from a couple of refurbishments I had done to my own apartment, this one was exactly the same as mine. The lightly furnished living room was neat and tidy. The things I was looking for were not here. I made my way toward the back rooms.

I had my first shock when I entered the room that, in my apart-

ment, was my study. Ferdi's walls were literally wallpapered with
pictures of me. There were no blank spaces at all. Some of them
had been made into decoupages, others had been enlarged. It was a
virtual temple dedicated to yours truly. Some of these photographs
I had never seen before. They had been shot secretly.

I turned to look at where Cüneyt was pointing when he said,
"Boss, look, you're naked in this one."

Yes, he had caught me naked too. In the bath, in my bedroom
standing in front of the dressing mirror, and in bed!

"Don't look," I said.

I could censor one, but what about the rest? If you looked carefully enough, there were plenty of naked pictures of me interspersed here and there. We stood in front of a gigantic Burçak
Veral collage coating all four walls of the room.

I found what I was really looking for in the room that I used as
my bedroom. It was a studio complete with technological devices!

Although I knew I was going to find something, not even I was
expecting this much. The ceiling, floor, and walls had been insu-
lated. There were five different computers connected to one huge
control panel that looked like those sound mixers in a music studio. All five computers were on.

On one of the screens you could see the entrance door to my
apartment. As far as I could tell, the camera had been hidden in the
gas meter box belonging to the apartment opposite. It had to be
one of those wireless cameras the size of a chickpea. I hadn't even
noticed it.

On a different screen was my bedroom. Judging by the angle of
the view, I guessed that the camera was near the window, inside
one of the masks on the wall. I had collected the masks from places
I visited; it was quite a collection, everything from an elaborate
Venetian carnival mask to primitive African totem masks. It was
perfectly understandable that I would overlook a camera placed

among the many beads, stones, and sequins that decorated them. One could also thereby deduce Satı had not been dusting them.

There were no displays on the other three screens, but each was labeled with a different room—one for the kitchen and one for the bedroom!

"Boss, this place is like a space station," said Cüneyt.

Dumbfounded, all three of us were trying to make sense of it.

What sort of a sick person could do all this? What was it he wanted from me? Why was he spying on me every minute, and why did he want to hear every word I said? What kind of fixation had I caused in him?

There were shelves of CDs, organized according to date.

My most private moments were all recorded here.

The CD of the night Hüseyin and I had sex was at the front, carefully labeled with the date and our names. It had been marked X, in red. He was categorizing scenes from my life in a manner similar to that used for the rating of movies, like 18+, etc.

I ran the formatting programs on all five of them to delete the systems fast. Still, it took a while, and then I shut the computers down.

I was going to destroy this.

All of it.

We started breaking the CDs, one by one. My hands began to hurt after breaking only a few, but the rage inside me outweighed the pain. I went on breaking the CDs with all the vengeance of someone determined on revenge.

Tarık stopped for a moment.

"*Abi*, we're smashing all these to pieces, which is fine, but what's it got to do with Hüseyin?"

"It's all the work of the same psycho!" I said, cracking the CD I was holding.

"So where is he, the psycho?"

"We'll find him once we finish here," I said, as I continued to break CDs with tremendous zeal.

We would, we'd find him. But just where was Wimpy anyway?

"Boss, shall we rip the pictures up as well?"

I hadn't thought about that. I'd have to think about it and decide what to do, and when. It would take hours to scrape those pictures off the walls.

"It took you long enough to get here."

I recognized her immediately. It was the girl with the bicycle. She stood there watching us, her arms folded, her shoulder pressed against the doorjamb. We'd been so busy breaking the CDs, and making so much noise doing so, that we hadn't noticed her arrival.

We stopped.

"It took you long enough to get here," she repeated. But we'd already heard her the first time.

She had a clear voice, with a bit of a sneer to it.

"The girl with the bicycle!" I said.

"Bravo!" she said mockingly. "You've finally passed the first part of the test."

What on earth did that mean?

"We left so many clues for you to find this place . . . But you kept getting stuck on other things."

She had big, cold eyes. She was arrogant.

"What is this?" I said. "A game of hide-and-seek? What are you trying to do? All of this, it's ridiculous! What do you want from me?"

The sentences, which I had begun yelling in rage, soon lapsed into desperation, until my voice finally cracked and trembled.

"A sort of payback, let's say," she responded.

This one was skinny. I could see the bones of her chest through her half-open shirt collar.

"Payback for what?" I said, squeezing my fist. "To whom?"

"You'll see," she said, with a calmness that got on my nerves. "Ferdı will explain it to you."

Ferdı would explain! My mad psycho!

"Where is he?" I said. "Where?"

"Part two!" she said, grinning. "You've got to find him . . ."

"We know who he is, his fingerprints are all over the place. The police will find him straightaway."

"Okay, let them find him, then," she said, with a confidence and ease that were enough to drive one up the wall. She turned her back to leave.

I couldn't let her walk out like that. I jumped on top of her. Her twiglike body was fragile. I thought I was going to pull her arm off when I grabbed hold of it.

"Where do you think you're going, missy?" I said, jolting her arm. "We're not finished with you yet!"

"There's nothing you can do with me," she said calmly. "My job is done . . ."

I could torture her and get her to talk, then hand her over to the police and have her questioned by the classical methods.

"Speak, *ayol!*" I said. "Where is Ferdı?"

"I don't know," she said. "You'll have to find him yourself."

There was a wary look in her eyes. I was sure she didn't know.

"Oh, there you are, sir."

And there he stood, Yılmaz Karataş, who had left his appointed spot without permission in order to follow the girl with the bicycle, and, having completed his tour, had arrived back at the apartment.

"I was looking for you. You weren't home. I saw the door open and thought I'd come in . . . I left you a note, did you get it?"

Yes, I had.

"What do we do now?" said Tarık.

I had no intention of letting the girl go. Detention by force was about to be added to my crime of breaking and entering. Since operation number two hadn't delivered the expected, conclusive results, I would have to come up with a new emergency plan.

I phoned Cemil Kazancı on his very private number.

"What's the matter? Is there a problem? Has our guy done something wrong?" he began.

No, I was pleased with Yılmaz. I just had a new request.

"I wonder if you could entertain a guest for me for a while, a young lady? Secretly . . . without letting her contact anyone . . ."

He surprised me by accepting without any hesitation.

"I'm sending her to you with Yılmaz," I said.

"You can't detain me," the girl objected when she understood what was going on. "You have no evidence against me!"

She must have memorized these lines for the police, which was hardly relevant under the circumstances, seeing as I was detaining her in a completely illegal way and handing her over to totally illegal people.

"Who's pressing charges?" I said. "You're my insurance, darling. Now, don't get cranky on us. We wouldn't want you to get hurt."

We tied the bicycle girl's hands and mouth with packaging tape so she wouldn't cause Yılmaz any problems on the way. I sent Cüneyt along with them just in case. I wanted to hand my safety deposit over in one piece.

I made Tarık swear every oath he knew that he wouldn't say a word about it to anyone ever, that he'd forget everything that had happened and wouldn't even dream of it in his sleep. Yes, I would keep him updated. I took his mobile number.

After sending everyone off, I went to my own apartment. First things first, I found the cameras. Then I proceeded to studiously crush them in a mortar. I derived inexplicable pleasure from grinding those cheap, buglike cameras to a pulp. As I bashed the pestle against the mortar, the mica, metal, silicon, and whatever else was in them shattered, making noises that resembled the screeching yelp of an animal, noises that were transformed in my mind into the psycho Ferdı's whining voice, begging for his life.

The listening devices were still in my home, but I had crashed his system so that they could no longer eavesdrop on me.

I could now go to the hospital to see Hüseyin. I could ponder what to do next, how I would pass the second part of the test, once I got there.

35.

*A*s I moved along the silent corridor of the hospital, I spotted Şükrü waiting outside Hüseyin's door. Okay, he might have chitchatted, giggled, and started getting a bit chummy with Hüseyin behind the bar, but still, two visits in a row in one day were a bit much.

He had seen me too. With his body slanted, one shoulder hanging low, the other raised high, his head thrust forward, he sidled along like a crab to meet me.

"Boss, we've got to talk," he said.

His voice was uneasy; so were his eyes.

Something must have happened to Hüseyin, but what? The doctor had said that everything was fine, that he was getting better. Had there been an unexpected complication? Was he in danger again?

The panic that had overtaken my mind must have shown on my face.

Şükrü took my arm; leaning against me, he started leading me in the opposite direction. He reeked of alcohol.

"Please," he said, "listen to me for a minute. I have to explain."

No, I wanted to find out, to see what had happened to Hüseyin immediately. I broke loose of his arm and rushed into the room, which now had a NO VISITORS ALLOWED sign hanging on it.

And froze.

Part two was already in production.

Poor, withered Hüseyin lay there with languishing eyes, drugged up and ready to pass out, and at his bedside, the psycho I was looking for: Wimpy Ferdı.

There was no one else in the room. Kevser and İsmail Kozalak, the safe hands into which I had entrusted Hüseyin, were gone.

"Finally," said Ferdı, his crazy psycho-man voice replacing that of my whiny neighbor.

Şükrü had followed me into the room and shut the door behind him.

"I can explain . . . Please!" he said.

Şükrü's new boyfriend couldn't possibly be my psycho Ferdı!

"What's going on?" I said.

I had been betrayed by my own employee, Şükrü, and those irresponsible parents Kevser and İsmail Kozalak had left their son in the hands of a psycho.

Psycho Ferdı had jabbed an empty syringe into Hüseyin's drip tube, and now stood ready to take the next step, his ink-stained thumb resting on the syringe press.

"Do you know what this is for?" he asked.

When the air bubble entering the vein reached the heart, it meant sudden death. The heart would stop. Even kids knew that.

I nodded.

"Good," he said, in an authoritarian voice that I found didn't quite suit his build. "Sit down and listen."

Şükrü held my arm again, and sat me down on the armchair this time, and perched on its armrest.

"Forgive me," he said. "I can explain everything . . ."

What was he going to explain? He was clearly collaborating with psycho Ferdı. He had been working for me for years and now he was repaying his debt with betrayal. He had sold me out. He had sold Hüseyin out. The guy was about to die. There could be no explanation for this.

"Remove the syringe first," I said, begging him. "Please . . ."

The edges of Ferdı's lips curled up in disdain.

"We know what you're made of. It's not worth the risk."

"What do you want from him? What do you want from me? Why is your house filled with pictures of me? You've bugged my house, you spy on me! What kind of a psycho are you? What the hell is your problem?"

I'd been beaten. I knew it.

I was about to cry.

"Easy does it," he said. "One at a time . . ."

Why didn't a nurse or caretaker come into the room to check in on Hüseyin, and see what was going on? Were we paying all that money to stay in a deserted hospital? What on earth had happened to their quality-certified service perfection? Scenes of nurses flirting with doctors, while those that weren't flirting chain-smoked outside and gossiped about patients, or crowded into a tiny room to watch the most shameless of gossip programs on a tiny TV screen, flashed through my mind. There had to be a reason why they weren't turning up. Okay, they may charge the price of a five-star hotel, but that shouldn't give them the right to act like one, leaving their patients for dead, completely unattended, all in the name of "not disturbing" their guests.

"All right, I'm listening," I said, banishing the nurses and caretakers from my mind. "Go ahead, tell me . . ."

"First," he said, "you've got to understand the situation. You've got to see the bigger picture. You are an arrogant fool blinded by details. The devil may very well be in the details, but you're missing the bigger picture."

My eyes widened; I waited curiously to hear what he would say next. He was in a mood for philosophizing.

"Who am I? Have you ever thought about that? Ever wondered?"

He was my nosy downstairs neighbor. His fingers were ink-stained and nasty.

"Yes, I moved in downstairs. I didn't even know you at first. But once I understood who you were, I thought highly of you, I saw that we had things in common. Then I began looking out for an opportunity to meet you, to talk to you. I kept trying to approach you. Did you pay any attention? Did you ever think about me? Let me answer that for you: no! You were so preoccupied with yourself and your own world! You lived in the cocoon you had built around you, thinking it would protect you. Closed off to the outside world, to those on your doorstep, to their problems . . ."

He was good at insulting me and he had the gift of gab. I was waiting for him to get to the point.

"But who am I? Who is Ferdı Aktan? Let me tell you . . ."

He was raised in an orphanage. There he was given a name and a surname. He had no idea who his family was.

"You can't imagine what it means to grow up without love," he said. "You always had people who loved you. There is no love in an orphanage. There's only one feeling: fear. Punishment, beatings . . . There's the hope that a family will come and adopt the cutest child among us, raise him with love, and there's jealousy of the ones chosen. Can you imagine what it's like waiting to be chosen, to want it so badly you could die? I don't think so . . . And not being chosen. No one ever wanting you. Feeling so much resentment toward the cute, the beautiful, the one that has a chance of being chosen. And if this is indeed a competition, seeking ways to eliminate the other contestants . . . Do you understand?"

I nodded.

"You've got a blank look on your face. Are you daydreaming again or what?"

"No, I'm listening," I said.

It was impossible not to listen.

"Have you ever visited an orphanage? Have you seen the looks on those children's faces? The fear in their eyes, the way they fawn all over every visitor for an ounce of attention they mistake for love? We were shameless in our attempts to curry favor . . . We'd do anything for a pat on the head, or, if we were lucky, a hug. And the grand prize was to be kissed! Even once was enough! We'd dream about it for days afterwards. It was a like a fairy tale that fed our fantasies again and again."

I was beginning to feel pretty rotten. The boy had a sad story. Still, it didn't give him the right to torture me or kill Hüseyin.

"And rape," he said. "You must have heard about it before. Everyone knows. No one lifts a finger. The abuse of juvenile bodies begins at a young age . . . Only the fit and the strong survive anyway. The rest just perish. No one even hears about them. The older kids rape the younger ones. Strangers visit every now and then, slip a few coins into the caretakers' pockets. It was fine by us. In fact, a lot of us liked it. Just think about it, getting close to someone! Being wanted for a moment, no matter how or why; being liked by someone! Ohh! It's an intoxicating feeling. The pain in your ass doesn't even matter. Someone wants you. You're being desired. It grows on you. And the more you want love, the more you want what you think is love: abuse! And every child in there is hungry for love. A vicious circle, right? But that's the way it is!"

I was moved to tears. I found it difficult to swallow.

"Hatice is from the orphanage too," he said. "The girl who dropped off the letter at Hüseyin's place."

So the girl with the bicycle's name was Hatice.

"They throw us out once we come of age. Hatice and I got thrown out on the same day. So you see, we share a common fate, hence our solidarity!"

I felt sorry for Hatice too. I hoped she wasn't being mistreated by Cemil Kazancı's men.

"We were lucky, because we were smart. We were curious and we understood at a young age that knowledge was valuable. We read a lot. We learned. We tried to educate ourselves by our own means. We did quite well. We were able to find ourselves jobs after we got thrown out."

An achievement certainly worthy of congratulations, I had to admit.

"Now, to get to the key matter," he said. "AIDS! The illness. You must know! After all those unidentified rapes, I, as you might guess, caught AIDS. Hatice's got AIDS too. Hers is from a blood transfusion from back when she was a kid. Her family abandoned her when they found out she had AIDS, saying they didn't want a cursed child. Actually, they hadn't wanted her anyway because she was a girl, so the AIDS bit just gave them an excuse to get rid of her. Another element of our common fate! We're carriers, for the time being . . . It's inactive . . . But you know, negative can turn positive anytime."

AIDS on top of the orphanage trauma; the picture was getting darker and darker.

"And what did I want? Attention. Whose attention? Yours. And what did you do? You treated me like a piece of shit. You ignored me, looked at me with scornful eyes, lifted your chin each time we met. You are so arrogant! Even right now! Look at how you're sitting!"

What was wrong with how I was sitting? My back was straight, as I was always careful to maintain good posture, my legs were crossed, perfectly parallel to each other, and my hands were on my knees.

"You're hilarious!" he said with the same disdainful curl of the lip. "You think you're Audrey Hepburn! The way you bend your neck, your hands . . . It's hilarious."

I leaned back and pulled my hands back onto my lap.

"All right, why me?" I asked.

"Why you? Good question. When I saw you, I knew you were the right person. You were successful, attractive, you had a wide circle of friends. You had created a sheltered, rose-colored, artificial world for yourself. You were the one. Let's say it was instinct. Our instincts are strong. Only those with strong instincts survive the orphanage. You can only succeed if you act upon instinct. My instincts told me you were the right one."

"The right one for what?" I asked.

"For my death . . ."

I must have drifted off at some point and missed something he'd said.

"This illness is killing me," he said. "I lose weight no matter what I eat, my blood cells are decaying and dying each day. I want to die without suffering, without agony. At your hands . . ."

That was going too far. The burden!

"I read a play," he said calmly, "called *The Zoo Story.*"

I knew the play. It was written by Edward Albee. Two very lonely men meet on a bench at a zoo and . . . Oh, my God, now I got it!

"One asks the other to kill him," I said excitedly. "Wanting to be a memory he would never forget all his life; at least in someone's head, to be a memory that would never be erased, that would always be remembered!"

"Bravo!" he said. "I knew you were smart. I want to live in your memory, in your fancy world. I want to stay alive in your memory after I'm dead!"

He was asking too much.

"Did you really need to kill Master Sermet, then poison Hüse-yin and now threaten to inject air into his veins?"

"Look, you don't understand," he said. "They are mere tools! Aren't we all going to die anyway? What difference does it make if it's a little sooner than later? We forget all about those who die nat-ural deaths. Think about it, how many people who died in their beds remain alive in your head? It's always the ones who die of un-natural causes that really stick with you, that always come to mind first, isn't it? Look at this way: I've given these guys the opportu-nity to be first in our memories, to take precedence. Besides, I mean, aren't they going to die anyway? I'm just fast-forwarding things a bit. I'm actually doing them a favor!"

Yes, he had had a tough life, but his frame of mind was totally sick. He was definitely crazy.

"Now I'm going to kill Hüseyin," he said coolly. "That way you'll find it easier to kill me. You'll believe that you have a valid reason to do so. It'll be revenge . . ."

Hüseyin's eyes widened in panic. Even though his body didn't respond, he was conscious. He could understand what was being said.

"Stop!" I said when Ferdı moved the syringe. "What about you, Şükrü? How did you become an instrument in all this?"

"I love him," he said, as if that were enough.

"What? You love him and you allow all this madness, these murders?"

Have you gone mad too? I wanted to add, but I didn't want to call him mad and cause provocation. I was buying time so long as we spoke calmly. I needed to do something, but what? The cards (that is, the syringe) were in Ferdı's hand.

"He explained it all to me," Şükrü said calmly. "I understand him. I tried to explain it to you, but you wouldn't listen to me."

I knew Şükrü wasn't very bright, but I'd never figured him to be this stupid. It had to be the side effects of the drugs he'd used in the past. He'd quit, been cured, and was clean. As far as I knew, he'd never used during the time he'd been working for me. He knew I wouldn't tolerate it, and that if he did, he would never set foot in the club again. But then, well, he would never set foot in the club again now anyway.

"Şükrü," I said. "We're talking about murder here. Not a *Pretty Woman* romance."

"I know," the idiot replied. "But I still can't keep myself from doing what he wants."

"Şükrü loves me," said Ferdı. "Try to understand instead of judging his passion. He's lucky to be able to experience such a feeling. How many of us have that opportunity, even once, in our entire lifetimes? Right, Şükrü?"

Şükrü nodded his head. This Ferdı was just like those nutcases who, having the gift of the gab, claim to be prophets and then brainwash their disciples and push them to their deaths with their eyes closed. Ferdı was the false prophet, Şükrü his brainwashed disciple. He listened to the words coming out of Ferdı's mouth as if completely mesmerized.

If this was a game, I was ready to play.

"All right, how do you want me to kill you, then?" I said, sitting up straight in my seat again, but without placing my hands on my knees this time.

"However you'd like, whatever is easiest . . ."

He clearly hadn't given this bit much thought.

"And what if I don't?"

"You will if I kill Hüseyin too," he said. "Ponpon is probably about to snuff it. I'm sure she's eaten all the chocolates. Isn't all of that enough motive for you?"

He gave me a nasty wink as he said "chocolates"; he was beyond contempt.

Yes, the things he said did provoke me, and they were certainly motives, but I didn't think I'd be able to kill someone with my bare hands.

"No," I said, determined. "I'm not going to do it. You can kill Hüseyin too if you like. But I can't kill you. I can't. I can't, *ayol!*"

Hüseyin's eyes widened even more. He parted his lips as if to say something, but the only noise he could make was a meaningless grunt. Was it normal for them to drug him so much?

Why didn't anyone in this hospital come to check on the patients? How much flirting could they possibly do without coming up for air? How many cigarettes could they smoke back-to-back? What TV channel went on for hours without a commercial break? What stupid program could keep its viewers glued to the screen, no matter how pathetic they were, for such a long time? In other words, where the hell were the caretakers and nurses? I had nothing to say for the doctors . . . I feel like it's acceptable for them not to be around. A moment's distraction was all I needed. Just a moment! The distance between us was short enough to deliver a blow.

"What did you say to his parents?" I had to buy time. Someone was bound to walk in. "How did you send them home?"

"We didn't," said Şükrü. "Hüseyin did. He said that you were coming and that you'd stay overnight."

"He insisted they leave before it got late," said Ferdı, picking up where Şükrü had left off. "He made our life easier. We hadn't really planned for tonight. Had we, Şükrü?"

"No," said Şükrü. "We just came to see if they'd used the cologne we prepared."

The cologne *they'd prepared*? Just what part of it had they prepared?

"Sulfuric acid," said Ferdı. "It doesn't kill. It's just good for the skin! But they didn't use it."

It seemed he wasn't satisfied with anything he did. He just

wanted more and more! To leave more of a trace, to be remembered more often, by more people, and with more hate.

"You're mad," I said. "You need treatment."

"Who isn't?" he said, with a sly smile on his face. "Do you think you're normal? There's no difference between thinking you're Audrey Hepburn and thinking you're Napoleon. Besides, the treatment would take too long. AIDS would kill me before they had a chance to fix me."

I didn't *think* I was Audrey Hepburn. She was just my idol. But I wasn't expecting him to understand that.

Suddenly the door opened and Gönül stormed in.

"Oh, my pups! Why didn't you let me knooow? I—"

Here was the moment I'd been waiting for. Springing up from where I sat, I shot out in a somersault on my hands, aiming for Ferdı's head. Bull's-eye. He tumbled over onto Hüseyin, with the syringe still in his hand. And I on top of the two. I quickly pulled the drip tube out of Hüseyin's arm. With my other hand I simultaneously delivered a choking blow to Ferdı's thymus gland. It wasn't difficult for me to trap his neck in a deadly scissor leg hold.

Not knowing what she had walked in upon, Gönül stood flabbergasted, unable to finish her sentence.

"Oh, my! Help! Help!" she yelled.

Someone had to have heard that. It must have echoed into the corridor.

Ferdı was already under my control when a nurse, followed by a husky caretaker, came in to scold us for making so much noise. Hüseyin was being squashed underneath us. Seeing as his life had been saved, getting a little squashed was nothing to worry about, really.

36.

It was sheer luck that Genteel Gönül had arrived. She had run into Hasan on the street and, Hasan being Hasan, he had told her we were here, and so she had come to wish Hüseyin a speedy recovery.

"Ay, my *abla*, why didn't you let me know?" she said in her own unique style of talking. "Okayyy, I ged id, you're fay-moos now. You won't have any-ting to do with us anymooore . . . But going into the hosp-it-aall and not letting me know. I'm a helping hand. Tank God I bumped into your Hasan and he told me. Or how would I ever have found out! I know I'm not reeeally your class or any-ting, but I believe a friend in need is a friend indeed. Wherever tere iz illness or a funeral, tere you'll find me. Good time Charlies are plenty. Tank God alllmighty I'm not one of tose."

I had never been so happy to see her. Besides, I knew she had a crush on Hüseyin.

Ferdı and Şükrü were arrested. I was going to do everything in my power to keep from letting Ferdı slip through the hands of justice on an insanity plea. I called all the psychologists and lawyers I knew. "Obsession," they said it was. It was more likely he would be sent to a mental institution for treatment than sentenced to prison. Like he had said, maybe AIDS would do him in first. I always opposed the belief of certain extreme conservatives who claim that

AIDS is divine retribution that has befallen homosexuals as punishment for their perversion. But there you had it, an irony of fate;
perhaps in this special case, AIDS actually was going to bring divine justice.

Ferdı, whom I couldn't bring myself to pity, had envied the
peaceful life I had created for myself over the years and had done
everything in his power to destroy it. In his efforts to deprive me of
my peace and comfort, he wanted to make those around me suffer
as well. After all, their suffering would be my suffering, and I could
never be at peace with myself thinking that their pain, or their
deaths, were all my fault. So the logic went.

Şükrü, who believed that with Ferdı he had found peace and
discovered the light of his life, needed serious psychological treatment as well. I didn't think I wanted to see him again. He had been
working for me all that time. I couldn't forgive him for what he
had done. I was going to have to find a new bartender.

Pulling out the drip tube in a single sudden move, I had ripped
Hüseyin's vein open. They stitched him up before he lost too much
blood. He's going to get better. He's getting his new car tomorrow.
He didn't borrow money from me. But of course I paid for the hospital expenses. In me he believes he's found the peace he's been
searching for. He intends to continue our relationship the way he
knows it to be. I don't. I'm going to have to give it some thought.

Süheyl Arkın has been released from the hospital too, but he
won't be able to prepare or present his show for some time. I
watched him being discharged on television. He said that once he
was fully recovered, and before he went back to work poking his
nose into all sorts of business, he wanted to go on holiday, something he hadn't done in years. Naturally this news appeared on his
own channel, not on any of the others.

I made sure that the girl with the bicycle, Hatice, was delivered
to the police safely. She'll probably be tried for collaboration.

Yılmaz was the one who turned her in. I don't know what explanation he gave them. He wouldn't be keeping watch at my door anymore.

Selçuk was furious at first when he found out about all I had done; but then we made up. He's always had a soft spot for me. I had a favor to return to the police. Cemil Kazancı saved my day. He and Selçuk are going to meet. In private. I'm organizing it. Apparently Cemil Kazancı wants to negotiate certain terms in a civilized manner. He had said that they could turn over certain wanted criminals who dealt in matters such as drugs, of which he himself did not approve. In return, the police would have to turn a blind eye to other, minor issues.

I bought know-it-all Melek a pair of red Converse shoes. I sent them to her with Hüseyin. Hüseyin was hesitant to give them to her himself, though, thinking it might give people the wrong idea, so he assigned the task to his mother. According to what Mrs. Kozalac told me over the phone, Melek was thrilled; she'd said she was going to prepare a present for me too, and that she was always ready to help whenever I needed her. Her mother, however, had apparently become suspicious as to why someone they didn't know would send her daughter a present for no reason.

In return for his assistance both on the night of the operation and with the Cemil Kazancı issue, Selçuk too deserved a memorable gift. I wondered if he, like Ponpon, would be expecting chocolates, the gift Ponpon had apparently, and longingly, expected from me for so many long years. I'd add a box of chocolates to his actual gift.

I finally got to speak to Gül on the phone. Hesitant and nervous, she told me that my dream man Bahadır really liked me, and that if I was up for it, they were proposing to have a threesome. I listened with my mouth half open, unable to believe my ears. They hadn't tried it before. She said she was ready to do anything to keep hold of the guy. The fact that Bahadır fancied me, and the idea of making love to him, were enough to sweep me off my feet, but I had a different sort of respect for Gül and I couldn't imagine myself in the same bed with her, sharing the same man. I thanked her and told her I would think about it.

I received an e-mail from my author Mehmet Murat Somer, from the land of sunny beaches, Rio de Janeiro, asking what had happened. "Have you sorted it out?" he asked. Of course, his life was bliss over there. When he got back, he'd augment all that had happened and write yet another novel.

And I was going to buy Ponpon, who would show reproach for days after hearing the end of the story, of which she was a part but did not actually witness, a huge box of chocolates from the Gezi patisserie. She'd tuck them in her mouth one by one, close her eyes, and find peace in the sweet flavor spreading across her tongue. "Chocolate is just such a marvelous thing. I think it is mankind's most important discovery. Believe me, it's better than sex, more effective—and, it's safe . . ."

Like she said, everyone loves chocolate.

Glossary

abi:	Short for *ağabey*.
abla:	Elder sister. Also expression of respect.
ağabey:	Elder brother. Also expression of respect.
ağabeyciğim:	The noun *ağabey* + dimunutive and affectionate suffix "*-cik*" (affectionate in this context) + possessive adjective suffix "*-im*." Would translate into English as "my dear/darling brother."
ayol/ay:	Exclamations traditionally used by women as well as effeminate gays and transgender women.
ayolcuğum:	*Ayol* + dimunutive and affectionate suffix "*-cik*" (affectionate in this context) + possessive adjective suffix "*-im*."
ayran:	Yogurt drink.
bey:	Mr., used after the first name.
börek:	Filled flaky pastry fried or cooked in the oven.
çörek:	A sweet or savory pastry.
effendi:	Gentleman.
gözleme:	Hand-rolled pastry filled with a variety of fillings, sealed, and cooked on a *saj*.
hanım:	Mrs., used following the first name.

hünkar beğendi/
  beğendi: Eggplant puree mixed with yogurt or
                      béchamel sauce and cheese, served with stewed
                      lamb meat on top.
kahve: Short for *kahvehane*, coffeehouse. A café open
                      only to male customers.
lahmacun: Round dough with spicy minced meat topping.
mantı: Dumplings with minced meat filling.
maşallah: "Praise be to God."
poğaça: Puff pastry.
rakı: Anise-flavored spirit.